THE THINGS WE DO THAT

THE THINGS WE DO THAT MAKE NO SENSE

STORIES BY ADAM SCHUITEMA

Switchgrass Books
NORTHERN ILLINOIS UNIVERSITY PRESS   DeKalb IL

Published by Switchgrass Books, an imprint of Northern Illinois University Press
Northern Illinois University Press, DeKalb 60115
© 2017 by Northern Illinois University Press
All rights reserved
Printed in the United States of America
26 25 24 23 22 21 20 19 18 17   1 2 3 4 5
978-0-87580-763-8 (paper)
978-1-60909-218-4 (ebook)
Book and cover design by Yuni Dorr

Library of Congress Cataloging-in-Publication Data
Names: Schuitema, Adam, author.
Title: The things we do that make no sense / Adam Schuitema.
Description: DeKalb, IL : NIU Press, [2017]
Identifiers: LCCN 2016021239 (print) | LCCN 2016028668 (ebook) |
  ISBN 9780875807638 (softcover : acid-free paper) | ISBN 9781609092184 (ebook)
Classification: LCC PS3619.C4693 A6 2017 (print) | LCC PS3619.C4693 (ebook) |
  DDC 813/.6—dc23
LC record available at https://lccn.loc.gov/2016021239

These stories appeared, in somewhat different form, in the following publications. My thanks to the editors for their support.
"All of Your Vanished Men" in *Glimmer Train*
"Peering through Blinds" in *Crazyhorse*
"Witch Whistle" in *New South*
"Gunplay" in *Indiana Review*
"Tracking the Jack Pine Savage" in *The Southern Review*
"Pink Blood" at *Green Mountains Review Online*
"Stone Dust" in *BULL*
"The First Seizure" in *North American Review*
"Last Year's Palms" in *Midwestern Gothic*
"Third-Down Conversions" in *Rio Grande Review*
"Virgin Lands" in *Hair Lit*
"Say Not Really" at *Cheap Pop*
"Light Years" in *Washington Square*
"Coronations" in *Knee-Jerk*
"Mercy Mercy Me" at *Sequestrum*

for Elizabeth

For ritual allows those who cannot will themselves out of the secular to perform the spiritual, as dancing allows the tongue-tied man a ceremony of love.

—Andre Dubus, "A Father's Story"

CONTENTS

THE THINGS WE DO THAT MAKE NO SENSE

ALL OF YOUR VANISHED MEN

The men in my family tend to disappear. Even before my dad vanished there was Uncle Glenn, on my mom's side, who worked as a petroleum engineer, requested a move to Kuwait, and writes home just once per year: a Christmas card with the words *Happy Hanukkah*.

Grandpa didn't truly disappear, but he became persona non grata when—at the age of seventy-three—he left Grandma for his occupational therapist, a fifty-year-old woman named Barb. He died two years later, and since he'd neither redrawn his will nor sold his cemetery plot, he lies buried beside Grandma this very day. There's a revisionist movement within my family that hopes to toss the whole episode down the memory hole.

But it's my dad I think about most as I cross the snow-cloaked street to the VFW. I had to park at the old water filtration plant because the lot at the club is full. The entire neighborhood seems to have turned out for the chili cook-off, just like last year, which was the last time I saw or heard from him.

This club—Creston Memorial Post 3023—hosted my sister, Donna's, wedding reception two decades ago. At one point late that evening,

Grandpa—gin-soaked, with a white gift bow atop his head—danced encircled by turquoise bridesmaids to the Billy Idol version of "Mony Mony." I was fifteen, and my dad and I slumped over in our chairs, all but pissing ourselves with laughter.

Dad was a lifetime member here before he disappeared. I suppose he's still a member. We attended the chili cook-off for the past three years, and though today might seem self-indulgent, like I'm just wallowing in memory, there's a point to all this. I'm not looking for nostalgia. I'm looking for clues—for any trace of his quiet plans.

There were no signs at this time last year. He and I drank six beers apiece before heading down to the canteen and drinking a few more. Someone upstairs announced his name as winner of the fifty-fifty raffle. The Captain came down and handed him his prize: a hundred and twenty-three dollars, all in fives and ones. He and I were already bombed. I was trying to scoop up some of the free popcorn but kept missing the basket and pouring it onto the floor. And he kept stumbling around the jukebox, looking for a Jim Croce song that didn't exist. Two weeks later Dad went underground.

The music hits me before the aroma as I step inside the building and climb the stairs. Jack Johns and the Bluewater Bluegrass Band are already underway. I enter the hall and look for a seat. Jack Johns leans toward his microphone, playing a resonator guitar, singing his take on "Ring of Fire." That's the theme for the event: heat. It carries over into the air itself, people overdressed and sweating like kids on a late-March playground. The event is open to the public, and the public has turned out, shoulders pressed together while seated on steel chairs at folding tables in the middle of the room.

More tables, maybe fifteen in all, line the cinder-block walls. These are the competitors: teams of two, standing behind steaming twelve-quart chili pots, peering into them every once in a while, stirring with glimmering ladles. The rest of the table space is devoted to upwards of three things. First, snacks: baskets of Cheetos and Fritos and tortilla chips. Maybe some toothpicked meatballs or cocktail weenies. These masquerade as accompaniments to the chili, but they're not. They're bribes, luring the attendees to spend their fifty-cent tickets on a cupful of the team's work, and, maybe, in the end, cast a vote in their favor.

Second, there are awards. Some are standing trophies. Others are plaques laid flat, declaring first-place and runner-up finishes at various competitions. Most are statewide or regional, bearing the distinct shapes of the Michigan peninsulas.

And finally, there is the paraphernalia—items that highlight the theme of each table, and often its recipe. "The women teams are good at that," said my dad last year. "The decorations and whatnot. Your mom would be good at that."

My parents had entered a surreal period of post-marriage, post-divorce companionship. They'd split up when I was in high school, and both remarried a few years later. By my midtwenties—while I was finishing my student teaching and starting to date Amy—they'd both divorced again. And then a year and a half ago I heard from Donna how Dad was hanging out at Mom's house a lot. The two of them would sit at the kitchen table playing board games and drinking wine and laughing about people they'd known in high school. They'd gone to high school together. They'd been sweethearts.

I visited Mom's one Sunday morning, and there was a Monopoly board set up in mid-game on the table. Three empty bottles of Merlot stood atop the refrigerator. She smiled as she spoke about the weather and a new rug she'd bought for the foyer. I returned a couple weeks later, and the Monopoly game was still there, a bit further along, with green houses and red hotels cropping up on some of the properties. Beside it were the reconstructed edges of a thousand-piece jelly-bean jigsaw puzzle. A hobby from their shared youth.

After removing my coat and scarf and draping them over a chair, I buy a bottle of Bud Light instead of some local craft brew like I'd usually drink. Bud Light was my dad's beer. There's no real clue here; I realize that. This is not an homage. I'm not "trying to be cute," as he would say any time I acted like a smart-ass growing up. But I'm going to retrace his steps as faithfully as possible because we usually discern secrets not with cunning but by stumbling over them. Bulldozers unearthing old bones.

That's how I learned *where* he is—a secret I'm still keeping myself. Today has nothing to do with *where*. He could be hiding in my basement for all I care. I just want to know *why*.

I walk sideways through the crowd, along the perimeter, scoping out the field. Most are the same teams as last year, their tables set up in roughly the same spots. There are the Horny Hunters, their table cluttered with framed photographs of the two cooks kneeling with rifles before eight- and ten-point bucks. The men wear bright orange today; their chili meat is venison.

There's Wolverine Wildfire, a pair of U of M alums decked out in maize and blue. They earned my vote last year, and not just because I'm an alum myself. Their chili had produced just the right amount of kick—a smoldering I could trace all the way down my throat.

A few tables down from them is a tandem named Dragonbreath with a medieval-inspired caldron of chili and one guy wearing chain mail over a blue sweatshirt. I don't remember their recipe, but I do faintly recall their being assholes and my dad saying something along the lines of, "Those boys are as dull as the toy battle-axes they're carrying."

The guy with the chain mail looks at me. "Come here," he says and hands me a Styrofoam cup of chili with a white plastic spoon. "Try this."

I take two spoonfuls, nodding my approval. "It's good," I say. "Almost all meat. Not much onion or tomato."

He leans toward me, his mail rattling against the table edge. "You want to know the worst thing about eating vegetables?"

I shake my head.

"Getting them out of the goddamned wheelchair."

I nod and take another, smaller taste of chili. "Good luck today." Then I set the cup down and move the hell on.

Across the room stand the Hula Girls, a pair of middle-aged blond women with faux grass skirts, Hawaiian print shirts, and chili made with pineapple. Inexplicably, the recipe won last year.

Dad had cast his vote for them. He'd always loved pineapples, and when I was a kid he'd buy one every week. One Christmas my mom gave him a stainless-steel easy slicer that worked like a corkscrew. He ran right to the kitchen, grabbed the pineapple from the counter, cut the top off the fruit, and then held the leaves above his head—a grin on his mustachioed face—as he wore the jagged green crown. Then he twisted the tool into the fruit and pulled five perfect, golden rings free from the shell.

Which is why, when he vanished, I figured he'd gone somewhere tropical: Guam or the Philippines. Maybe the Hula Girls' recipe had triggered something in his brain, and weeks later he was lying on the sands of a tranquil coast, eating pineapples with the juice running down his chin and onto his bare, tattooed chest. But I've seen nothing so far today that would explain why he'd instead chosen the desert, someplace as desolate as the apartment he left behind.

It took us a few days to even realize Dad had gone. He'd failed to show for his weekly Saturday game-night visit to Mom's. That following Tuesday, with still no word from him, she called his landlord, explaining Dad's high blood pressure and convincing the man to go check on him. The landlord found an apartment containing only three cardboard boxes stacked in the middle of the living room. Each was taped shut and labeled: one for me and one for Donna and a smaller one that read JAYBIRD—his nickname for my mom.

Taped to the bathroom mirror was a note:

No foul play. Did no crime. No woman involved.

He didn't sign it "love." He didn't even sign his name. But the bit about "no woman involved"? That was his final message to Mom.

I continue to retrace the day of last year's chili cook-off, my pockets full of cash. I have enough to sample all these recipes five times if my stomach's up for it. I approach the stage and watch the band for a few minutes. Jack Johns is singing "Lonesome Road Blues," breathing heavily and wiping his brow with a little red cocktail napkin. Only after he finishes do I notice the team to the right of the stage—a team not present at last year's competition. A team of nuns.

The two wear modest black habits, white aprons, and large wooden crosses around their necks. A handwritten sign hanging from their table reads OUR LADY OF THE SNOWS. Atop their table stand a few votive candles, a gold chalice, and three trophies. One of the nuns—much older than the other—sees me staring at the trophies. "Not every reward is in heaven," she says, stirring her pot. "Most, but not every."

I nod, sipping my beer, taking this all in. "You must be good."

She gazes at the chili while she stirs. "Because we use buffalo instead of beef."

The other nun, a woman in her twenties who appears strangely tan—orange like one of my high school students—stands up from her folding chair. "That's the secret," she says. "Almost everyone uses beef. And the palate grows numb." She nods toward the pot. "Until it finds us."

Of course I'm as mystified as anyone would be by these sights: the trophies, the chalice, the orange skin. The very existence of a chili-cooking team of nuns. But they weren't here last year. Their presence today offers no answers regarding my dad.

"I'll be back with a ticket," I say. "I promise."

I glance at my watch. The tasting begins in twenty minutes. I approach a table helmed by a team of actual veterans from the club, young men back from one or both of the wars. Jesus, they look like kids from my geometry class—baby-faced, their chins free of stubble. The table is lined in red-white-and-blue bunting and balloons. One of the vets stirs the chili, holding a wooden spoon with his prosthetic hand.

I'm pretty sure it's a different team than the vets who competed last year. For one thing, they seem much younger, though that's just a mirage, like the illusion that this year's crop of homeroom freshmen is more childlike than last's. They're always the same. I'm the one who's older.

There could be a lead here. If the sight of young soldiers makes me think these things, what might Dad have made of them? Maybe they reminded him of himself or of friends from *his* war. Maybe they dredged up the stories that Donna and I had grown up with, the mythology of our parents' romance. Dad in boot camp, forced to stand before the other recruits and eat—literally chew and swallow—the love letters from Mom that she'd suffused with Chantilly perfume. The Noritake china that he'd bought in Okinawa—in that interlude between Vietnam and marriage—which he'd shipped home so that a family they'd not yet conceived could dine once a year on its blue floral print.

I set down my empty beer bottle and walk over to where the Captain, an old VFW executive, sits behind a lockbox and a mammoth roll of tickets. I hand him a ten-dollar bill. I'm going to try every recipe in the room. I'm going to taste myself sick.

The Captain is actually a retired chief petty officer. He served on a minesweeper during the Korean War and earned his nickname at the club because of the blue-and-gold ball cap he always wears that reads USS MOCKINGBIRD AMS-27. "You want to put into the fifty-fifty raffle?" he asks.

"What the hell," I say, handing him a five. "Let it ride."

Might as well go all-in on this reenactment. See if Dad passed any of his luck on to me. He'd always been a small-time gambler with that kind of near-luck that made other men jealous. He'd once gotten five of six lotto numbers and won a few grand. Another time he'd found an engagement ring along a trail while hiking in the Porcupine Mountains. The stone was missing, but the setting was worth a few bucks.

He used to say he'd burned up all his bad luck when he was nineteen, during that stay in Okinawa. He'd lost a drunken bet that he could never actually remember and woke up the next morning with two huge tattoos on his chest: a grasshopper on each pectoral, facing one another, with boxing gloves on their front legs. He used to wash the car in the driveway with his shirt off, and when we were kids Donna and I would beg him to flex his chest to make the hoppers fight.

A few months ago, Donna referred to the tattoos. "At least we'll be able to identify him if he turns up dead somewhere." She still wanted to call the police and report him as missing, but there was that note in his own handwriting.

"He put it right there," I said. "There's been no crime."

But she was convinced of violence—homicide, suicide. If anything, all I could imagine was a term I'd learned from a book I was reading. The act of faking one's own death. Pseudocide.

She's talked about hiring a private detective and always seems to be waiting for me to say I'll chip in for the fees. But even before I found him I didn't share her morbid curiosity. I'd been more focused on Mom and her grief during this kind of third divorce she was going through.

She slipped into a quiet devastation with Dad gone. She's worked third shift for years, cleaning office buildings at night, but instead of sleeping till noon upon returning home, she lay on the couch and drank Merlot while watching the *Today* show. For a while Donna and I took turns visiting her a couple days a week. A month after he left, that Monopoly game was still set up on the table. The puzzle half-finished.

We'd usually sit in silence, staring at the TV, avoiding the topic always floating there between us like sunlit dust. Then one day Mom finally asked, "Did he ever say anything to you? Did you know anything about any of this?"

"No," I said, and it was true. He'd never talked about going anywhere, seeing anything. He had no dreams that we knew of. No close friends. No hobbies or passions. He had his pension, a small apartment, shelves of military fiction and history, and a storage unit filled with empty Bud Light cans. When he'd reach five hundred cans he'd haul them to Meijer, cash in the ten-cent refunds, and buy more beer.

So Mom and I just sat there, watching TV, while fruit flies hovered over the glasses of yesterday's wine.

I have fifteen minutes to kill before the tasting officially begins. I slip down the back stairwell, into the quiet and dark coolness of the private canteen. The sudden silence is a relief. Like all lifetime members, Dad has his own chair somewhere in the room, a little bronze engraved plate screwed to the top: *Rick Carroll, First Sergeant*. Maybe I'll look for it later. It's probably stacked in the dim back corner, behind the service branch flags and the bingo cage.

I come down here every once in a while by myself. The beer's a buck fifty, the hot dogs are fifty cents, and it's a good place to grade AP Calculus exams. Even when I'm not grading I sometimes come here alone to watch football and sit among the ambient chatter of old men. I'm no good with people my own age. I'm best with teenagers and the elderly.

There's a smattering of men at the bar, and the bartender, a woman in her sixties named Gloria, is making a cocktail. "You a member?" she calls to me as I approach.

She doesn't remember me. And just from the sight of me—maybe my weak, doughy chin or the sweater I'm wearing—she can tell I'm no military man. "Auxiliary." I reach for my wallet to show her my card.

She shakes her head. "Don't need it. What are you drinking?"

I order a pitcher of Bud Light, and while she turns to the tap I head over to the pull-tab machine near the bathrooms. I slide in a five-dollar bill and buy ten tickets. One of the men at the bar turns on his stool. He wears a red flannel shirt and a gray goatee. "That fucker's been laying eggs all week. If you win anything I'll change my name to Sally."

I sit beside him, and Gloria serves me the pitcher with a small glass. I pay her, pour myself a drink, and stack the lotto tickets in front of me, just to stare at them a bit.

"Well, you going to open them?" asks the man.

I take a sip and shake my head. "Then the fun's over." I rarely gamble and don't know why I bought them—don't know why I bought the fifty-fifty tickets. It's not really about studying Dad's luck. I just love this moment—the teetering rush of even the smallest suspense. If I ever meet another woman and we have a son, I want to teach him two things: first, how to score a baseball game; second, how to appreciate anticipation. The darkening skies before a storm. The heady restraint of Christmas Eve. These unpeeled tickets are like that faint high of a wine's bouquet. They're like lingerie.

"It's better to wait a few minutes," I say.

The man turns to his whiskey. "You can do that because you're still young. I prefer to know shit bang that I lost."

I'm not young anymore, but I accept the compliment, even as it sends my thoughts in the direction of my students. Every year another class graduates, and they seesaw there on that thrilling cusp of commencement, hugging and crying and pumping their fists in joy. And every year I'm jealous as fuck.

It's been a half decade since my last relationship. Amy was a linguist who moved to Bilbao to study Basque, and though we'd lived together and planned to marry, she called one night to say she wasn't coming back. Since then I've just sort of waited for some other woman to appear—the worst kind of suspense.

As I refill my glass of beer, still staring at the unripped pull tabs, I have to admit that this is probably something I've inherited from my dad. Imagine the anticipation he must have had swirling inside him. What sort of commencement could be more breathtaking than a step off the edge of one's earth? Last year, when the two of us were down here getting drunk, he was celebrating his send-off. A bon voyage party I didn't know I was throwing.

When we left that afternoon, he glanced up the street and then down it, before saying something about *his* dad—my other grandpa. "Except for the war, my father lived his whole life in this same square mile." He shook his head a little and smirked. "Two different houses, but the same square mile."

I'm not much better. Though I was born in North Carolina, when Dad was still stationed at Cherry Point, we moved to Grand Rapids when I was seven, and I've lived here ever since. Other than a few quick trips to Ontario, I've never left the country. I don't live in Bilbao or speak Basque.

I have to be careful here. A few more drinks and I could easily surrender to the flood of self-pity that's always straining the hinges of that gate in my brain. Weight gain. Hair loss. Three-year sexless streak and a piece-of-shit Corolla.

Which is why a part of me gets it—the allure of vaporizing and rematerializing, leaving one life and starting fresh and unknown in another. When Dad disappeared and I first went online to research this sort of thing, I found and bought a book called *American Vanishing Act*. It's pretty hard core, aimed at people who are running from the law or trying to escape an abusive relationship. There are whole sections devoted to destroying credit cards, using toilet-seat covers, and adding long-grain rice to a car's radiator fluid so a person can't get behind the wheel and chase after you.

Again, none of this relates to my dad. But it sent me to a world of fantasy for a few weeks, and I started imagining a pure, blank start of my own—to the point where during spring break I hiked out into a state game area north of town, pitched a tent, and just played make-believe for five days. One morning I woke to a pelting sound on my nylon roof. I crawled out into the dirt, and there across the creek were two boys with handfuls of stones. They dropped them, scooped up their fallen bikes, and disappeared into the brush.

So yeah, there's still a part of me that thinks about Dad and wants to be like Donna, shouting, "What do you mean there was *no crime*? He left his loved ones!" But then I wonder what the hell he owed us—two thirtysomething children and his longtime ex-wife. Why should we hunt him down with *our* handfuls of stones?

Long story short: when—just yesterday—I discovered where he was living, I decided to keep it to myself.

I glance at my watch and drink quickly. They're about to start upstairs. I begin pulling the tabs from each lottery ticket, looking for three of a kind. My first six tickets come up empty. On the seventh I win a dollar. The last three are losers as well.

I stand, my pitcher still half-full. "Beer's yours if you want it," I say to the man beside me. "So's the dollar winner. Use it to buy another ticket. The grand prize."

"Keep the ticket," he says. He curls his wrist around the pitcher and drags it toward him. "I got better odds with this."

I ascend the bare stairwell once more. The air is seasoned with the tang of peppers and spices. The Bluewater Bluegrass Band is hip-deep in a patriotic medley. They transition seamlessly from the "Marines' Hymn" to Lee Greenwood's "God Bless the USA." Revelers sit at center tables with white sauce-stained cups scattered about.

I buy another beer and begin to make the rounds, starting with the Horny Hunters. The venison is tender, but the overall product's too soupy. I approach Dragonbreath but take a pass. I've already tasted it. I know it's low on vegetables. And Wolverine Wildfire lacks the heat it had last year when I gave them my vote.

My tongue slightly numb, my head a bit high, and my stomach roiling with beer and stew, I pay visits to several other teams, mostly locals and club members without trophies and paraphernalia, who've brewed up solid but forgettable recipes. One's heavy on beans. Another is vegetarian. Yet another tastes oddly of licorice.

I skip the nuns for now. Their table has a crowd encircling it, and the two of them have sweat dripping down their faces. I approach the Hula Girls, who have slipped on white T-shirts that feature illustrations of slim, bikini-clad bodies on the front—neck to thigh—creating an optical trick as they stand in front of the white cinder walls. One of them smiles and jokes with a customer: "Don't laugh! I used to have a figure like this!" Their recipe is complex and delicious, and though a fruit-laced chili will never win my vote, Dad would have loved it once more.

A few tables over stand the young veterans, who grin and shoot the shit with those they serve, scooping generous helpings up to the brim of every cup. And I have the urge to talk to them—to talk to them the way I can talk to my students, about college and movies and football. My students laugh at my jokes and shake my hand at the end of the school year and invite me to their graduation open houses. I can't talk to anyone else in this way. Amy used to say it was a little weird, and maybe it is. But it's a hell of a lot easier than talking to a guy my age who's married with three kids and a house in Ada or East Grand Rapids. Or worse yet, someone from my high school days who sees me at the grocery store and wants to catch up. No, I'm clearly not a distance runner anymore—just look at me. No, I haven't played guitar in years.

A sixteen-year-old kid who walks into my classroom in September? Shit, to him I've always been the guy I am now. No shame in that. But that kid's got years to figure out the truth, which is that tragedy isn't what you are. It's what you *were*.

I look away as the veteran serves my chili. I'm afraid I'll get caught staring at his prosthetic hand. So I gaze at the red-white-and-blue balloons behind him, take my chili, and taste.

For the first time there's a trace of what I've been looking for, a trace of what the event promised: heat. There are more beans than I'd like, and it's a bit heavy on the garlic, but there's at least enough afterburn that my beer can't extinguish it. There are also some chunks of kielbasa, like the kind Dad's dad made at his old meat market on Bridge Street.

When Dad said that last year—about Grandpa living his whole life in the same square mile—I thought at first it was a missed clue, that Dad was taking this fact to heart and was inspired to move away himself. But he'd traveled the world as a Marine. It had nothing to do with him. Only now do I believe those last words were a kind of advice, encouragement. It was a warning directed at me.

The other thing he left me was that taped-up box in his empty apartment. When I'd brought it home and sorted through it, I'd hoped to find some object of sentiment. Something from his youth or mine. A Father's Day card made from construction paper and stickers. Or maybe something serious, like his dress blues. Instead there were some artifacts he'd collected over time, like an ivory shoehorn and a German trench knife, though neither were part of our own family's history. Mostly the box contained books: a few dozen on history and some novels. One of them was Keegan's *The Face of Battle*, which gave me pause because of a slip of white paper hanging from between its pages. I sat on the couch, beside a table lamp, and inspected it: a Burger King sales receipt he'd been using as a bookmark. He'd bought a Whopper value meal with a Dr. Pepper. At the top was the date: January 25 of last year—the week before he'd left.

Once I realized this was the book he was reading before disappearing, I started flipping through it, looking for marginalia or something else hidden between its pages. A cocktail napkin. A pressed flower from a woman he'd once loved.

But there was nothing. I closed the book and stared at its cover without really looking at it, my mind playing with that worthless clue of knowing he'd eaten one night at the South Leonard Burger King. I turned the book slightly, and the sheen from the lamp picked up something on the dust jacket's gloss. There were indentations—handwriting—as if the book had been used as a hard surface for paper and pen. I sat up and raised it closer to the lamp, turning it more until I could distinguish a few numbers and words: *3884 Blue Mesa Drive*. It took all of ten seconds for me to google it and find a matching address in Somerton, Arizona, just a few miles from the Mexican border. At first I thought that was the key—Mexico—and that he'd had some real danger to escape. But then I realized Somerton was just south of Yuma, home to the Marine Corps Air Station, where they based harriers and an aggressor squadron of F-5s. Where Dad had been stationed when Donna was born.

I checked satellite imagery of the address before switching to street view. The house was a brown ranch with a brown lawn and a single tree of a kind I didn't recognize, nothing native to the Midwest. There was also a satellite dish, a red pickup, and a sky so blue it felt like cheating.

I knew the image was probably several years old, from long before he'd moved to this place, if he had indeed moved there at all. Even so, I zoomed all the way in on the image, staring at the dark pixilation of the living room window.

A young woman with jet-black hair and a toddler on her hip walks over to that young veteran with the prosthetic hand. She kisses him on the cheek and whispers something in his ear, making him nod. And I admit that which I've sort of known for a while now. Dad didn't leave because he was in some physical danger or had creditors to evade. He was scared of falling back in love with Mom. He was hiding from *her*.

Jack Johns is singing: *"Off we go, into the wild blue yonder."* The crowd around the nuns has thinned. The older nun pats her face with a white towel and then slips it around the back of her neck like a basketball player coming off the court. I hand them one of my last tickets. "Saving the best for last," I say, trying to smile.

Two men walk off with their chili, and now I'm alone, at that table beside the stage, with the nuns. Neither of them acknowledges me at first. Then the older one glances up, dark rings circling her eyes. "Have a little snack first." She nods at a bowl of round, bite-size tortilla chips on the table.

"No thanks. I'm pretty full."

She drops her eyes, shakes her head slightly, and picks up a single chip. "Cleanse the palate," she says. She looks up again and reaches over the table, holding the chip out to me—not toward my hands, but higher, toward my mouth. And without thinking I'm opening wide, extending my tongue a bit, where she gently lays the chip. I close my mouth but never take a bite, letting it slowly dissolve. The band begins playing "This Land Is Your Land."

I look down now for my serving of chili and notice there are no more cups or spoons. "Are you all out?" I ask.

This time it's the younger nun who shakes her head. Her skin is so smooth; I try not to look at it. She picks up the gold chalice that stands amid the candles and trophies. Then she scoops it into the pot and pulls it out, rivulets of chili running down the side. She holds the chalice before me, and the older nun nods. "Drink up, my son."

I set down my beer, grasp the chalice with both hands, and raise it toward my mouth, pausing for a moment to stare into its darkness. I don't want to sip yet—I want to linger in this moment—so I keep my mouth closed and let the chili accumulate around my closed lips.

Then I gulp. Some of it spills down my cheek and trickles toward my ear. The taste is rich and earthy; the buffalo makes all the difference. But then the taste disappears, replaced by heat. It gradually warms my tongue and then travels like a thin flame down my throat. I can feel it in my stomach. My lips go numb.

These are the things we do, and they make no sense. They endure over time or are tossed down the memory hole. I'm not going to commit pseudocide, but days from now I'll commit to leaving, like Dad and Grandpa and Uncle Glenn, resurfacing elsewhere.

So forgive us, Mom—all of us. All of your vanished men.

PEERING THROUGH BLINDS

The blinds were open after dark, which I hated, because people could see inside my house from the street or sidewalk. I'd come home late from a client meeting and now sat on the living room sofa to watch *SportsCenter* with a bottle of beer. The moment I'd entered the foyer, Abby had said hello, brushed past me, and hurried out the door to grocery shop, desperate for a little fresh air after being home all day with the baby. Our three-month-old, Victoria, lay asleep in her upstairs nursery.

I watched the Lions recap—another loss—forgetting that the time change had occurred a day earlier, the clocks turned back, and the November dark came so early again. When I eventually looked up from the TV, the front windows were black with nightfall. I stared into them, trying to see if anyone was out on the street staring back at me. At first I only saw my reflection and the mirrored light from the room's lamps. Then my eyes refocused, and I looked through the image of myself. The streetlight by the curb glowed orange, creating silhouettes of the sycamore branches clustered around it. I stood to close the blinds, and the streetlight died out.

I'd noticed this before—usually when I went for late-night runs through the neighborhood—how certain lights blinked out every few minutes and returned maybe thirty seconds later. I still don't know why this happens.

As I pulled the cord to lower the blinds, the front yard filled with a curving river of new light—headlights from two turning cars—that shined into the living room, bent over the room's corners, and rounded out over lampshades and end tables. The two cars pulled into my driveway.

I closed the blinds and walked quickly to the side door of the house. A horn moaned. It was like a kid half-awake with the flu, long and low and ending in a sort of breathlessness. It returned immediately, someone pressing their hand down hard on the steering wheel and holding it there.

The side door opened and Abby plunged inside. She looked over her shoulder, into the dark, and screamed. "Stop fucking following me!"

I pushed past her, slammed the door, and turned the dead bolt. "Who is it?" I asked. My limbs went heavy, my heart electric. The horn never stopped.

Abby stepped past me and opened the door again. She stuck her head out into the night and yelled. "What's your problem? Fucking leave!"

I grabbed her arm and wrenched her back into the dimly lit hall, turning the dead bolt again with my free hand. Her face was flushed, and her hair hung over her wet, red eyes.

"What the hell," I said. "Who is it?"

She kept silent for a moment, staring at the door and listening to the horn. "Go out there," she said quietly.

"Oh my God! Go where? Who is it?" I stepped around the corner of the hallway and into the kitchen, grabbing my phone off the counter.

"Oh shit. Shit," she said. "I don't know." She took a huge breath, her eyes widening with the inhalation. "They cut me off in the Meijer parking lot, and I flipped them off. That's all I did. It was dark. I didn't think they could see me."

"I'm calling 911," I said.

"No," she said. It was almost a whisper. "Go out there. Do something."

I rubbed my eyes with one hand, still holding the phone, ready to call. "What am I gonna—?"

The horn stopped.

In the sudden rush of silence, I slipped the phone into my pocket, thinking they were leaving. Abby and I stared at each other, unmoving, listening for the sound of the car backing out of our driveway. But the engine murmured at the same pitch, and through the low, ragged hum we heard the voices of two men.

We ain't going nowhere.

You got to apologize for that rude gesture.

Even though muted from the closed door, their voices seemed to pour inside as if through a screen, a veil of mesh anyone could punch a fist through.

"You have to do something," said Abby.

Come on out, sweets. We just want to talk.

I turned the lights off in the kitchen and dining room, and Abby followed me as I crept to the small, hexagonal window next to the china cabinet. Two dark profiles stood beside a pickup truck. Their shadows stretched over the driveway, and the beams of the headlights seemed to shoot from their hips and burn sharp light into the garage door. Above them, in the sycamore branches, the orange streetlight—which had been illuminating their truck—blinked out again, making the sidewalk, the sycamore, and a small pocket of the neighborhood vanish. The truck's yellow eyes were all that was left. No one in the neighborhood had turned on their porch lights. No one stood outside to witness the commotion.

Come on out, honey. I just want to show you something.

One sat on the truck's front bumper, and the other set his palms on the hood and propped himself up backwards to sit on it. All the time in the world. He put his hands behind his head and reclined a bit. I crouched lower so I could gaze high above the driveway, waiting for the orange streetlight to return, and pulled my phone from my pocket, ready to call.

The man hopped back down off the truck and opened the driver's side door.

We'll stop by later to tuck your sweetness into bed.

The other man climbed into the truck before it backed out into the road. Then it revved its engine and squealed off, the horn blasting one last time so that its sound trailed after them and hung in the dark like exhaust.

I felt light-headed, my arms and legs numb from adrenaline, and kept staring out the window. The streetlight flickered back on.

I stayed up that night peering through blinds—from the nursery, from our bedroom—waiting for the truck. Abby coaxed me into lovemaking, wanting to rescue the night. We usually kept the lights on because I liked to see her body. But that night I kept obsessing about the tiny slits running across the closed mini blinds, feeling like everything in our lives could be seen from the street. So we made love in the dark, which ruined everything.

I tried to sleep but couldn't. I walked downstairs to the kitchen, pulled a knife from the cutlery block, and later slipped it into my nightstand drawer. Abby and Victoria slept undisturbed, never knowing I had spent much of the night pressed against the blinds with one finger gently lifting them to peek out. Abby never knew I had stood in the kitchen at three thirty in the morning gripping steak knives, slashing at imaginary men. She wasn't there when my limbs were light again, my heart beating in perfect rhythm with my steady breath. But that's for the best, because I'm sure as she slept she never dreamed I'm the type of man who has to stand in dark kitchens, practicing such things.

WITCH WHISTLE

We awoke in predawn darkness to the wind-splitting screams of bombardment. Bits of brick and mortar sprinkled down on us. Dirt misted our skin. The oil lamps swayed—orange globes that sent shadows lurching over the walls, even though most of us kept still and just lay there, five-deep on the concrete platform of the Metro station.

I jolted upright, my hair tangled and hanging limply over my face. I was nine then, and in those early months of the war Mom still brushed out the snares each day, checking for lice and trying to hold back my bangs with a half-rusted hair clip she'd found on the sidewalk. There were days when this was the only time she'd come close enough to touch me.

Dozens of us sprawled over each other like felled dominoes. At first I thought Grandma was still asleep beside me. Her eyes remained closed. Her head sunk into a burlap sack that had once held rice; she'd stuffed it with crumpled newspapers to make a pillow. I lay back down and pulled the soiled blanket over my head, tenting it by pulling it tight with my feet and my raised hands. It shielded me from debris without the smothering feeling against my face. But the air beneath felt earthy and damp, like a cellar of overripe potatoes.

Grandma was awake. Her hand crept over the floor, beneath the blanket, and squeezed my knee, softly at first and then tightly as the ground again shook. "Come here, Rosario," she said.

I emerged from my blanket to the dim light and faint sewer smell of the platform. Grandma's eyes were now open and glassy. Stray hairs like torn cobwebs floated from her headscarf.

"Come here." She reached under my armpits and dragged me over the small space between us. "My God girl, come here!" Then she pressed my face into her chest with one hand and grasped my back with the other.

Someone among the mass of huddled bodies broke into hysterical sobbing. I began crying through gritted teeth, wiping my tears against Grandma's shawl. A rough, heavy hand patted the top of my head, and when I peeked up Grandpa was yawning, propped up on one elbow. Even in the low light his bald head had a sheen to it. He lit one of his remaining cigarettes and spoke in the lull between bombs. "The milkman's here," he said, because lately the bombers only struck in the nothing hour before first light. All the better to evade pursuit planes. All the better to extract fear. They arced the night just before most of Madrid awoke, when our sleep was deepest and we'd allowed ourselves to fasten onto dreams.

Another witch whistle cut through the air. I looked up, as if to the sky, though there was only the dark, curved ceiling of the Metro tunnel. I clutched Grandma's hand with both of mine and squeezed. Grandpa had told me that the Germans designed the tail fins to make the terrible noise ("They're a clever people. Ah yes, how clever") and that if you could hear it clearly then it was already far away. "A bomb's faster than its whistle," he'd said. "If one hits you, you'll never hear it anyway." He'd said this with a smirk and a shrug.

So this was how our days began. Trembling in the light of tiny, oil-soaked suns.

There were maybe fifty of us there underground. All were strangers except my grandparents, my mom, and my baby sister, Ana, who was a kind of stranger to me then because she was still too young to speak or walk. Most of the people, like us, had moved to the Metro because Nationalist artillery had devastated their homes. A few were farmers from the south who'd escaped the advancing Moors and thought they'd find refuge in the city, the poor fools.

The only men with us were elderly, except for one middle-aged peasant with clubbed feet. The rest, like my dad, had been swept into the militia. He was a leatherworker who'd made wallets and handbags, until that July when union leaders had ordered him to report to headquarters. They issued him a rifle and sent him to the barracks. I'd seen him just three times in five months, and not once since the shell had ripped through our roof. Sometimes, when Grandma wasn't using it, I rubbed my cheek against her burlap pillow. It felt like the stubble on Dad's neck and chin.

An old man haltingly stood up from the sea of bodies and leaned against the curved, poster-covered wall. "The swine," he muttered. He jutted his chin upward. "They shall not pass!" he shouted, though he was as blind to the sky as I was.

A stretch of near calm soon followed, long enough that I thought the new day's bombs had stopped. From down the dark platform came echoed footsteps and the quivering, staccato breaths of someone who'd been bawling. The orange light first revealed my mom's face, which had the sallow, chapped look of an apple just before decay. She was twenty-eight. Whenever Ana awoke crying, my mom would scoop her up and walk her away from everyone, pacing down near the shadowy vestibule.

Ana squirmed in her arms. Her once soft, round cheeks—now tear-streaked—had begun to sink recently so that she seemed, at times, more like a shrunken adult than a baby. Mom approached all of us and then slumped against the curved wall, not unlike the old man, before unbuttoning her blouse and lowering Ana to her breast. Ana screamed, twisting away as my mom palmed the breast and moved the nipple over Ana's lips. That there were dozens of us who might witness her nursing meant nothing anymore. In the daytime? Perhaps. On the street, under the sun? Sure. There were still times for modesty.

But in the dark, during the bombs, this was a different place—all of our faces blackened with dirt and our noses filled with the scents of urine and excrement. We scraped strange, cold stew from tin pots. Drank dirty water from Rioja bottles. Dug fingernails into our scabies and ringworm.

Even then, as my mom tucked her breast back under her blouse, there was a child my age in the fetal position, its back to me, who'd kicked away its blankets and was naked from the waist down. I couldn't tell if it was a boy or a girl.

Beyond the child, the train tracks disappeared into the black mouth of the tunnel. The trains still ran, though not at night, and I wondered how far the tunnel stretched. Maybe to France. Maybe to the sea. Dad was fighting just a few kilometers away, his unit supporting an International Brigade in the University City. I didn't comprehend the actual distance until Grandpa explained that, were there no barricades or checkpoints, we could have walked there in half an hour.

In the middle of the night, when even anxious mothers slept, I probably could have stolen a lamp, shimmied down to the tracks, and hiked into the darkness. I didn't understand the map of the city, but I believed the line might lead to the university buildings, to a place a few kilometers beyond, where I could stare straight up and know that my dad slept on a patch of earth above me.

Mom remained against the wall, bouncing Ana slightly in her arms, singing, I assumed, a lullaby into her ear. I wondered if it was one she'd sung to me or if she'd chosen new songs for a new child.

Posters stretched in both directions beside her, plastered so tightly together that they hid most of the white wall tile. Because of the tunnel's curvature the posters leered over us. They were like the ones on storefronts, signposts, and alleyways throughout the city. The clenched fist of the Republic. *They shall not pass!* A trade union image of a winged man rising to the sky to slay bombers. Another with close-up photographs of eight dead children. *Killed by rebel bombs in Madrid! Innocent victims of the enemies of Spain!*

One showed militiamen in blue overalls and side caps firing their guns from behind an outcrop. One lay dead, sprawled backward, blood pooling onto the dirt. A woman in the same blue uniform knelt above him, aiming with her right eye closed, a rifle stock braced against her chest. Smoke poured from the barrel. A thin beam of fire ran off the edge of the poster, toward an enemy I couldn't see but assumed she'd shot dead.

The bombs returned. They struck closer now, their screams shorter and the blasts a series of quick, terrible concussions that made one of the lamps swing, fall, and smash onto the platform. I shrieked and tucked myself into Grandma's body as the glass shattered into a puddle of flame. Two boys ran over with blankets and swatted at it till it choked and died.

For a while I kept still, a tear running down my nose and hanging there on the tip. Grandma's eyes squeezed tightly in an asterisk of creases. She kept murmuring something—the rosary perhaps, though we were at war with the church. I sat up again to check on Grandpa. He had reclined and gone back to sleep, his chest rising and falling, the extinguished cigarette still lodged in his lips.

Soon the bombs became more distant. I rolled back to my own little space of floor, feeling hollow in my chest and stomach and arms. It was more than just hunger and more than the wrung-out sensation that follows crying. It was closer to the fever dreams I'd had that past spring, when I'd seemed to float above my bed.

I removed a torn paper sack from underneath my blanket and poured out the contents. They sounded almost musical even as they tinkled onto the concrete: eight piano keys, five white and three black. I arranged them in order on the ground—from C up to G—and then leaned over them, hands arched and fingers curled the way Grandma had first taught me. She'd once made me hold two oranges over our decrepit piano, which my dad had salvaged from a bankrupt nightclub. But I'd found these keys amid the burned-out husk of a baby grand that lay, inexplicably, in the middle of the Gran Vía.

Once arranged, I settled in to play a simple, childish melody called "Cloud Baby." Mom had sung it to me for years, from when I was Ana's age until I was seven and had become embarrassed by it. I heard the words and notes now in my head. *There are clouds so high they caress the morning sun. There are clouds that make the purest mountain snow . . .*

A tiny lightning bolt struck my jaw, making me wince and stop to press my left hand to my left cheek. The tooth pain had started a few days earlier, for no reason I could tell. When it came to blocking out the sound of bombs, it was the only thing stronger than my imagined music. I'd told no one, convinced that Mom would make Grandpa find some pliers and pluck it free. The pain ran from my chin to my ear, lasting a minute or two, and when it receded, the relief was so sudden that the pain seemed make-believe. I leaned once more over my false piano.

When the day's bombardment finally stopped—when the lamps stopped swaying and the ceiling stopped crumbling—I gathered up my keys and dropped them into the sack.

"They shall not pass," said the man against the wall, mumbling it this time. It was dawn, yet we all curled beneath our filthy blankets again, into each other's stinking bodies, hoping for at least one more hour of sleep.

• • •

So you'll forgive me if I never take the subway. Next year—1987—it will have been twenty years since my husband, daughter, and I moved here to Chicago, and I've still never set foot in its subterranean realm. Even now, walking down Michigan Avenue, my chest tightens when I pass the gray stairwell leading down beneath the streets. And elsewhere in the city, whenever the "L" roars and clatters overhead, I stare at the sidewalk, watching the flicker of sunlight and shade until it's passed. The sour breeze from any passing train is enough to bring back those curved Metro walls, the creeping claustrophobia.

That next morning I squinted from the pale December light as Grandpa and I climbed the stairs and emerged at street level. The wind raked my face, and I clutched my collar to keep the gusts from slipping beneath my sweater. Grandpa walked with his hands deep in his coat pockets and his tweed flat cap pulled down toward his eyes. "Time to hunt and gather, eh?" He winked at me. "We'll try to make it a game. You should be playing games anyways, like other little girls. Even in this winter of shit."

Grandpa was a retired stonemason who'd cheered the rise of unions. When the war broke out in July, he'd said he'd like to kill a fascist himself, in the middle of a bullring and with the same methodical ritual. A lance behind the neck. A couple of banderillas. Then a sword between the shoulder blades, plunged right through the heart. "Or maybe I just get a gun. I don't know. But I'll do it in a bullring."

By December, however, he'd turned cynic, awaiting the eventual fall of the city. Grandpa had long since made it a game. He smiled unhappily when reading of Franco's advances. He chuckled and shook his head while squatting on our cold platform, boiling coffee with lumps of candles. And at night he slept soundly, never rolling over or flinching until the bombs arrived at dawn.

The two of us headed down the Gran Vía, taking our ration card to the trade union headquarters for a loaf of bread. The rest of the family remained in the Metro. Grandma washed clothes in a tin bucket of gray water. She'd traded an egg to a jaundiced old man for his half-used bar of soap. Ana had fallen asleep in my mom's arms just as the rest of us underground had awoken. The two of them had been fused together since the fighting began. Mom had suffered three miscarriages in the eight years between my birth and Ana's. She used to cling to me that same way, especially after the failed pregnancies. Walking me to and from school each day. Watching me from the rocking chair until I fell asleep at night. But now she allowed me to accompany Grandpa on these errands. He'd laid out the case beforehand, saying how the dangers of random daytime shelling were infinitesimal compared to the dangers of darkness, bacteria, and stagnant air in the tunnel. But she'd barely needed convincing, merely nodding and stroking Ana's hair while he'd talked.

A tram rumbled past us, its windows filled with faces. It was almost impossible to imagine people still having jobs, commuting past trucks crammed with troops headed for the front. Past overturned automobiles. Past gaping urban craters where exposed cables dangled like ripped tree roots.

Another tram passed. It was the first time I'd seen a woman as conductor, though that soon became ordinary because—like bread and coal and clean water—we had a depleted supply of men.

Grandpa stopped abruptly on the sidewalk to fish a newspaper out of a garbage can. He checked the date. "It's today's," he said. Then he rifled through its crinkled pages, looking for announcements about new food shipments. With our ration cards we could get our hands on some staples: rice, beans, coffee, canned milk, a little sugar. And once a week some fish and a hunk of cheese. The black market had gouged prices. Some people faked illness for extra supplies. When Grandpa scoured the newspaper like this, he was looking for ads about meat, which he craved like tobacco and wine.

Disappointed, he folded the paper under his arm. "The good news," he said, "is that we still have the factories. The bad news, of course, is that Franco has the farms."

"We could always eat smokestacks," I said.

I'd heard him make this joke before, but it startled him to hear it come from my mouth. After a pause, a huge grin spread over his face, and he patted me on the cheek with his calloused hand. "I bet they're delicious," he said. "A little salt. A little olive oil. You've got a meal."

We continued walking the Gran Vía. As grim as things below had become, my throat always tightened when I scanned the aboveground panorama. White buildings torn in half like soldiers themselves, their bricks ripped off, their splintered guts spilled out. They reminded me of my pine dollhouse, which my dad had bought second-hand and restored for my fifth birthday. If I'd have dropped it from a balcony, it would have exploded this same way. The street seemed filled with giant, disintegrated dollhouses.

"Does the whole city look like this?" I asked.

"Oh, no." Grandpa smirked. "No, no, no." He pointed vaguely east. "Salamanca? Untouched. And you know why? It's teeming with Franco supporters. Aficionados of fascism. They're the ones hurling firebombs from building tops when the airplanes come." He gestured to the east again, this time cursing them with his hand made into the sign of the horns.

Amid the motor traffic were peasants—streams of them, with donkeys pulling carts piled with trunks, mattresses, and children. The city had barred horses from the streets a few years earlier, but it couldn't stop the flood of animals now brought in by refugees. Other than stray cats and dogs, I rarely saw animals, and though I wanted to approach and pet the donkeys, the peasants' desperate faces kept me away.

Though only a few blocks' walk, we passed destruction everywhere on our way to the breadline. Half the stores were boarded up, and out front of many others the shopkeepers swept up broken glass. Charred fire escapes dangled from apartment walls. Boys played hide-and-seek among piles of rubble. And in the middle of the street lay half a mannequin—just the waist and legs of a naked plaster woman. I didn't even see a clothier nearby.

Shrapnel had pockmarked nearly every building in some way, which made our discovery all the more miraculous. At the corner stood Optical America, and in its window stretched a display of eyeglasses, the delicate lenses of every pair still flawless. If I'd been a rich woman instead of a dirt-streaked girl, I'd have bought every one of them and locked them in a strongbox. Reflecting that weak December sunlight, they resembled jewels or precious metals. Too rare to actually exist.

The queue for bread was surprisingly short, though Grandpa fidgeted with his hat in his hands for most of the wait, uncomfortable, it seemed, with being the only man in line. He made me hand them the card and hold the bread. The top of the loaf was perforated with the UGT stamp for the General Union of Workers. And though it quickly cooled in the brisk air, it had come fresh from the oven and managed to warm my hands for at least a little while.

We had no interest in immediately returning to the dank tunnel so we wandered the streets for about an hour, surveying the damage but also looking for anything familiar and unchanged. We walked down Calle Montera to the Puerta del Sol, where a group of girls about my age laughed and spun tops beneath an acacia tree. Bookstalls sold everything from comics to magazines about movie stars. And one vendor still sold lottery tickets, promising riches to those of us with nothing but bread.

Even so, much had changed. Gone were the men who'd sold the treats Dad used to buy me: popcorn and carobs and sunflower seeds. Instead, old women spread their wares out over the pavement. Russian-style fur hats emblazoned with red stars. Hammer-and-sickle badges. The red-and-black hats of the anarchists. Nearby, shoeblacks shined the boots of militiamen. A little boy with a broken broom handle aimed it at the sky, making bullet and explosion sounds.

Grandpa and I wandered east, to the Prado, where we watched volunteers remove painting after painting and load them onto trucks. The art was escaping to Valencia, the way the government had one month earlier.

A few blocks farther we paused at the edge of Buen Retiro Park, where a vast flock of sheep grazed alongside rumbling buses and honking automobiles. Grandpa shook his head. "Where am I, Rosario? Have I finally gone senile, or can you see these things, too?"

I saw everything. I just didn't know, sometimes, how to feel about it. Grandpa talked about fascism and communism. How people all over the world were watching. Some had come to fight for us and some to fight against. I didn't know what that meant or where all these people actually were. I thought of them as living in the sky, like the bombers but also like ghosts. Invisible angels and invisible demons. I wondered if my dad saw them.

When he was last home on a forty-eight-hour leave, he'd curled his arm around my neck, pulled me to his chest, and kissed the top of my head. "When I'm gone," he'd said, "Grandpa's in charge. But you're our second lieutenant." And a warmth as if from a tiny hearth had grown in my stomach and spread through my body. I smiled and hugged him back and kept smiling after he'd left the room. But a month later, standing amid sheep and traffic and low, gray skies, that statement cast more shadow than warmth. I couldn't have explained it then, but I'd begun sensing awful new truths. If I was our number two, it was only because Grandma was lost to fear and Mom was lost to Ana. And if Grandpa was our leader, then we were no different than those grazing sheep, scrounging in circles, heads down, on an urban island.

Eventually he and I ambled back to the Metro, but not before he paused outside of a café near the Telefónica Building. He nudged me with his elbow and pointed at the window. "What do you see in there, Rosario?"

I cupped my hands to the glass, my breath fogging it before I got a good look.

"See the clothes they're wearing?" asked Grandpa. "The slick hair? Those are journalists. French and English and American. They're here every day, drinking beer and eating steak. You know why they're in Madrid?" He leaned forward and lowered his voice. "To write about us."

I stepped away from the window. The smell of the food triggered a fresh hunger, and I wanted to get back to our family with at least our loaf of cold bread.

Grandpa lay his hand on my shoulder as we walked on. "You know all those bedtime stories you've always heard? Did you ever make-believe you were one of the characters? Because that's what's happening right now. You are a character to those men. They're telling *your* story. Or they think they are. And when they're finished, guess what? They're getting the hell out of here."

As a nine-year-old these words struck me terribly, though not the way you might think. I took them to mean that these men were literally writing about *me* somehow, and in the weeks to come I felt like everything I did was being watched, recorded, and would be told to the outside world. And the whole time I wondered, what was there to say about me? I was a girl in a tunnel whose dad was a hero. Write about him. Write about the other soldiers. But me? I lived underground. Like a mole, though not as blind.

Perhaps I'm just like those reporters. It took decades, but eventually I got out as well. My husband accepted the position at Northwestern, to teach Iberian literature, and we arrived in July 1967 knowing little about the city. Franco did not rule here; that was enough.

And we had no idea the mayor was to unveil a new fifty-foot Picasso sculpture just weeks later, but we took a bus that day from Evanston into downtown and then spilled out into Daley Plaza with thousands of others. I remember the gasp through the crowd when the enormous sheet of blue-green fabric fell away. My daughter, who was eleven at the time, said the figure looked like an insect. But I saw something else: a ruined giant, formed by the twisted remains of *Guernica*.

Grandpa and I returned that day with the bread, which all of us ate with tins of herring, and that night we slept until the bombs returned again. "Please, God," said Grandpa, "don't let them hit the brewery."

They fell in a distant part of the city and lasted for so short a time that I never even set up my piano keys. Afterward, none of us felt tired except for Ana, who'd slept right through the action. The rest of us shifted uncomfortably under our blankets. Grandma's hands began to tremble. At first they seemed victim of only a mild palsy but soon nearly took flight, shaking so much that her arms quivered at her sides. She squeezed her eyes shut, sat on her palms, and a few minutes later the hands fell still.

Later that night we huddled in a tight circle to keep warm. In the dark Metro, while most of the people fell back to sleep, Grandpa quietly read aloud from the newspaper he'd found in the garbage can. My stomach dropped when I recalled the journalists in the café, but I said nothing and tried to listen.

We always enjoyed hearing what films the cinemas were showing. Of the few remaining open, most had turned to Russian propaganda pictures. *Battleship Potemkin*, that sort of thing. But a couple still featured American movies so long as the stars were known sympathizers of the Republic. Bette Davis in *Special Agent*. *Love on the Run* with Joan Crawford. Anything with Errol Flynn.

Mom gently lay Ana in a nest of blankets and then sat behind me, brushing my hair while Grandpa continued reading. Grandma told him not to read stories about the war, which left little else besides weather reports. He started reading how the Moors were checking the mouths of dead villagers, searching for gold-capped teeth, which they'd smash out with their rifle butts. You'd have thought Grandma had been electrocuted.

She shoved her open hand against his face. "In front of a child! Are you deranged? There aren't enough nightmares for real you need to read nightmares for fun?"

She gave him a pass when a later war story bordered on—if not comedy—at least the absurd. Our troops had surrounded Nationalists trapped in a mountain monastery near Andújar and the only way the enemy could supply them was to airdrop live turkeys burdened with provisions. The turkeys thrashed their wings, dying on impact, of course, but slowing just enough to protect the supplies. *"It is believed,"* Grandpa read, *"that the turkeys' own meat was still edible when cooked on a spit."*

We all laughed. The thought of those frantic wings! And the rebels, resorting to such primitive methods! But when we quieted down, my mom spoke. She'd been vigorously brushing my hair so that it hurt, in a good way, but then suddenly stopped. "The poor birds," she said.

Grandpa scoffed and waved her words away. "They were fascists of the animal kingdom." He smiled. "Aiding and abetting the enemy."

I expected him to say something about dead women, dead children. Hold his hands out to the side and pretend to weigh the comparative tragedy like a scale. But he stopped teasing, and Mom soon resumed work on my hair. I stayed silent, my head rhythmically tipping backward with the tug of the brush. I closed my eyes, relishing the sensation.

Grandpa gathered the pages of the newspaper, folding it back into its original form, and stared at the front page. "There are things you women should read on your own time. About what's happening in the University City."

When he said "you women" he meant the adults. And when he said "what's happening" he meant the battle that my dad helped wage.

"All right," said Grandma. "Enough."

"They're fighting for each building and each room. Using encyclopedias for sandbags."

Grandma slapped his arm. "Enough!"

I felt Mom's warm breath on the back of my neck, but she stayed quiet.

Grandpa tapped another page with his index finger. "Well, you'll approve of this. They've printed one of the speeches by La Pasionaria."

I'd seen La Pasionaria once in person. Dad had pointed her out on the street, before he'd been drafted and before the shell hit our house. She'd stepped out of a dark unmarked Cadillac, a breeze catching her black dress so that it unfurled like a muleta. She had the sturdy frame of a peasant but with that brightness of eye that suggested great intellect. Flanked by guards, she strode toward the doorway of some government building and disappeared. My dad raised his fist in salute.

"This is from July," said Grandpa. He cleared his throat and read. After a few lines he paused, took a deep breath, and continued. *"The whole country is shocked by the actions of these villains. They want with fire and sword to turn democratic Spain, the Spain of the people, into a hell of terrorism and torture. But they shall not pass."*

He struggled to keep his voice lowered in the dark tunnel.

"Young men and women, sound the alarm. Rise and join the battle."

The newspaper trembled. Grandpa's hands shook, though differently than Grandma's.

"Women, heroic women of the people. Remember the heroism of the Asturian women. Fight alongside the men to defend the bread and tranquility of your threatened children. Soldiers, sons of the people. Stand firm, as one man, beside the government, beside the workers, beside the People's Front, your fathers, your brothers and comrades."

In 1975, when Franco finally died, I found the entire speech in a book and copied it down on lined paper. With my husband and daughter both out running errands, I read it aloud to myself, in front of the bathroom mirror of my Evanston home, projecting my voice as if a crowd of thousands fanned out before me. And I did that every year on the anniversary of Franco's death for about five years before stopping for some reason. Partly I did it to celebrate the new Spain. But partly I did it to recreate that feeling I had when I was nine, hearing Grandpa read La Pasionaria's words to our small family circle.

Even as a child I understood them. They were spurs in our sides. They were a call to arms.

Buses of two kinds rumbled down the Gran Vía. The first were double-deckers filled with militia—men in blue overalls and caps, each with a white blanket rolled over his shoulder. People on the street raised their fists, shouting, *"¡Salud! ¡Salud!"* as the soldiers returned the gesture.

"Rosario."

The other buses teemed with women and children. The word *Evacuation* loomed across the windshields in huge black letters. Few of these people spoke.

"Rosario! Over here."

Grandpa sat on a sidewalk bench, waving me over. He held a fluttering newspaper—the new day's paper—which he'd found in the street, its pages only faintly smeared with horseshit. I approached and stood over him, leaning on his shoulder for balance. Between the roaring buses, my poor night's sleep, and the coffee Grandma had made me an hour before, my whole body seemed to vibrate like a tuning fork.

Grandpa's eyes had grown wide. He jabbed the page with his finger and showed me an advertisement:

WE ARE HAPPY TO REPORT THE SLAUGHTER OF 350 COWS AND
1000 SHEEP.
TODAY THERE WILL BE MEAT IN ABUNDANCE.

"That's a kilometer north," he said. "I'm going to get us some beef. You stand in line for the potatoes." He handed me our voucher. "You know the way."

My stomach swooped. We'd never separated before. I shook my head. "I'll go with you. Then we'll get the potatoes together."

"They'll be gone by then." Grandpa stood and patted me on the cheek. "You'll be fine. You're a big girl. And I'm sick of standing in food lines with all of those women. It's widow's work."

"But you're *going* to a food line," I said.

"It's different with meat." He held his hand flat out in front of him. "You see that?" His hand trembled but not like Grandma's last night and not even like his own while he'd read the speech. "I also need some medicine. For that." He winked at me.

I didn't know what he meant; I didn't know he was ill.

"Where are we meeting?" I asked. I wanted to hide my fear so I added, "If I show up by myself, Mom will kill me."

"And your grandmother will kill *me*." Grandpa pointed over his shoulder, to the Telefónica Building, which was still quite new then. The first European skyscraper. An irresistible target for bombers. "Be back at nine. Check the clock on the tower. We'll meet right back here and return together."

I swear to you, the moment he left my tooth began hurting—only dully, but enough. I headed west along the street. I wanted to get the potatoes and get back to where I could at least see the Metro stairs. I wouldn't really be alone if I could see the path to my family.

A block farther ahead lay a dead horse beside a toppled cart. I saw no blood and couldn't tell if it had died from a bomb or something else. A peasant stood weeping over the horse while a nearby policeman looked up and down the street, maybe hoping for help with the enormous corpse. Hungry dogs would circle it shortly. Women, too, who'd strip the carcass with kitchen knives and mix the meat with lentil soup. Widow's work.

A half hour later I slung our sack of potatoes over my shoulder and lugged it back toward the Telefónica Building, where the clock read eight thirty. I set the sack down, leaned against the wall of a bombed-out pharmacy, and took a deep breath. The stairs to the Metro lay about a hundred meters off. If anything were to happen now, like a Nationalist artillery potshot, I could make it safely down to the others. Even if Mom still clung to Ana, I'd find refuge in Grandma.

I ran my fingernail along the brick wall, picking at a bullet hole while raising my closed eyelids to the sun. My tooth pain had ebbed; my vibrations had stilled. If a journalist were writing about me now—a photographer putting me into focus—let him write. I sort of posed against the wall, aware of how I might look to someone, like the actress playing the spy, beautiful and strong. The blue sky brought an illusion of tranquility the way winter sunlight brought one of warmth. For a while, before our air defenses had strengthened, we'd been afraid of blue skies. But at moments like this even the sun seemed on our side. It was easy to heed La Pasionaria's call. I could rout Franco's forces right alongside my dad.

A half-hour wait to a nine-year-old was no different then than it is now. I itched to move. When two young militiawomen ambled past me, I barely hesitated before following them down the sidewalk.

They appeared to be eighteen, nineteen years old. They wore crisp overalls and cartridge pouches that bounced on their hips as they walked. Their short hair was oiled and parted beneath their caps. Struggling with the potatoes, I marched in their wake, drawing close behind them. One had penciled eyebrows. The other smoked a cigarette, blowing smoke from her nose.

I wanted to know their destination. I wanted to see others like them. Militia units were often organized by kind. A battalion of teachers. A battalion of barbers. There was even one made of footballers and matadors. I suppose I hoped that, by following these two, I'd find a battalion made entirely of women—young and modern and armed to the teeth.

They walked for ten minutes, oblivious to the citizens—elderly, especially—who craned their necks and stared. I struggled to keep up, the potato sack chafing my shoulders, until they paused just outside the Plaza Mayor. White leaflets lay scattered about the street and sidewalk. More rested on rooftops and in trees. The militiawoman with the cigarette bent down, picked one up, and read it. Then she removed the cigarette from her lips and touched it to the paper, producing a thin tendril of smoke.

A tram approached, and the woman let the leaflet float to the ground as she and her friend ran off to catch their ride. They climbed aboard, sat toward the front, and then disappeared among the morning traffic. I strode to where they'd stood and picked up the same leaflet. A burn mark—small and black and perfectly round—punctuated the end of the sheet's lone sentence:

UNLESS THE CITY SURRENDERS BY MIDNIGHT
THE BOMBARDMENTS WILL BEGIN IN EARNEST.

Nationalist airplanes must have dropped them that night. I folded the leaflet and thrust it in my pocket to show Grandpa, and the thought of him made me realize how far I'd wandered from the Telefónica Building. I'd lost track of time and began jogging back the way I'd come, my shoulders burning, potatoes thumping against my back.

Looking for a shortcut, I turned down a narrow backstreet lined with cramped apartments. Winter-naked plane trees bordered the curb. Their mottled bark reminded me of blistered skin, and though similar trees lined prestigious thoroughfares across Madrid, I'd always found them ugly.

I'd barely stepped onto this street when the witch whistle cut through the sky. We humans have reflexes, like any other animal. Mine dropped me to my knees at the first instant of sound. The sickening noise resonated between the buildings, and I curled into myself, hands over head, the potatoes falling and rolling in all directions. Eyes closed, teeth gnashing, I waited for the bomb that would butcher me.

The sound stopped, replaced by a scream. One story above me, a graying woman in a housedress and apron shoved open her balcony doors. The scream was a man's, gushing out of the darkened space behind her—a horrifying wail that lasted for several seconds, stopped for breath, and then returned again.

"You goddamned monster," muttered the woman, brandishing a mop like one would a sword. She reached over the balcony railing and began swiping the mop at a tree that grew right alongside her building. After a few thrashes she flushed a bird from the branches—a brilliant blue parrot. It launched upward in a commotion of feathers before settling into a graceful circle overhead. Then it rose—camouflaged against the sky—and flew out of sight over the rooftops.

The man inside continued screaming. "It's all right, Mateo," said the woman, turning toward the doorway. "She's gone again."

The woman glanced down and noticed me there on the street, shambling on my hands and knees, gathering up potatoes. "Are you okay?" she asked.

I met her gaze briefly and nodded. The screaming stopped.

The woman set her mop down, held the railing with both hands, and peered down at me, lowering her voice as if in conspiracy. "That thing's been stalking our neighborhood for days. I don't know if she was a pet or escaped from the zoo. Either way, I'm going to assassinate her."

I only half listened. A part of me still expected the silver glint of bombers overhead.

"Sounds like the real thing, doesn't it?" said the woman. "I guess if they can talk like humans, they can talk like bombs. Mateo can't tell the difference."

"Who's he?" I asked, climbing to my feet.

"My poor son. The one you heard. He's back from the front with shrapnel wounds." She shrugged. "They're not bad. They're not the real harm. You heard the real harm." She shook her head and stared at the tree. "Every night he goes crazy at the sound of bombs. And now, in the daytime, we have this. A blue devil, torturing him with a trick. I've asked the police, I've asked passing soldiers, 'Please! Will you shoot this bird?' They won't do it. I don't know why."

I took a deep breath, filling my lungs with that pure oxygen of relief.

"I'm going to get seed and make a trap," said the woman, smiling faintly. "Then pluck her and boil her and feed her to my son. We'll call that justice."

"Yeah," I said, and at that moment a distant bell began to peal—once, twice—before I understood. "I have to go!" I yelled, grabbing the sack, abandoning the woman, and charging down the backstreet toward the Gran Vía. The bell chimed nine times, but even after the final strike a resonance wavered in the air behind it. Like a comet's tail. A ghost of sound.

I continue down Michigan Avenue—an American Gran Vía—to meet my daughter for lunch. I'm around the same age now as Grandma was then, although the New World has kept me young by comparison. I have mostly American problems these days. My husband used up all the hot water for the shower. I have a hard time finding good asparagus at the grocer.

I pass the Wrigley Building—that early skyscraper with its glazed terracotta facade, its stoic clock tower. And believe me when I say that it's not merely a sibling of the Telefónica Building but a fraternal twin. From the corner of my eye it's nearly identical. And even with a lifetime between the me of now and the me of then, I can so easily convince myself that it's a target, that the firebombs are imminent.

Fifty years is a long time, though some memories are so intense they're like focused sunlight through a magnifying glass. My daughter did that as a girl—burn small, smoking holes into gum wrappers and leaves. Whenever I hear the word *concentrate* I think of it just like that. Memory sharpened to a thin blade of fire.

Back in the tunnel, the day's last train blurred past. A sleeping man near the platform edge tucked in his legs, sensing the hundreds of tons rushing just past his feet. I sat cross-legged, wrapped in a blanket, my half-frozen hands floating just above my piano keys.

The tooth pain had returned, spreading deep into my jaw and down the left side of my neck. Sometimes it pulsed like a heartbeat, and sometimes it rolled in and out like waves. At its crest, I clenched my teeth and squeezed my eyes shut, waiting for it to pass. I was ready to tell Grandpa and have him wrench it free, but I wanted to wait until tomorrow. In a few hours the clocks would read midnight—the deadline that Franco had put in the flyer. I'd confess my pain in the morning.

I couldn't concentrate enough to play imaginary songs. I repeated an exercise Grandma had taught me, pecking at a key like a hen biting grain. Grandma and Mom sat over by the curved, poster-covered wall, peeling potatoes with dull paring knives.

There was, of course, no meat. Grandpa had arrived that morning to find the number of slaughtered animals just a fraction of that which had been announced. Any meat once available had been snatched up already. He'd spent much of the day sleeping and now loitered alone down at the darkened vestibule near the stairs. As for Ana, she slept beside me. Sometimes her eyes moved beneath their lids. As she dreamed, they looked like tadpoles swimming just below the surface of a pond.

Grandpa emerged from the darkened end of the tunnel, teetering on his feet as he approached me. "Are you okay?" I asked. I still wondered if he were ill. "Is your hand all right?"

He smiled and stretched the hand flat out before him: still as stone. "All better," he said with a wink. "Got medicine. Good medicine." He reached under his coat and removed a bottle with a brown label that I couldn't read or understand. A small amount of clear liquid swirled along the bottom.

I nodded, but at that moment a bolt of pain sent me lurching forward and cupping my hand around my jaw.

"What's the matter?" asked Grandpa. He knelt down beside me and Ana.

"My tooth."

"Here," he said, uncapping the bottle. "You're going to sip this and hold it in your mouth so that it washes all around your hurt tooth." He tilted it toward me. "Don't swallow, all right? You do not want to swallow. It will burn, but you will hold it there in your mouth for a few seconds until the medicine starts to work."

I glanced at Mom. She and Grandma sat and peeled in their own world of talk. She hadn't brushed my hair yet tonight.

Grandpa poured the liquid into my mouth, where it collected against the back of my cheek and burned my tongue. "Just a few more seconds."

I nodded, my eyes watering.

"Now spit it back in here," said Grandpa. He pressed the bottle against my lips and I coughed it back into the glass. "Good," he said. "It feels numb, no? It feels better?"

I nodded. It did feel better. My whole mouth seemed to float away from my face. Grandpa smiled. Then he tipped the bottle to his own mouth and drank what remained.

"How dare you!" yelled Grandma. I hadn't seen her approach, but she stood over Grandpa now, slapping his head repeatedly. "Where did you get that?"

He smiled, oblivious, it seemed, to her strikes. "I wandered by the Hotel Gaylord," he said, "where the Russian officers stay. There was an open truck and many bottles. They won't miss one or two."

Grandma smacked him again. "You act so brave, like some bullfighter. But you're only bolstered with booze." She turned her back on him and returned to her work. She hadn't seen me take my sip.

I lay down beside the piano keys, enjoying the relief, and immediately fell asleep without meaning to. I awoke, as always, to the bombs, though this time the very air in the tunnel felt different. I hadn't slept long; it was nowhere near morning. The tunnel shook in a continual quake, the explosions right overhead, erupting in a tower of sound. Large tile fragments fell from the ceiling and smashed on the concrete. The oil lamps flickered. An old man rushed past me down the platform. That's when I noticed the eerie green light pouring from the street level down the stairwell. The man ascended the steps and returned seconds later. "They're torching us! Everything's burning with green fire!"

The newspapers spoke later of calcium bombs, which the planes used like spotlights to illuminate their targets. They'd unleashed a new weapon. The green soon turned red as incendiary bombs turned the streets into tributaries of fire. Everyone underground instinctively pushed deeper into the tunnel, away from the stairwell. My mom swooped in and snatched Ana up off the floor. Fleeing to the extent that they could, she and Ana were absorbed by the refugee mass. I sat there, watching them, waiting for Mom to turn around and check on me—to at least motion for me to follow. But I'd already lost sight of her.

Grandma was catatonic. She sat with her head swiveling, her mouth moving but making no sound. Grandpa tried to pull her up, but he stumbled on his own precarious legs, too drunk to function. I crawled over to Grandma, shoved my shoulder under her armpit, and lifted until the muscles in my legs burned. With both of us on our feet, we stumbled toward the panicked crush of the others.

I don't know how long the attack lasted. If I had to guess—a gun to my head, if Franco had put his own sidearm to my temple—I'd have said two or three hours. But it may have been minutes. They may have bombed all night. The fire spread so rapidly that we couldn't tell if it still rained from the sky or had simply fed itself into a monster.

I sat against the wall, hugging my knees to my chest, under a strata of collective shrieking and weeping. I couldn't see Mom or Ana or Grandma. Grandpa sat beside me, staring at the floor, neither awake nor unconscious.

Sometime a little before dawn, when a few of the older boys got up to investigate, I stood and followed, and no one told me not to. A sweltering orange light illuminated the stairwell so that it seemed we were approaching the firebox of some enormous boiler. We climbed the stairs, into a winter night of blazing heat. It was impossible to tell where buildings began and ended because entire city blocks were consumed by sheets of fire. Crazed silhouettes staggered down the street, past automobile carcasses, swatting at flames with shovels and rugs. A man threw his coat over a little boy whose shirtsleeve had caught fire. In the distance, a bucket brigade had formed to save the Telefónica Building.

Swarms of families had poured onto the streets, abandoning their homes with a few possessions gathered in their arms. A little girl with a doll. A man with a stack of books. An old woman held a caged canary. I stepped deeper into the chaos. Along the curb lay a pile of four dead women. Farther down the sidewalk, men had spread out blankets and begun to lay bodies side by side.

Chicago refers to its Great Fire, but its witnesses have long since passed, making it history. Making it a fairy tale. Mrs. O'Leary and her mythic cow. But I've seen what happens when a city's set aflame. Franco taught the godless children of the Republic all about the church by giving us its Sunday school version of Hell. Walls of fire pressed in on both sides. Ahead, somewhere, lay the University City, where an inferno between us now made the distance between my dad and me seem unfathomable.

And behind me? Did a hand clasp my shoulder? Did a voice shout my name? I stood there, dumbstruck by ruination, expecting at any moment for my mom or my grandpa or just some stranger from the Metro to emerge, seek me out, and drag me back to safety.

But no one did. I stared until my eyes burned—as if staring at the sun—and then returned to the tunnel myself, seeing the afterimage of fire with each blink in the darkness.

The sun itself rose about an hour later, and those of us in the tunnel still strong enough to help climbed the stairs and took to the streets. Grandpa and I joined them. The aftermath revealed an urban massacre: blackened cement, smoldering brick. A city cremated.

The dead still lay on blankets along the sidewalk though they'd multiplied terribly, shoulder to shoulder for a half block, some of them tagged for identification. The living didn't look much different. Many huddled half asleep in the doorways of the less-damaged buildings. The rest of them managed to work. With stained faces and tattered clothes, women and children formed a human chain to remove debris, passing brick after brick down the serpentine line. Others used the wreckage to build roadblocks and fortifications. There was the sense that Nationalist tanks would roll in any minute. Elderly men in berets tore cobblestones from the street with pickaxes or bare hands. Little boys hauled broken concrete in soapbox carts.

I made my way toward the human chain. "Let's go over here," I ordered Grandpa. I hadn't slept all night but felt alert and determined.

"No, no," he said. "Rosario."

I looked back over my shoulder.

Grandpa closed his eyes, sighed, and gestured me toward him with his index finger. "That won't feed you, will it?"

I stopped. "What?"

"Do those women have water to share? You going to fill your belly with brick?" He approached and lay his hand on my shoulder. "What little food this city possessed is now burnt, buried, or being hoarded as we speak. Let's find what we can."

He turned and walked in the other direction, and I'm ashamed to say I followed.

But we didn't get far. Most of the roadways were blocked by either collapsed buildings, legions of workers, or a crush of wanderers fleeing the city center. People in the throng began to fear our very gathering. "They'll be back soon, and they'll aim for the crowds!"

We edged along the Puerta del Sol, Grandpa scanning the area, though I had no idea exactly what he hoped to find. He acted as if we might stumble upon crates of ripe oranges or turn a corner to discover some forgotten trove of pork. And all the while we flowed down the street in a current of human commotion, everyone equally desperate for shelter and food.

The crowd bottlenecked at one point, and people pressed and fell into one another. Grandpa called back to me as we started to separate. "Hold onto me, Rosario!" I reached between bodies and hooked two fingers into his back pocket, and we traveled onward like that, toward our nowhere destination, to our nothing goal.

Several minutes passed with this thread of connection between us. So many men and women pressed against him that he never detected the absence of my touch. I don't know how far he traveled before realizing I was gone. But amid the sirens and the shouting and the city's great endeavor to conquer the fire, I gently released my grip, lifting my fingers out of Grandpa's pocket and watching him disappear ahead of me as the crowd sent us in separate directions.

I could have worked the human chain like the women. I could have dug up cobbles like the men. When I shoved free from the crowd, stumbling into an alleyway, I didn't know what I planned on doing.

A soldier sprinted past me, and in the blur of his passing he resembled my dad just enough to make my empty stomach clench. I bent over and began retching. I was certain Dad was dead. There was no way he could have survived the night. All of the practice I'd had imagining him—and imagining me walking through tunnels to find him—allowed for a perfectly clear picture of him now. He lay in a trench, his skin blistered and black, tagged like those bodies that stretched down the curb.

I was wrong. My dad had actually survived the onslaught, though it would be days until we would learn this. In fact, he survived the entire war, dying instead nine years later in an auto accident near Segovia. But at that moment I knew next to nothing. I merely *saw* everything. I simply *felt* a great deal as I drifted down the alleyway, heading west, as aimless as when I'd been latched onto Grandpa.

The alleyway—quiet in comparison to the rest of the world—crossed an avenue before continuing on. I followed it farther, its cold, shadowy route like some narrow stream cutting through the city. And that's when—ahead and above, alighting on a fire-escape clothesline—the parrot appeared.

I reacted first to its color. Among the ash and soot and the alleyway's garbage, its blue feathers looked obscene—rare, like those untouched eyeglasses I'd discovered—but also gratuitous, especially on that morning.

The parrot shrieked. Like before, the sound was not animal nor human but utterly mechanical. The witch whistle. A bomb splitting the sky. I covered my ears, and when it fell silent the parrot briefly looked at me and cocked its head before taking flight. The goddamned thing might have winked.

It should have been dead, drowned in liquid fire. Every one of my senses said it was unnatural. But I followed it around the next corner and found myself on the same quiet backstreet as yesterday. The mottled plane trees. The apartments with their balconies. I remembered the woman and especially her son. I bent over again and retched.

The parrot settled into one of the trees, and I slowly approached, holding my stomach, scanning the ground for potential weapons. If the soldiers wouldn't shoot it, then I'd rise and join the battle. I picked up a chunk of brick, stood beneath the branches, and launched it. I missed and the bird barely flinched. I found a rock and tossed that. Another rock. A piece of scrap metal.

It witch-whistled again. The blue devil's call.

"Shut up!" I screamed. A searing pain ran from my jaw up to my skull.

The parrot fluttered to the next tree and made the sound once more.

"Shut *up!*" I strode to that tree, found the perfect round stone, and when I threw it my shoulder burst into pain. The stone sailed past. The parrot again took flight.

Did the journalists witness this? Were they watching and taking notes? I'd have loved the next day to have been in the tunnel, to have had Grandpa reading us articles from the newspaper and to hear him tell of a girl trying to kill some escaped mimic. I'd have given anything to hear Mom's reply, to know if this time she would dare say it.

"The poor bird."

Because I'd say nothing. I'd merely scoop and serve us all our evening lentil soup, which I'd flavored with the meat of my first fresh kill.

GUNPLAY

W e'd always had guns. By preschool we were lying on our bellies in the basement rec room, propped up on elbows, aiming with one eye shut at our Magic Shot Shooting Gallery. We bought wooden popguns during vacations on Mackinac, firing white thread with corks on the end. In the summer, we pointed lime-green, rocket-shaped water pistols at each other and at cousins and at those kids who lived across the street.

Our grandparents had few toys at their house, but they had this: an Astro Wild West skill-action steel bank. A little cowboy stood inches across from a brilliant silver six-shooter that was three times his size. The gun was spring-loaded and fired the black pennies we'd find in their green shag carpet. We'd shoot, and if our aim was true, the cowboy's hat would fall back, his hands would rise up in surrender, and the penny would disappear in the hollow of the bank.

By first grade we had our own six-shooters, glinting cast iron with revolving cylinders and break-barrel action, that we pulled from front pockets and aimed at our dad. Soon after, he was buying us toy firearms

made of gunmetal gray plastic that looked legit but just clicked weakly
in our small hands. Our squirt guns became more serious, too—bright
orange Colt .45s with invisible cracks, the water running down our
wrists and forearms. In the August heat, pre-pubescently sweating along
our hairlines, we'd get thirsty, stick the muzzles in our mouths, and pull
the triggers.

Sometimes there were no guns. We'd return to school or be grounded
or have to visit old aunts. So we'd improvise. We'd shoot stones from
homemade slingshots, hurl army-green water balloons, or nail two rulers
together to make swords. At restaurants we'd fish for the little sabers in
Mom's martinis, sliding the olives off and licking the gin from the plastic.

Or we'd mine the other available toys to make guns from Legos. Guns
from old Duplos. Guns from Tinker Toys and Erector Sets. We once saw a
kid at the grade-school playground holding his sister's Barbie by the torso,
bending her at the waist, and aiming with the barrel of her long, slim legs.

Third grade, fourth grade. The guns evolved. They were now more
like the ones Dad used in Vietnam—M16s and M60s. We held the
triggers down, and they rattled away on automatic, our invisible enemies
convulsing before they dropped.

We had cap guns, of course. You always carried the .45 revolver with
the paper strip caps. And I'd choose the .38 with the red eight-shot rings.
We'd smile through the sting of rising gray smoke. You'd set an entire roll
of caps on the sidewalk, and I'd lug a fieldstone over from the front-walk
landscaping. When I dropped it, the flames licked our ankles.

All guns. Every gun. Winchesters, AK-47s, and cadet military rifles.
Pump-action shotguns. Uzis and Tommy guns. Berettas with safety darts.
Key-chain Derringer flashlights. Lazer Tag blasters. Luger cigarette lighters
we'd steal from Uncle Don's pockets.

Night would fall and we'd slip inside to play with the Nintendo Zapper
that shot something invisible when we fired it at the TV. Or we'd play with
our G.I. Joe figures, arming them with their own bazookas and grenade
launchers, their thumbs sometimes snapping off when we forced the
weapons into their tiny hands.

Of course, by then, anything was a gun. A curved piece of driftwood.
A Windex bottle. The caulking gun in the toolshed. We raced electric slot
cars just so we could hold the yellow pistol-grip controllers with the black

cords dangling down our arms. Hair dryers. T squares. And as a last and humiliating resort, a gun from our own thumbs and forefingers.

Randy DeWitt's dad tried selling us a blowgun at his garage sale, but the thing left us cold. It looked like a pool cue and had no grip, no hammer, no sight. Randy tried to tell us about poison-tipped darts, but we needed shells and powder. We needed bullets.

Once—once—there were real guns. Memorial Day, 1986: Dad brought us with him to Dick Brewer's cabin up in Shelby for the old Marine get-together.

They fired everything from Remington 788s to .44 Magnums at a line of bowling pins. And then you and I were finally handed real firearms. Dad stepped toward us with a couple of .22s. He handed you the pistol and me the rifle and told us to never tell our mother. And though we missed the Mountain Dew cans we were aiming at—probably missed entire cornfields and hillsides in the distance—we'd felt the recoil and smiled away the pain and could finally say, Hell yes, we knew guns.

A little later in the day, with Dad taking a piss and getting a beer, Dick Brewer waved us over to where he stood in the field. He shushed us with a finger up against his lips and raised his gun with the other hand: a sawed-off 12 gauge he'd recently obtained. You shook your head at first, looking over your shoulder, waiting for Dad. But I shamed you in some way, and you followed my lead. We took turns shooting it, once apiece, with Dick Brewer a foot behind us, catching us under the armpits after the blast.

All of this was twenty-five, thirty years ago. I'd forgotten these things—all of the guns—until yesterday, sitting beside you at the funeral. While you stared at the carbon steel box with Dad's body inside, my gaze floated upward to the wooden crucifix above the altar.

I envisioned turning the cross sideways, clutching the transverse beam, resting the top against my shoulder, and pointing with the long post.

Imagine the firepower of such a weapon. Imagine there were a target at which to aim.

TRACKING THE JACK PINE SAVAGE

In the fathomless woodlands of northern Michigan,

there's a predator more fearsome than wolf or bear.

I should know.

I spent a boozy, bloody night in his wake.

by

Jason DuPont, writer at large

Arbuckle Magazine

Vol. 65, no. 11

H is sleeve tattoos make his skin a kind of camouflage. The blue and black inks—skulls, fangs, and Gothic scripts—overlap the way leaves do, the way pine needles do, so that when the daybreak sun cuts through the trees he almost disappears on the trail ahead of me, amid the latticework of sun and shade.

His name is Donnie Sarver and he just might be marching me to my death. I think I've angered him. I think I've *infuriated* him. He keeps a rosewood-handled folding knife in a sheath on his belt. Last night he illustrated its sharpness, holding a limp, unfolded cocktail napkin out in front of himself and slicing it into ten neat ribbons without the slightest tug or tear. So perhaps his early morning plans include bleeding me out over a hemlock stump and then weighing down my corpse with heavy stones. He says the bogs here aren't deep in terms of water, but their mud could suck a body down below, leaving no sign beyond an earthy, satisfied belch.

I'm exhausted is the problem. I'm overreacting, I know. We've been up all night despite drunkenness, the hangover burning off before it ever had sleep in which to settle. I'd feel better now about Sarver if he seemed just the least bit foggy of mind. But from his eyes I can tell his concentration is sharp and cold like his blade. Meanwhile, I have no idea where we're headed and my face is slightly numb. My breath escapes me in a white plume. It's early September, but the first maple leaves have already gone red.

He pauses now as we enter a shady grove of white pines. When he turns his head back to me I think he's going to speak, but he only covers one nostril to blow snot out the other. Then he continues on through the trees.

My God, the pine needles underfoot! No synthetic material from all the world's science mimics the luxurious cushion of pine forest floor. I could lie down in them right now. Scoop up handfuls in a pile to make a pillow.

Sarver hasn't spoken since we left the cemetery at about six thirty this morning, while it was still dark, and drove us to this stretch of state forest. I can't read this man's mind. Not after yesterday. Not after last night. For Sarver is what, here in the Upper Peninsula ("da U.P." in local parlance), they call a Jack Pine Savage—a man of the Great White North still hell-bent on conquering it, whatever that means in the twenty-first century.

None of this was planned. None of this article was ever supposed to be about Donnie Sarver, the pageantry of his annual fistfight, or the death of his once bride-to-be.

I'd arrived here in Michigan thirty-six hours ago to fish the Two Hearted River, a Type 4 trout stream a little east of here that was immortalized in the short fiction of Ernest Hemingway. Go ahead and laugh; I don't blame you. What half-assed Nick Adams hasn't dreamed of wading its waters? And if you know anything about Hemingway then laugh all the more, because you know the fiction is actually based on the Fox River, twenty-five miles to the southwest. My editor said the same thing. But that's my angle, I explained. It'll be a city-slicker-plays-outdoorsman piece where I'll fish the *actual* Two

Hearted. See how it compares. I'll quote from young Hemingway's letters, maybe snag a few fish, and—like the river—my narrative will meander a bit but eventually lead to something vast and deep and pure, like Lake Superior. I actually said this.

That was before I met Donnie Sarver. Were they contemporaries, he and Hemingway would have either formed an instant kinship or immediately come to blows. (Sarver would have decimated him, by the way. Broken a chair over Papa's skull and then pissed on the carcass.) Among his many tattoos, he has, on his chest, nineteen tally marks representing all of his fights, all of his victories. He'll add to them, he says, until he runs out of skin.

We spoke further of his tattoos last night, when we were still half-sober and he was still half-reliable as a narrator. On his right forearm there's an outline of the Upper Peninsula, a shape that's ubiquitous up here but that most Americans don't recognize when they see it and don't miss when it's absent from a US map. There's a wolf on Sarver's left delt. Antlers on his right. At Rusty's Tavern, he pulled down the collar of his T-shirt to reveal, high on his chest, the words I AM SUPERIOR.

"Who is?" I asked. "You or the lake?"

And he grinned wide. "Both, motherfucker."

Sarver's smile made me think I had permission to ask what followed. I pointed to some more text—the only ink on his throat—which read, in plain letters, JANE. "What about that one? There's got to be a story there."

A wave of contempt crashed over his face. He leaned toward me, resting his elbows on a tabletop rubbed smooth over a century by the arms of men like him—other Jack Pine Savages. "That'd be your pot of gold, wouldn't it?" Then he smiled again, but his upper lip curled over his incisors like a dog pulling a chain taut. "That could be your goddamned thesis statement."

I didn't fully understand him then. But through the ensuing hours, leading to our current pine forest trek, I'd learned enough about Donnie Sarver to decode his snarling response, his hatred of grand theories. It translates roughly, to this:

You are an outsider. You are a writer, stealing stories not your own, which you will smuggle home and sell for profit. What's worse, your home is New York City, and the only thing worse than New Yorkers are the little jag-offs around the country who buy your magazine—delicate, effete men who will read your article amid ads for TAG Heuer, Gucci, and Chivas Regal. Among

columns opining on the width of lapels, the mysteries of tantric sex, and
the essential oils of upscale shaving creams. Outsiders who, like you, might
contemplate coming here. And if anyone should understand my feelings on
outsiders, it's you, who witnessed my wrath just today. So tell me, what makes
you think you can point at the name JANE *on my throat and still leave this*
northern town unharmed?

This northern town is Haymaker, and what I witnessed was a fight.

That might seem redundant given the name, though I'm told Haymaker earned its moniker not from knockout punches but from lies. In the 1870s, the founders of this place advertised cheap land for farming and hoped the name would entice folks to settle here and try their hands at agriculture. When those folks discovered the land was all forest, marsh, or sand—and the winters long and brutal—they about turned their pitchforks on local officials. Lucky for them, a lumber mill soon arose. The ancient forests fell. The "boomtown days" arrived. Donnie Sarver traces his lineage to those old lumberjacks. Their grit infuses his DNA, forming a man whose attitude is equal parts "can do" and "fuck you."

Two days ago I secured the last room at a tumbledown establishment called the Black Birch Motel. Unbeknownst to me, I'd arrived in the midst of Boomtown Days—an annual festival of the town's lumber heritage—and the place was full of visitors. But you see, visitors are okay. Visitors they like. Nowadays, the main industry here is tourism: camping, fishing, and kayaking in the summer; snowmobiling all winter long. Sarver makes money off these people, of course. "Trolls," he calls them, because they live "under the bridge"—under the Mackinac Bridge. Donnie owns a towing service and body shop, and more than a little of his livelihood depends on broken-down minivans filled with luggage and kids. Even he can see the need for tacky gift shops, ice cream parlors, and *temporary* lodging.

But here's the thing: it may have taken well over a hundred years, yet at some point Haymaker did become enticing to outsiders who wanted to come here and *stay*. Doctors from Chicago's Gold Coast. Lawyers from Grosse Pointe. Wealthy suburbanites began purchasing beachfront property, erecting lake houses and summer retreats. Artists and writers arrived and built isolated cabins. Retirees swept in and opened bookstores, for Christ's sake. Coffee shops.

Sarver finally decided enough was enough. He'd long known of a loophole in the local lawbooks, a relic of the roughneck era stating, in essence, that two men with an honest dispute could settle their differences with their fists. No weapons, of course. No outside interference. And a court case in the 1940s had upheld the law, an attorney comparing such occurrences to the old pistol duels of French noblemen.

So four years ago, Sarver posted orange signs on streetlamps and telephone poles throughout town, declaring that newcomers were not welcome and issuing a duel of fisticuffs at high noon on the Saturday of Boomtown Days. A transplant to Haymaker accepted the challenge, and the two clashed on the hallowed battlefield of the gravel parking lot behind Gassy Charlie's Filling Station. A crowd of men and boys watched and cheered. A police officer even monitored the event. During this one special ceremony each year, the cops condone it, issuing not so much as a fightwite.

Needless to say, our man emerged victorious from that first sanctioned duel. The loser—having taken his beating—was allowed to stay. And thus was born an annual spectacle known throughout these parts as Donnie Sarver's Welcome Wagon Shit-Kickin'.

I discovered it by accident while shopping for a fly rod and flies at the local outfitters. The guy at the checkout asked me, "You headed to the scrap?" Upon reading my confused expression he briefly explained it all to me: the history of the fight, the intent. Even sketched a map with directions on the back of my sales receipt, showing me the way to Fitzgerald Point Lighthouse. When I turned up I saw the lighthouse was a gorgeous ruin at the tail end of a snaking two-track. White paint had flaked off it for decades, and the roof had shed dozens of its red shingles, which dotted the ground like autumn leaves. But the seventy-foot tower still gleamed under the pale sun and loomed over the boundless waters of Lake Superior. Sarver knew what he was doing when he chose this locale. Since that first year at the gas station, he'd learned what any great showman could tell you: that spectacles deserve majestic backdrops.

A crowd of perhaps forty had gathered to watch, including Haymaker Police Chief Lenny Boston and an old physician named Vernon Brewer whom everyone (of course) called Doc.

I got my first look at Donnie Sarver then. Early thirties. The aforementioned tattoos. A jittery energy as he jogged and hopped in place. He's got the kind of hair so black it looks blue, like Superman's in the comics. And though not a large man, by any means—just under six feet tall and lean in a T-shirt, jeans, and work boots—the guy's flat-out ripped. He removes his shirt, and you can't help but think of Brad Pitt in *Fight Club*.

Again, showmanship. Theater.

His opponent was Jimmer Nixon, a twenty-nine-year-old cement mason from Ohio who claimed his parents and grandparents were born in the U.P.—he'd spent summers here as a boy—so he was hardly some outsider.

But Donnie's philosophy is pure and unshakable. "If my daddy was born on Mars, that don't make me a Martian."

A bearded fireplug named Ray Valentine served as the master of ceremonies. He glanced at his watch, stepped between the two combatants, and called out, "It's high noon, everybody! Time for a shit-kickin'!"

The crowd formed a circle around Sarver and Nixon, and I squeezed into the mass of bodies for a view. The bearded guy yelled, "Commence!" and Sarver shot forward like a bottle rocket. I could almost see the sparks trailing behind him, the explosion when he struck. They exchanged punches and then he connected, with two sharp jabs to Nixon's forehead. The other man dropped low, looking to make some sort of leg takedown that he may have learned in high school wrestling. Sarver retained balance on one foot long enough to begin punching downward on the back of Nixon's neck. The blows made a sickeningly wet and heavy sound, like a meat tenderizer. Nixon released Sarver's leg and was trying to crawl away when a raised knee to the jaw sent his eyes rolling back in his head. The police chief jumped in then and split up the men. Old Doc literally tossed a white towel.

Nixon had paid his dues. He'd endured Sarver's draconian hazing and was now free to stay. As the cheers filled the skies above Fitzgerald Point, the show ended the way it reportedly always ends: with Sarver looming over his opponent and happily shouting, "Welcome to da U.P.!"

This happened only yesterday, but my lingering skull rattle—from booze and fatigue and the disorienting sea of trees—makes it feel like this happened eons ago. I'm on a journey only fathomed by means of wormholes. Space-time.

The trail dips down into a ravine where a quick-moving creek roils over the remains of a collapsed footbridge. Sarver eschews the bridge, hopping across a couple of slick, flat stones at the water's surface. I follow and lose my balance, plunging my right foot into the creek. As we continue, my sodden shoe drips and turns heavy with mud. I'm craving black coffee and breakfast meats.

I need to sop up the alcohol coursing through my veins. After the Shit-Kickin', Donnie invited everyone out for a drink and announced the first round was on him. I followed the caravan from the lighthouse to Rusty's Tavern, abandoning my plans to fly-fish that afternoon, hoping instead there was a story in this warrior xenophobe. The river could wait.

From the outside, Rusty's looked more like a ramshackle hermit den than a saloon, and inside it featured honest-to-God dirt floors. But the bar was well stocked, and the beer was cold, so the rest seemed more than sufficient. At first I hung around the periphery, watching and listening as Sarver held court. He grinned, sang, and told filthy jokes, still riding the postfight high. He did, in fact, buy everyone a round—maybe twenty-five people—and many soon returned the favor by ordering him shots. Whiskey replaced adrenaline, and he barreled on as the center of attention. He talked about the time a jack went soft while he was underneath a Silverado; it nearly crushed him to death. About the time he was helping a friend haul ammonium nitrate and detonation equipment to a quarry and he was nearly arrested for transporting "weapons of mass destruction." And the time he took a stick to the head playing hockey and lost his sense of taste for a month. ("Well all's damn if spaghetti don't feel like a mouthful of worms!")

Next he claimed his pickup was struck by lightning while he and his buddy were driving to Escanaba. "Every hair on my body stood on end. Scotty's right arm was hurting bad, and that's how he ended up with that lightning scar that looks like cedar leaves. We drive into town to find the hospital, and when I park and take the keys out, the goddamned truck's still running! Running on thunderbolt fuel!"

All the men gathered round him cracked up and pounded the table. A heavyset guy named Merle said, "Come on now, Donnie, that's just stupid. No way that fucker kept going."

And Sarver said, "Well, I might be stupid, but you might be fat," before howling in laughter and throwing back another shot. After clattering the glass down on the table he surveyed the room, and that's when he noticed me standing against the bar. He squinted in a way that revealed curiosity and bewilderment. Then he pointed and motioned me over.

Now, I'm not a brave man. God knows how I'd have fared if I'd lived through selective service like my father and his father before him. I marched right over, though, as if my responsiveness would lessen my punishment. Clearly we were heading to round two of the Shit-Kickin'. *Welcome to da U.P., Mr. DuPont!*

The other men turned and, with rapt attention, watched me approach. They could tell in an instant I was some sort of troll, even if my bridge was the Brooklyn instead of the Mackinac. I stood across the table from Sarver, hanging my head a bit.

He tucked a cigarette into the corner of his mouth and lit it. "You in town for the festival?"

I told him not really. I was actually here to fish.

"You don't look like no fisherman," he said, and the men around us laughed. When I told him I was a writer they laughed harder. "You're one of those, huh?" said Sarver. "Here to grow a beard and write the Great American Novel like all the rest?" And when I mentioned this magazine he smirked and said he'd never heard of it. "But maybe you want to write an article on the G.O.A.T., huh?" He stood up and raised his fists over his head. "You want to write about the Greatest of All Time?"

He curled his arm around my neck. He handed me a shot. And somehow, even amid the party atmosphere around us, the two of us began to talk. I asked questions and he answered most. When I first asked about the JANE tattoo, his reaction suggested I might well be a goner. But over the ensuing hours and innumerable drinks, Donnie peeled back his defenses and told me her story.

Seven years ago, Jane Bannister's Ford Taurus plowed into an oncoming lumber truck, accordioned like a crushed aluminum can, and burst into flames in the roadside gully. She was twenty-three. It was her dad's birthday, and she was headed to her parents' place in Brimley for a little party, driving south through the forest on M-123, a two-lane highway heavy with summer tourist traffic. She was running late and was stuck behind a plodding RV that was hauling a trailer burdened with kayaks, mountain bikes, and camping supplies. The curve ahead was blind, and when she tried to pass, the lumber truck emerged from the bend in what must have seemed like a storm of steel and gasoline. This all happened outside a town called—I shit you not—Paradise.

Sarver hadn't purchased a diamond ring. Couldn't afford one. But he'd planned on proposing two weeks later, during a camping trip they were to have taken to the Porcupine Mountains. For a guy already known for his benders—who'd spent a few nights in the Haymaker drunk tank before this incident—it's impossible to describe how blindingly intoxicated he became for the next several days. He has no memory of the funeral and could not tell you where in the cemetery she lies under a stone. He came to one morning on his apartment floor, stumbled into the bathroom, and glanced at his ashen face in the mirror. That's when he noticed the throat tattoo of her name, which he also didn't remember getting. And he began weeping there in front of the mirror, not only for the loss, but for the drunken mistake. "I should have had it written the other way," he said. "It's for *me* to read, not anyone else. But every time I shave, every time I brush my teeth, I look in the mirror and the word's backward. How fucked up is that?"

They'd met at a bar in Marquette. She was a college girl majoring in biochemistry and—in almost every way, according to Donnie—out of his league. "I fell so goddamned hard for her. I knew I didn't have the mind power of most of the guys she knew, but I said to her, flat out, 'Janey, I will steal your brain's heart.'"

After her death, he almost joined her. He'd planned it all. He would disappear in the forest and smear his naked body with a concoction of honey and raw beef. He would commit suicide by bears. And in his will he would state that any remains should be cremated and the ashes buried in a dune graveyard so that the sands would shift and someday scatter him over the entire peninsula.

As he continued, I began to understand the rage. I could make sense of why he left that poor Ohioan, Jimmer Nixon, in a heap.

But Sarver claims he's always been like this—a son of a bitch with a hair-trigger temper even as a kid. He refused to talk about his childhood other than revealing how classmates used to call him Donnie McNasty, which he liked. Yet I try to imagine him during that brief stretch when he and Jane

Bannister were together. How did his world turn on its axis when Donnie Sarver was—for all intents and purposes—softened by the glow of love?

A little after two o'clock in the morning, he and I stumbled into his pickup and headed to the cemetery. We wove between lanes, then dipped onto the gravel shoulder and back again. Even now, during this endless woodland hike, I'm paranoid that we killed someone last night—clipped some teenager walking home from a friend's house and left him dead in a gully like Jane.

A part of me still thinks I'm as good as dead, too. It only makes sense that he'd snuff me out. We've all experienced morning-after regret, but what—to his mind—had he done last night? He'd let me glimpse his world. He was going to let a national readership learn of the life he so protected. In the cold sobriety of first light, he must realize he'd broken the fighter's first rule. He'd let his guard down.

We'd spent over thirteen hours at the bar. *Thirteen hours.* Some of the men from the Shit-Kickin' went home and came back again, but others stayed the entire time, too. We played cards and pool and watched college football. I don't remember the tragedy of my final bar tab, but I do vaguely recollect using the magazine's credit card. Sarver's knife might ultimately cause me less pain.

The path of our conversation remains blurry in memory, but at some point late in the evening I convinced him that we must visit Jane's grave. I think I actually said *he* must visit it, but I realized what I was doing, for I was just lucid enough to see this article unfolding before me and wasn't above giving the narrative a little nudge. Lakecrest Cemetery was only three blocks from Rusty's, but Sarver had never gone back since the unremembered funeral.

He very rightly asked, "Why would I do it tonight, with some New York asshat I don't even know?"

And I think I said something about her "story." *This would be a chance for you to tell Jane's story.* It's a miracle he didn't gut me right then.

But it had worked. Or something had. Asshat or not, he said I reminded him of a little cousin with whom he'd once been close. And I'd impressed him with my headful of NHL trivia. I'd made him laugh when I'd sung "A

Boy Named Sue." Maybe he realized he was already in too deep, having told me so much of their history. In any case, he agreed.

So we parked out front of the cemetery's locked gate and scaled the fence with all the grace and decorum of two ham-fisted orangutans. Sarver somersaulted over the top and crashed onto his back. I'd grabbed a flashlight from his glove compartment, and when I shined it on him he lay there giggling with his eyes closed. "Throw some dirt on me, DuPont. Just bury me where I'm laying."

He made more jokes as we crept through the grounds. I held the flashlight except for when he snatched it from me, held it up under his chin, and made faces and sounds like a ghoul. From the looks of the slanted, moss-caked stones, we seemed to be wandering over the oldest plots in the cemetery. Birth dates—where still legible—harkened back to the mid-1800s. "Lot of these are my people," he said. "Even the ones I've never met. But *I* sure as shit ain't going to be locked in some cemetery cage. Burn me up, brother. Scatter my ass to the wind."

He grew quiet, though, when the stones turned newer. Polished granite. Laser etchings. We split up to search, and since I had the flashlight, Sarver just sort of wandered around, flicking his cigarette lighter along the edge of the property. When I found her grave, I waited a few moments before calling him over. It was a modest white stone, nearly flush with the grass, displaying JANE NICOLE BANNISTER, her birth and death dates, and an etching of an angel with a cross. "It's here, man," I finally said.

He looked up, his face a shadowy orange before he flicked off the lighter and disappeared in the gloom. I heard him approach, his boots scattering early autumn leaves. When he sidled up next to me, I held the flashlight beam steady, letting him stare and soak it in. His rough fingers reached for the stone but stopped just short of touching the angel and cross. For several moments he said nothing, but eventually he turned his head and spat. "Her mother," he mumbled. "The world's great whore." He grabbed the flashlight and aimed it down at the grass. "She's one of them Jesus freaks. I ran into her about six months after the crash. We was at the grocery store and she come up and said something like, 'I can tell you're all angry, Donnie. I can tell you want to explode. But you got to let go,' she said. 'You got to *let go and let God*.'"

Sarver ran his fingers through his black hair. "I almost shot her dead."

I prepared to leave then, but soon after that Donnie started wandering along the edge of the property again. He carried armfuls of branches and leaves—making multiple trips—and dumped them in a pile beneath a looming oak tree just a short ways from Jane's grave. Then he knelt down with the lighter, cupped his hand around the flame, and lit a fire.

I'd known him by then for about fourteen hours, plenty of time, I figured, to make the following assumption: Donnie Sarver was going to burn that fucking cemetery to cinders.

I panicked. I started looking for those spigots they always have where people can water their hanging flower baskets. But in a moment Donnie sat down cross-legged next to the fire and simply stared at the flames as the leaves lit and the twigs began to snap. The deep night had turned cold, and though I hesitated, I soon sat down beside him and did the same.

His face looked swollen. At first I figured it was puffy from emotion, like he was holding back tears. Then I realized he resembled a boxer at a postfight press conference. He'd taken more shots from Jimmer Nixon than I'd realized. Staring into the fire, he could have used a pair of shades.

I was still nervous, expecting a cop to see the flames, smell the smoke, and figure at the very least we were a group of high school kids getting stoned. But sitting there, growing warm, the fatigue of the night began to hit me and I relaxed. Donnie seemed almost calm himself. When he began speaking, it came nearly as a whisper. He didn't talk about Jane, God, or fistfights. Not car repair, whiskey, or thunderbolt fuel. Instead, he described how, as a boy, he'd ride his bike south of town to swim alone in Little Deep Lake. How he and his cousin would catch panfish in Oslo Creek. How his dad would take him camping, and the only thing better than the afternoon hikes was the sensation of waking up in the morning with the blue nylon of their tent overhead—the warm, plastic smell of it—and the gentle sound of falling beechnuts plunking the surface. Bacon and eggs would be sizzling outside. And he would hear his dad shuffling a deck of cards—over and over again, just shuffling the cards to pass the time and relax. "That, for him, was a vacation."

I nodded. I recognized the solemnity of the occasion. And so I broached the subject delicately. "Is he dead, too?"

You have to remember: *thirteen hours!* We'd been drinking at Rusty's for thirteen hours! This is not how I normally talk. A part of my brain was so absolutely focused on being polite and respectful—you have no idea! But when I went to say something along the lines of, "He sounds like a good man" or "Those are great memories to have," it came out just like that. Wham. *Is he dead, too?*

Sarver exhaled deeply, a backwoods yogi. He seemed perfectly tranquil as he stood up, turned to face the gargantuan trunk of the two-hundred-year-old oak tree, and began pounding the fuck away on it—with both fists, like it was a heavy bag. There were two or three, what I would call, "primal screams." I should have run away, realizing I was probably next on his hit list. But instead I tried to make him stop. Blood streamed over his fingers and down his wrists. I wrapped my arms around his waist, tried to pull him back, and for the only time that night—and not from the booze, mind you—I blacked out. I think it was a one- or two-second blackout. Boom. Now I'm on my back, by the fire, with no memory of him hitting me. I probably would have stayed that way were it not for the fact that my left elbow grazed the coals. I got up, rubbing my arm, and staggered a few steps before settling down on one knee, my head pounding, the cemetery shaking.

Sarver stopped, returned to the fire, and sat down again, frothing like an exhausted horse. When he finally began wincing—presumably from the pain in his fists—I felt it was safe to timidly approach. I sat with the fire between us and waited for him to speak.

"You going to write about this?" he asked.

"About what?"

"Shit, man." He shrugged, staring at the fire. "All of it."

The wood had broken down into those winking embers that, when you toss a fresh log onto them, immediately set it ablaze. Pure potential energy. Hungry ambition. That's when a fire gives off real heat and will last you through the night.

A shaft of light breaks horizontally through the trees. I squint with my good eye, the other one blurry from Donnie's punch. The trail begins to climb and turn sandy. I stop, rest my hands on my knees, and gasp for air. A string of spit dangles from my lips. It occurs to me I forgot to cancel this morning's plans with my fishing guide.

"We're almost there," he says, and it feels like the first thing he's said in hours. The blood on his hands has dried and looks almost like stains of chocolate syrup, as if he were merely a little boy who'd eaten his sundae with bare hands.

As we climb the hill, the trees around us appear much larger than what we'd passed through before. When I say so, Sarver nods. "These are old growth. Never been harvested." I ask if these are jack pines and he says no, the jack pines were farther back. They're the pioneers that rise up after logging or fires.

I see my connection. My pot of gold. My goddamned thesis statement. "Like you?" I ask.

He looks back at me and smirks. "Nice try, but get the fuck out of my head." He flashes me a middle finger. "Here's *your* Rorschach test, DuPont. What do *you* see?"

I hear Lake Superior before I see it: the melodic drone of whitecaps. Then it's there, over the crest of the hill—cobalt blue and big as the universe. The early sun—fresh from dawn—shines just above the horizon, casting our shadows due west down the dune. They're maybe twenty feet long. Sarver raises his bloodied fists over his head, watching his shadow grow. "You're the tallest man in the world," I say.

He nods. "Greatest of all time."

PINK BLOOD

Linda Selig opens her hope chest and reaches inside, fumbling beneath the linens and quilts until she finds the plastic baggie full of baby teeth. She winces while shifting her knees over the hardwood floor and then closes the chest in a cedar-laced sigh.

There are twenty teeth inside, and all of them were Jordan's. He's their firstborn, and when Hannah came three years later and Chloe ten years after that, Linda and John were so swept up in the day-to-day that they forgot to save most of the girls' teeth. Linda usually swapped out dollars beneath their pillows and flushed the teeth down the toilet.

An airplane growls somewhere overhead. Linda stands and stretches her back. Her bedroom blinds are open. The sun has set, and eventide has settled over the small cemetery on the corner. The buildings next door to it are dark, except for the barbershop, where pockets of disinfecting blue light wash over the combs. Linda pours the baby teeth into her palm.

There is a bright blue vein that runs down Jordan's forehead, above his left eye. It was there when he was an infant and has never gone away. Over the years, as his mess-ups turned to broken rules and eventually broken laws, Linda would stare at the vein, to remember.

John gave up on him years ago. "Kid could slit his throat with a safety razor. Or someone else's."

When Jordan was nine he and Brandon Sellars spray-painted the misspelled word ASSHOLL on trees throughout Jaycees Park. A few years later he was suspended for bringing a knife to school, caught because he'd carved MY BLADE WAS HERE on bricks and tiles throughout the building. And when he was fifteen he and two older guys who'd sometimes buy him beer were arrested at the industrial park trying to steal pallets of aluminum platforms to sell for scrap. They were parts of a playground structure that a charity was shipping to Guatemala. Jordan was charged with misdemeanor petty theft and served probation.

There were fights, but Linda didn't know the details. He'd dropped out of school by then and was working part-time jobs at Home Depot and then the car wash. She was still convincing John to let him live under their roof.

Jordan would come home with dried blood on his face or bruises on his hands. Then he'd sit at the kitchen table to make himself a peanut butter and jelly sandwich, slipping potato chips between the bread slices—the way he'd done as a boy—so that it would crunch with each bite. Or he'd roll his old BMX out of the garage and ride slowly back and forth down the sidewalk, making U-turns in the driveways of empty homes.

She taught him how to ride a bike when he was five—there, across the street, at the little cemetery. Years later, John called it bad luck. They'd taught the girls in the church parking lot, and they'd turned out fine. Hannah made honor roll this semester and is working her first job, standing alongside 28th Street after school, wearing a yellow T-shirt, waving at cars, and holding a sign for one of those cash-for-gold places. And across the hall from Linda, Chloe has just run into her bedroom and begun jumping on her trundle bed while speaking to stuffed animals in baby voices. Twenty years ago that rhythmic squeaking of bedsprings would have come from her and John, in that respite between wedding and pregnancy, when sex was more elation than release.

Jordan is now nineteen, and tonight—a few hours from now—he will enter the gates of Jackson State Prison for what Linda hopes is only five years but could be ten. Last fall, after a Lions game, he and three other guys from the car wash stumbled out of Ford Field and trailed a man in a Packers jersey for eight blocks. When the man cut through an alley toward his hotel, Jordan and the others beat and stomped him. Smashed bottles over him. Cut his face with brown glass.

The man was Kevin Vaughan, a forty-two-year-old father of three from Marquette who'd become separated from his friends in the crush of exiting fans. He was comatose and paralyzed when loaded into the ambulance. Surgeons removed sections of his skull so that his brain wouldn't swell. Linda saw this on the news.

She refused interviews—after the arrest, during the trial. After Jordan was convicted of assault with intent to do great bodily harm. On the day of the conviction, she came home from the courthouse and wandered into the backyard. She doesn't remember the actual moment when she lay down beneath the magnolia. It was just days past its full bloom, and the grass beneath was covered in pink flowers. But she does remember slowly arcing her arms above her head, slowly scissoring her legs in the grass, making a shape like a snow angel amid the blossoms. And she remembers John, standing and staring in the driveway, horrified.

So what would he think of this?

Linda closes her hand over the teeth and squeezes them—kneads them beneath her fingers like a palm full of gravel. She opens her hand again. The roots of some teeth are tinged pink with old blood. She pinches one between her right thumb and forefinger and slips it into her mouth like a pill. It rests on her tongue, and in the seconds before swallowing she searches for its taste. There is something in this pink blood. Something faintly umbilical.

STONE DUST

On the day I was born,

God was sick,

gravely.

—César Vallejo, "Have You Anything to Say in Your Defense?"

The pool water dripped from Luke's hair and chest and legs, dotting the concrete and vanishing seconds later under the Mexican summer sun. He reached behind himself, grabbed the white towel draped over the lawn chair, and wrapped it high around his midsection, covering his growing belly and the surgical scars on his lower back. He still had the arms of a pro ballplayer and looked good in a T-shirt, but when he took his shirt off he couldn't stand the sight of himself, even peripherally. He reached down by his feet to grab his cigarettes, lighter, and a glass of white tequila with ice.

The patio roof of Casa Isabela overlooked two blocks of Old Town neighborhood, and beyond it, down the steep hill, lay the churches and bars and finally the ocean waters of Puerto Vallarta. For the past three days Luke had sat here, watching the horizon but also watching the neighbors in the foreground. Smiling men with machetes acting out swordfights with one another. Children in school uniforms playing *fútbol* in the street. Women raising their nightshirts over rooftop toilets. Above them all, clay roof tiles slid earthward like old-age skin.

He sipped the drink, set it down, and lit a cigarette. The downstairs stone-carving studio was quiet. Esteban and Omar had set their tools down hours ago. The noise now came from the drug dealers on the corner. Stereos played American hip-hop while crewmembers took turns on motorcycles, roaring up and down the brick hill. Last night, Luke had borrowed some of the orange foam earplugs from down in the studio to sleep.

A hummingbird appeared among the red potted azaleas beside him. It levitated, moved backward, and then darted forward again, its beak and tongue shooting from the sweetness of one bloom to another. In the brief moments of hovering, its dark green feathers gave off a dull sheen and looked like the scales of a fish. Seconds later the bird and the rhythm of its wings evaporated, like everything else in this heat.

Footsteps rose from the stairs. Omar smiled broadly, a highball glass in each hand. "It's happy hour."

It happened every evening at this time—Omar emerging with a vodka cocktail mixed with whatever fresh juice Lalo, the cook, had made earlier that day. The first night it was kiwi green. Last night, a muddy tamarind. Tonight's drink looked like the evening horizon.

"Mango," said Omar.

He handed one of the glasses to Luke, who now sat with a drink in each hand and the cigarette hanging low off the corner of his lips. "Good thing my wife's not here to see this."

Luke set the new drink down by his feet, saving it for the ritual. It was one Omar claimed to perform every nightfall, watching the sun set over the darkening ocean and holding off on the first sip until the top edge of the sun—the final, slim arc—disappeared completely. Then they would drink. Right now, the very bottom was just starting to slip away.

And when, these past nights, it had disappeared entirely, the club down the hill seemed to sense it. The place was called El Party, and it emitted black light at dusk, glowing there across from Parque Hidalgo and the twin steeples of Our Lady of the Refuge. Luke had passed it yesterday. A gleaming spiral staircase led to the second-story dance floor lit by tiki torches beneath a thatched roof.

He finished the tequila—ice hitting his teeth—while Omar paced back and forth behind him, looking down at the street and a motorcycle rumbling past. Luke waved him over with his free hand. "I got a question for you."

Omar pulled a matching white lawn chair over and sat beside him.

Luke nodded at the pot of red flowers. "Lots of hummingbirds around here, *sí*?"

"*Sí*," said Omar, wiping condensation from his cocktail and then drawing his dampened fingers over his mustache. "Especially early in the day."

All three levels of the open-air casa were filled with sculptures, many of them by Esteban but most by Omar, who was the place's caretaker and artist in residence. Sandstone. White and red limestone. Alabaster, volcanic basalt, and assorted varieties of marble. Luke found the works throughout the house—in the kitchen, the dining area, and several sculptures here, along the pool and beside the red Mayan hammock. Many were nudes or abstracts, but Luke had noticed at least three hummingbirds done in bas-relief.

"Do you know what kind? The species?"

Omar reclined in the chair with one hand scratching the back of his head. Luke figured he was in his late forties, maybe fifty, but he was lithe and trim and ran three miles every afternoon in the heat.

"My wife loves the things," said Luke. "She has feeders on our patio back in Michigan. I just want to know the name because she's going to ask."

Omar nodded. "Berylline? I think?"

"Berylline?"

"*Sí*."

Luke shrugged. "Sounds good to me. I don't know shit about birds."

Omar glanced at his watch and checked the horizon. "I love them." He darted his hand forward and backward and smiled. "Drink nectar all day to get that quick. Always close to starving."

"That's rough."

Omar's brow creased. "I think they—how you say it? Hibernate."

"Oh yeah?"

"*Sí*."

"Huh," said Luke. He wanted to say something else but failed. Instead, he braced himself on the arms of the flimsy chair and limped to the iron rail overlooking the street, where he tapped his ashes over the edge.

"You want a cigar?" asked Omar. "No Cubans where you live."

Luke stepped gingerly back to his chair, his left hand half covering his belly. "Cigars are for celebrating." He shook his head. "No. I'm good." Then he sat, nodded toward the horizon, and picked his mango cocktail up off the floor. "Here we go."

Omar smiled and held his glass so that it almost touched his lips. Seconds later the last of the sun slipped beneath the sea. They drank.

After a few moments of silence Omar rose and walked across the patio to his two-room living quarters. He returned with an olivewood recorder and stood in back by the hammock, playing a sweet, high-pitched tune. A few minutes later came the dance-beat throb of El Party down the hill, faster than the beat of Omar's song. Faster than a grown man's pulse.

Stone dust poured into Luke's bedroom through the wooden slats of the balcony door. It mixed with blades of sunlight and in the dimness became a glowing smoke. The casa's windows were without glass or screens. Huge cockroaches and tiny lizards sometimes scurried up the cool brick walls.

Luke lay in bed with two pillows propped under his head and another smaller one tucked beneath his knees. An open book rested on his chest. Esteban and Omar were working in the outdoor studio, two floors beneath the balcony. The sky filled with the buzz, whir, and metallic shriek of their tools: pneumatic chisels, diamond saws, disc sanders, masonry drills, and old-fashioned chisels and hammers. Luke had arrived only four days ago, but already the din had blended into something resembling white noise, which actually made it easier to read. They would break at noon, but the light gray dust would continue falling. It settled over his bedroom every morning, and every afternoon while they ate lunch the housekeeper, America, made it all go away with Pine Sol and a mop.

A ceiling fan twirled overhead, and a small box fan stood on the bedside table blowing directly onto his face. This wasn't merely to fight the heat; Luke used fans year-round, even in Michigan. In the winter he'd sleep with the blankets tucked under his chin and a fan on the floor, tilted upward so that it would send cool air rushing over him without chilling Shannon. He needed the fans not so much for coolness but simply for the touch of the air itself. He could never explain it to Shannon, how it soothed him. Growing up, his family had owned a cabin in Escanaba with a creek running through the property, and when the windows were open, the water's soft gurgling would lull him to sleep. It was like this but different, like the creek but with air instead of water and touch instead of sound. The comparison never quite worked when he described it aloud.

Beside the box fan were a half-filled bottle of orange Gatorade and the near-empty bottle of white tequila he'd drunk from last night. Luke took a quick sip from the tequila and several swallows of the Gatorade, some of it trickling down his chin and making a small orange stain on the chest of his white T-shirt. He'd felt dehydrated every day since his arrival. His urine had turned the color of rust.

Luke returned to the book, a history of the British Army during the Battle of the Somme. Over a million casualties. Two men killed for every centimeter of ground gained. He usually preferred mysteries, but these statistics and the graphic descriptions of wounds made Luke feel oddly relaxed. He liked reading about soldiers. In the US, football players were the athletes with warrior status, but he'd felt hints of it as a starting pitcher, standing on the mound with two outs, a runner in scoring position, and forty-thousand fans either on his side or at his throat. His career in the majors may have been cut short, but it had been long enough for this kind of understanding. It made his back pain and lifeless foot—at least once in a while—seem worth it.

Like all power pitchers, the incredible torque from his legs and midsection had been far more important than the actual strength of his arm. During thirteen professional seasons of throwing low-nineties fastballs—thousands upon thousands of them—the contortions had slowly ground down the cushions of his spine. The slow burning pain of degenerated discs turned sharp and debilitating one night in Kansas City, culminating with the trainer escorting him off the mound, back to the locker room, and sending him to the hospital for tests. The results showed hernias of the L4 and L5 discs, and though he didn't know it or believe it at the time, an eclipse had occurred, a sudden darkening of the atmosphere when things should have otherwise been light.

The initial surgery was an apparent success, but two months later came a recurrent herniation that damaged the peroneal nerve running down his right leg, leading to a chronic foot drop. In addition to the renewed spine pain, he was suddenly unable to flex his right ankle and toes. He walked with a limp—a fresh affliction.

What followed was a life beneath the umbra. Chronic pain. Unpaid bills. Depression and rage and fists sent through kitchen drywall. Crying daughters.

Luke was thirty-one then. He'd spent ten years in the minors and just three in the bigs, and he passed those early retirement days on the couch watching cartoons or reality shows or old movies—anything but sports. His short stint in the majors had still qualified him for lifetime health insurance and a pension of over thirty thousand a year. So they could live, he and Shannon. But it was a type of life.

And even cheap booze got expensive after a while. Luke drank to blunt the pain, and he drank to sleep. He'd drink to work up the nerve to make phone calls to old teammates or his brother or even his parents. He'd drink to brace himself for Julia's T-ball games or to slow his heart when it raced at random times. And he drank to create that gentle, temporary bubble of happiness that he sometimes needed to prove to Shannon and the girls that he *could* be happy and to prove that—should they ever have any ideas about leaving—there existed still some residue of a normal husband and father.

Two years of that and now four days of this: drinking in Mexico, where he'd come at the invitation of Esteban, an old friend. A baseball friend, with all the old baseball memories to rehash. Luke was thirty-three now, walking with a cane like an old man and drinking out of mourning. With orange Gatorade on his shirt and the grit of stone dust in his teeth.

His phone vibrated in his pocket. It was Shannon. They hadn't talked since she'd dropped him off at the airport in Detroit. He'd only sent her a quick text that night, telling her he'd arrived safely.

He sat up a bit, wincing at the sharp sting in his back, and answered. "How's my favorite *gringa*?"

"Oh my God, I can barely hear you. What's that noise?"

"The guys working in the studio."

"How can you stand it?"

He eased his legs over the edge of the bed, braced his free hand on the headboard, and stood to walk out of the room and into the hall. His brain trilled from the tequila, the roaring tools, and the images of soldiers' mangled bodies lingering like a broken-off dream. "That better?"

"Much." She asked about the weather and the house and how Esteban was these days. "Probably not worth asking how your back feels?"

"Probably not," said Luke. "How are the girls?"

"My mom just took Julia to swimming lessons, and Brie is sitting here at the table with a coloring book. Summer break's so far, so good."

He nodded and took a few steps down the open-air hallway, imagining the girls playing out front of his little blue ranch in Allegan County, which they'd bought mainly for the land and the open solitude of neighboring farms: corn, wheat, soybeans. But with each year the sprawl chewed up more of it: highway, mall, tribal casino.

Luke peered down at the street. Omar's beat-up blue pickup was parked below, the bed weighed down with a pile of huge jagged rocks that would someday be smoothed and shaped and displayed.

Neither he nor Shannon spoke for a few seconds. He closed his eyes and raised his face to the sun. A murky orange like an egg yolk flowed beneath his lids. A disc sander screeched in the distance. "Have you talked to Jimmy or Tom or anyone?" asked Shannon.

Luke opened his eyes. "Not worth talking about that either."

Jimmy and Tom were old friends trying to help him get work. Jimmy taught civics at Grand Haven High School—Luke's alma mater—and they needed a JV coach. And Tom had a Suzuki dealership out on 28th Street and thought his customers would love the idea of buying a car from a former Tiger, from a local boy who'd made it to the local big-time team.

"We'll figure that out when I get back," said Luke. "I need to think some more."

"Your birthday's in five days. I take it you won't be back by then."

"No," he said. "A little after that. Just a little."

"Are you safe there?"

"Am I *safe*?" He glanced down the road to the lonely phone booth and empty benches, where it was too early in the day for motorcycles and loud music.

"Because of the drug wars," said Shannon. "And the travel warning. They just said a big cruise line is cancelling calls in Puerto Vallarta."

"That's all bogus. At least around here." And it was true, according to Omar, who said even the dealers on the corner were just teenage delinquents. Harmless if you stayed out of their way. "It's like when we used to tell people we lived in Detroit and they feared for our lives. People here are pissed about the American media coverage," said Luke. "There was one murder a few months back, and I guess it had nothing to do with drugs.

The locals are terrified that travelers are going to overreact and stay home. Esteban says the only unsafe thing here is the tourist industry."

Brie was saying something in the background. Apparently she wanted to say hi to him but then she didn't. He heard her grab the phone and then set it down on the table in a loud clatter. Shannon picked it back up. "She wants lunch now so I have to go. What time is it there?"

"Almost noon. Just an hour difference."

"You're not drinking too much, are you?"

"I'm not drinking as we speak."

Luke said he'd call her in a day or two and then slipped the phone back into his pocket. A few beads of sweat had formed on his forehead. He retreated to the dark bedroom, closed the door, and then lay down, wincing as he shoved the extra pillow beneath his knees. The box fan chilled the sweat on his brow, and he closed his eyes for a few moments, taking deep breaths through his nose as someone outside switched to the pneumatic hammer.

A few minutes passed. Luke turned to his side and reached for the tequila. On the brick wall just above where the bottle stood was a brown-green lizard. It was only about two inches long and it remained frozen against the wall for several minutes, its right eye staring at him. Luke slowly reached his hand up so that it lay flush against the brick, beside the lizard, and he waited. After maybe five or six or seven minutes, the lizard began to walk across the wall and then over the top of Luke's hand, its tiny claws leaving indentations smaller than freckles on his skin. Minutes later, with the lizard now at the far end of the room, the feel of those miniscule pressure points remained on Luke's palm.

Even in the dark brick kitchen, the sun at high noon diffused through the louvered doors and windows to create a pleasant glow. Lalo, in his bright white smock, leaned over the counter and removed the lids from two steaming chafing dishes. Luke shambled toward the table, only vaguely hungry for lunch, and made room as America bustled past him with her curt and customary "Hola, hola" as she carried the bucket and mop into his bedroom. He should have hidden the tequila.

Lalo nodded at Luke and waved his hand toward the food. This afternoon it was a boiled chicken dish, along with the usual rice and beans topped with crumbled queso fresco. Luke filled his plate, and Lalo brought over a small glass pitcher of the day's fresh drink: a pale green limeade with somersaulting bits of pulp. It would go well with vodka at sunset.

Omar arose from downstairs, his clothes covered in dust, his hair shooting out in all directions from having blown it clean with the air compressor. He approached the food, smiled, and gently patted Luke on the back. Esteban followed, his build and overall persona filling up space in the kitchen the way it once had in dugouts and locker rooms. He was in his midfifties now, his hair gray and his goatee silver, but the shoulders revealed by his tank top proved he could probably unload the rocks from Omar's truck with little trouble. He put a dusty arm around Luke's neck. "What we got today, Boss? Pollo Lalo? This stuff melts in your mouth like chicken ice cream."

Luke was eighteen when they'd first met, recently drafted out of high school by the Brewers and sent to Low-A ball to pitch for the Beloit Snappers in the Midwest League. Twenty-five guys from all over the US and Latin America, all of them eighteen, nineteen years old and every one of them believing they'd make it to the bigs, even though the odds were something like one percent, a number Luke didn't learn until after retiring.

There was a joy to it then, even on stinking, sweltering twelve-hour bus rides crisscrossing the Rust Belt and Corn Belt: Peoria to South Bend to Battle Creek. Even when the bus caught fire once. Rockford to Clinton to Cedar Rapids. Even when a flipped semi spilled a thousand gallons of milk over the highway and jammed traffic for hours. The guys just grabbed balls and gloves, hopped off the bus into the grassy median, and played a few games of pickle under the Midwestern sun. Low-A ball was sort of like summer camp.

So much so that guys like Luke were prone to the soft and quiet loneliness of it. That's where Esteban had come in. He'd spot a guy like Luke, take him to a diner one morning in Burlington or Fort Wayne, and ask about his parents, his hometown, about the girl who'd just broken up with him over the phone.

Esteban had come from a family in San Diego who owned a successful architectural sculpture and restoration business, and though he'd apprenticed in that field growing up, he'd abandoned it by eighteen for baseball. He'd had a solid major league career as a back-up catcher for five franchises. And like all catchers Luke had ever known, he understood the game better than anyone else on the field.

Seven years later, Luke found himself playing AAA ball in Toledo after being traded to the Tigers and floating between the Florida State and Eastern Leagues. The team had tanked that season, and the next year they brought in a new manager, and who should it be but Esteban, who by now had a reputation as a fixer, a guy who could work well with egos and locker-room politics and make a team work. It was Esteban who'd encouraged him to develop a split-finger fastball, an addition to his arsenal that, in two years' time, led to Luke's promotion to Detroit. They'd kept in touch over the ensuing years, talking technique in the off-season but also occasionally meeting up for dinner or even to go hunting in the U.P.

But Esteban had grown tired of the minor-league grind and being passed up for promotion, so he'd settled down to help his sister run the family business in San Diego. He also purchased this place, Casa Isabela, named after his only daughter. He'd spent childhood summers at his grandparents' in Puerto Vallarta and had bought the casa to serve not only as a vacation home for himself but as something he rented out to everyone from sculptors to study-abroad students to guys using it for bachelor parties. Right now the only guest was Luke.

Esteban had called him last month. "Something in your voice, Boss. Something says you need to take a break and clear your head before you break your head."

They sat beside each other now in the dining area, which was open to the sea air and had a distant view of the ocean. Esteban manned the head of the table, chugging a bottle of water. A shelf behind him displayed marble bowls and figurines. Omar ate across from Luke, his head bent low toward his plate, eating with absolute focus. Luke stood up, walked to the refrigerator, and returned with a bottle of beer.

"You still dehydrated?" asked Esteban. "Switch from that to this." He raised the bottled water. "Beer only makes it worse."

"I've been drinking Gatorade," he said and he unconsciously touched the orange stain on his shirt.

Esteban watched him for a few seconds, then started eating. "You should come down to the studio a little later and see what we're working on. Got a show at a gallery next month. Down by the marina." He pointed his fork at Omar. "This guy's making flowers. Unbelievable. Sandstone petals thin as paper. I'm afraid they'll break if I even look at them."

Omar stifled a grin and shrugged, sipping his limeade.

Esteban took a large bite of chicken and nodded at Luke. "What you been up to this morning?"

"Reading." Luke shook his head slightly. "My back's been bothering me."

"You should get out and walk around," said Esteban. "Even with the pain and your foot. Stretch it out. Get the blood flowing."

Luke nodded, staring out toward the ocean. "I'm going out this afternoon. Maybe to the Malecón. It's tough walking here with all the hills and cobblestones."

"You should go to the beach," said Omar.

"You should," said Esteban. "Swimming would be good for you. The pool upstairs ain't bad, but you need the buoyancy of salt water. Get you feeling fresh and right. Your mind, too."

Luke took several swallows of beer. "Beach is pretty far away."

"Take a cab. Omar or me will call one for you. It's a quick trip."

Luke nodded. He'd eaten little but felt full.

Esteban picked up a chicken bone, sucked at the marrow, and set it down to lick his fingers. "You get out. You see some sights. And you clear your mind. Then, tonight, you and me, we have some dinner. There's dancing in the *zócalo* tonight. I know where we can watch from a balcony and eat great ceviche. And we'll talk about whatever you want. Like our beautiful wives and children. In my case, grandchildren."

Lalo cleared their dishes and then presented a platter of watermelon wedges. He picked up a shaker from the table and sprinkled salt over the wedges, then stepped around the table to the corner where a small tree grew out of a large clay pot. Luke had seen the tree, of course, but had never really noticed it. He'd certainly never noticed until now that it bore fruit. Lalo reached overhead and plucked a small lime from a branch. Then he returned to the table, sliced it in half with a paring knife, and squeezed the juice over the platter.

Luke grabbed a wedge and took a bite. The sweet, sour, and salty began as three distinct flavors, but by the second bite they mingled into a taste he strangely enjoyed but couldn't quite describe. Like sweetened seawater. Like sugary sweat.

He stared at the lime tree, a bit disbelieving. Any time he wanted he could just walk up to it, from inside this house, and pluck fruit from a tree.

• • •

Luke pulled the massive wooden door shut behind him so that it echoed down the narrow street. From here, the casa was a windowless wall of bricks, like a fortress, with locked gates that Omar opened only when he had a delivery of stone. Luke stepped out of the shade, just to test the heat. He'd brought the wooden cane he'd purchased a couple days ago at a souvenir shop down the road. It had cost him seven hundred pesos, and he was sure he'd been ripped off, but he'd never liked haggling, and aside from food and drink it was the only money he'd spent since arriving. The seller seemed to claim it was rosewood, but Luke spoke little Spanish and didn't care all that much about specifics. What he liked was the amber-colored snake carved into the shaft, its head serving as the handle and its body coiling downward to the cobblestone street. He'd never before walked with a cane because of all of the decrepitude it implied—he'd certainly never use one back home. But the rough terrain of these streets called for some sort of aid. And so what if it was an affectation? Like some goddamn staff from mythology. So the fuck what? Luke had laid low all morning—laid low for two years—and he felt like striking out this afternoon with a rosewood snake in his fist. He was in Mexico. It was almost his thirty-fourth birthday. And he hadn't liked the way Esteban had been treating him like a child at lunch.

The midday sun struck down on him like a blade. As a Michigan boy he'd always thrived in the cold, wilted in the heat. Luke stepped back into the shade to lean against Omar's pickup. The tires looked half-flat, exhausted by the weekly loads. Beneath a windshield wiper was a photo of a woman in a purple bikini, an ad for an escort service. Luke's eyes lingered over it for a few seconds. He reached for the cigarettes in his pocket before realizing he'd left them in his bedroom, up a flight of stairs he had no desire to climb. He also had the urge to chew tobacco, a habit Shannon had broken him of years ago because of her disgust at Mountain Dew spittoons lying around the house. But tequila would be vice enough this afternoon. He started down the street, headed to the OXXO, in the direction of the drug dealers on the corner.

On the day Luke had arrived, Esteban had warned him to avoid the corner. "Just go around the block the other way. Even if it's a little longer. The Canadians next door always want to call the police on them, but that'd just make things worse. They're harmless little *pendejos*, but no need to pick at their scabs, you know?"

But there were three reasons why, on this afternoon, Luke had no plans to go around the block the other way. First, every step mattered when it came to walking with a cane, a dead foot, and a couple of ramshackle lumbar discs like the ones working to keep him vertical. Shortcuts mattered.

Second, these tough guys weren't going to mess with a cripple, even an American with a smirking, puffy white face that they'd probably like to cave in with their heels. At their age it was about wanting to slay the lion, not kick the one-eyed cat. You rise up by taking down kings.

And last, Luke kept thinking about his birthday. Thirty-four equaled midthirties. A lot of guys might not give much thought to this age, but for professional athletes, your midthirties were when you started flinching and looking over your shoulder for the Career Grim Reaper. Teammates gunned for your position. Opponents smelled blood. And management started checking for the end-date of your contract.

Even now, removed from the game, Luke sensed a shift with this new age. He could be walking without a cane right now, striding confidently down the cobblestone street, and these dope dealers would still just shrug him off. A man too young to frighten but too old to be an actual threat. If Luke feared anything about their youth, it was not its latent violence. It was the health of that youth. The confidence of that youth. To them he was invisible, and there's nothing to fear when you're invisible except the danger of never being visible again.

It was just as bad around young women. If he was in Grand Rapids he'd sometimes drop by a bar downtown for a quick drink or two and— if he were already seated, his limp unnoticed—a woman in her early or midtwenties might strike up a conversation. He was an easy target for their flirtations: too young to be a full-on creep and too old to actually stand a chance with any of them.

Luke passed by the dealers now, looking straight ahead down the road, the cane clacking with each step. He didn't want to fully ignore them and seem arrogant. He glanced to his right. There were seven or eight of them wearing *fútbol* jerseys or muscle shirts, smoking cigarettes and laughing at jokes Luke couldn't understand. They sat around a silver pay phone on some wrought-iron benches that may have once belonged to a park. Their hair was gelled back or else cut short and combed up into black thorns.

An approaching roar made Luke shuffle to the roadside, and seconds later one of them came squealing around the corner on a bright green ATV, two wheels leaving the ground before skidding to a stop in front of the others. The tallest and oldest-looking of the group approached the rider and playfully shoved him off the seat to take his place. The rider shoved back. Then he noticed Luke, who was staring and leaning on his snakewood cane. The young man gave a quick lift of his chin in acknowledgment, and Luke replied with a half nod before hobbling along.

He passed a few stray chickens and then a small dog barking behind an iron gate, the bars spaced wide enough that it could have simply stepped right between them but never did. An old man approached from the other direction, a drooping plastic grocery bag hanging from his grip. The two of them nodded as they passed. Luke recognized him already as a neighbor on this street. He figured the man recognized him too—the lame *gringo* leaving the high brick fortress.

Luke turned the corner and began the descent. The cobblestones dropped at what seemed a forty-five degree angle; the handle of the cane pressed into his palm as he fought against them, against gravity and a sinewy fear. He veered off to the sidewalk, which he tended to avoid because the curbs were often over a foot high.

At the corner he squeezed past a taco stand where a group of construction workers stood eating their lunches, the air seasoned with grilled beef, cilantro, and spilled Coke. It gave way to the fumes of traffic, and even at a green light Luke worried about being too sluggish to react should a bus or taxi careen toward him. His right foot flopped along as usual, like a half-dead fish in the sand, and the heat and noise raised his pulse in a way that flared up his back pain. There were pharmacies all over town, and he wondered if it were possible to get any narcotics. But pills had always made him nervous. An uncle of his had accidentally overdosed on methadone when Luke was a boy. The good and bad that came from pills always seemed to come too easily.

When he finally reached the OXXO store, Luke slipped through the glass doors into the glorious chill of air conditioning and squinted beneath the fluorescent glare. His pulse slowed, and he breathed deeply as he took a large lemon-lime Gatorade from a cooler and clacked over the white tiles to the cashier. The liquor stood on shelves behind the register. Luke pointed at a pint of white tequila on the lowest shelf. He couldn't remember the name and was too far away to read the label. The cashier's hand hovered over the shelves as he waited for Luke to acknowledge he was getting warmer.

"*Blanco*," said Luke. "*Sí*." He nodded and kept pointing.

The cashier said something Luke couldn't understand.

"*Pequeño*," said Luke. "A little one." He leaned his cane against the counter and used both hands to mime something small. The cane fell over, and he struggled to bend down and pick it up off the floor. He'd been buying cheap tequila to save money but also to keep himself in check. The bite and burn of it kept him from drinking too quickly, and its morning aftermath from drinking too much.

With his cane in his right hand and a brown paper bag in his left, he wandered south in the direction of the Malecón. He had no destination, but he knew he couldn't return to the casa right away. Esteban might say something. Something about getting his mind and body right.

Luke passed El Party, the nightclub that sent waves of bass up the hill every nightfall. It was quiet now, and there was nothing to see except the silver spiral staircase near the entrance. He imagined women in stilettos and mini dresses coiling up the narrow steps.

He considered finding a place to sit on the Malecón, to watch the sand sculptors or just stare at the sea. But there'd be too many tourists, too many college students. Too little shade from everything bright.

That's why it made so little sense when Luke settled on crossing the street and resting at the park, which was nearly all concrete and flagpoles. The slim shadows beneath the palm trees offered little relief, but he eased himself onto a bench anyway and removed the Gatorade from the bag.

Nearby, an old woman tossed bread to gulls. A man with stooped shoulders and knotted fingers plucked a guitar. A pack of teenagers walked past in school uniforms: the boys in white polos and navy shorts, the girls with short skirts and high socks. One of the boys held a plastic water bottle up to his mouth like it was a microphone. He closed his eyes and sang falsetto while wiggling his hips. It was to make the girls laugh.

Luke sipped the Gatorade. His shirt was damp with sweat, sticking to him, and he became more aware of the rolls of fat on his stomach. In one of the only deep pockets of shade, beneath the park's largest palm, a young couple was making out, touching each other's faces. The woman's skirt rose up her leg as she leaned further into the man. This, too, had come to Luke with age—an appreciation for a young woman's skin. Her thigh looked as smooth as the inside of a seashell.

It had been two months since he and Shannon had had sex, and three months since the time before. When they'd fight—even if it was about money or parenting—the subject of sex always arose. He'd say she was cold, uncaring about his injuries, and was sickened by his fat and lameness. And she'd say something like, "You're only ugly when you hate yourself."

Luke sipped some more until the bottle was half-empty. Then he glanced around the park for any police, opened the pint of tequila, and poured half of it into the Gatorade. He tilted his head back and swallowed, feeling the heat of the day on his face, squeezing his eyes shut against the sun.

Machine noise cut through the windows and walls, shocking Luke out of sleep and onto his feet. His ankle buckled, and pain flashed through his back. He held himself up against the closed door, staring at his bed for a moment, and then scanned the room for the light on the walls. At first he thought it was morning and the sound was from the studio. But orange rays slipped through the window slats, the way dust did in the morning, and he realized it was verging on night. The noise returned, a motorcycle howling back up the street.

Luke rubbed his eyes, inhaled deeply, and then patted his hair down where he felt it sticking up. He opened the door and walked to the railing overlooking the neighborhood. The motorcycle had turned around and was making its run again. The green ATV followed in its thundering wake.

More than pain, more than confusion or fatigue, what he felt was a cavernous thirst. He staggered to the kitchen for water but stopped when he noticed Esteban reclining on a sofa, watching the news in the adjacent living area.

"How's it going?" Luke said.

"For me or for Calderón?" The Mexican president was on TV, speaking at a podium adorned with the eagle coat of arms. The footage was spliced with images of the northern border. Stacks of seized brown packages beside a display of automatic weapons. *Federales* in black ski masks patrolling the streets. Esteban hit mute. "Missed you at six thirty."

"What was at six thirty?" asked Luke, and immediately he remembered their dinner plans. "Oh shit, I'm sorry."

Esteban stood up and walked to the kitchen. He ran his hand along a large limestone abstract that stood in the corner. "I knocked on your door."

"Yeah, I fell asleep."

"You fell asleep, huh?" said Esteban. He opened a bag of chips that was on the counter. "Or you get struck by some white lightning?"

Luke grabbed a glass from the cupboard, filled it at the water cooler, and drank it down before replying. "Same time tomorrow. On me."

"On you?" Esteban sauntered back to the sofa with the chips. "Maybe I'll order some lobster. Maybe some caviar will wake your ass up."

Luke clenched his jaw and headed up the staircase to the patio. A cockroach slowly climbed the wall, and for a second he thought about smashing it with his bare hand. But instead he just winced and dragged his dead foot up the steps.

The sun was straight ahead—huge and orange and floating just above the sea. Omar stood silhouetted beside the pool, watching it. He turned at the sound of Luke, and immediately a grin spread over his face. He waved him over. "*Ven aquí*. Hurry." He held a glass and handed it to Luke. "You almost missed it." And he patted Luke on the shoulder before jogging down the stairs to make another drink.

Luke held the cocktail up to the fading light. It was pale green—the limeade from lunch. A slice of lime floated on the surface. He took a sip and immediately felt a glimmer of clarity cut through the murk of his brain.

Beside him, on a wooden pedestal, stood a sculpture carved from dark gray basalt. It resembled a huge avocado except for the top, which had a vaguely shaped head and arms and large breasts, like a primitive fertility icon. A second stone—smooth and round—was set in a hollow in the center, to act as the fruit's seed, or maybe an embryo.

Luke lay his hand over the second stone and felt it tremble. The motorcycle and ATV took another pass, and he couldn't tell if the earth had really shook or if he'd imagined it—the trembling coming only from his hands or maybe the sensation between his eyes. He had a vision of the vehicles going by again and again, shaking the house until all the sculptures fell to the floor and smashed. He took another sip of his drink as he walked to the back of the patio. Then he leaned against the railing overlooking the street, staring at the group on the corner. Fucking tough guys. Fucking punk-ass *cabrones*.

The glass was almost to his lips again when Omar, who had quietly returned, noticed and scolded him. "No, no, no! Wait for the sun!"

Luke pulled his arm down, spilling a little of the drink on his leg. "Sorry. I wasn't thinking."

The sun was already half buried in the horizon as they walked back toward the pool and the avocado sculpture. They settled into chairs, abstaining from speech, watching the sun vanish. When it was gone, they drank. Luke's thirst still burned in the back of his throat. "This stuff's dangerous. I could drink it all day, like Kool-Aid."

Omar nodded slightly, still staring at the afterglow. "Did you swim today?"

Luke shook his head. "No, man, I didn't swim." He stood from the chair, leaned back a little to stretch his spine, and shambled once more to the back of the patio, overlooking the darkening road. A streetlight shone above the drug dealers, some of whom were now shirtless. Lean and tattooed. He didn't know why, but Luke wanted them to notice him, to see him staring from his perch. He'd lock eyes with them. Maybe wave at them in the dusk.

"What are you doing?" Omar came up behind him, grabbed him by the elbow, and led him back toward their chairs. "Stop looking over there. That's the ugly side." He swept his free hand toward the purple sea and sky. "This. This is your view. You stare at this."

Luke gripped the taxi's door with two hands and pulled himself out of the low backseat. He grabbed his bag, paid the driver, then squinted against the shining white beach that unfurled to the south.

For a moment he considered lying. He could sip a margarita at a hotel bar and just tell Esteban that he'd spent the afternoon floating in the surf. But Esteban would somehow know and call bullshit, like always. Luke had been trying to play nice, to take him up on all of his suggestions and invitations. To be less of a prick. It had been his experience, with both Shannon and his closest friends, that complaints about chronic pain were good for only a short period of sympathy before they went rotten. Now he was to keep that mess to himself.

He'd been here for a week now, and the past few days had settled into the relative pleasure of routine. Luke would wake, pour some coffee laced with cinnamon, and read in bed for an hour with the fan blowing on his face and dust streaming through the balcony doors. Then he'd spend some time downstairs in the studio, watching the guys cut stones. Esteban was working on something abstract, shaped like a crescent. Omar continued hand-sanding his delicate flower petals, individual pieces he would later arrange in pinwheeled layers to make a plumeria bloom.

They continually offered Luke a block of stone. "Put some goggles on and go raid the tools," said Esteban. "I'll show you how they work. See what you can find inside this rock. Maybe you got a knack you don't know about."

But Luke would just smile and shake his head. He joined them every day for Lalo's lunch before exploring a little more of the city alone, walking a little farther each day, pushing his body and building his strength. In the evenings he and Esteban would tour some galleries, wander through shops, or listen to mariachi down at the amphitheater. They'd eat a late dinner someplace downtown and talk a little about family, a little about baseball, but Luke always steered the focus elsewhere, to the city or to sculpture. Esteban would have a single glass of wine or bottle of beer with his meal, and though nothing was ever said, Luke felt compelled to show a similar restraint.

He set out now across the soft sands of the beach and immediately struggled with balance. He'd left the cane back in his room, thinking it would be worthless on this terrain. But this was far worse, and he immediately headed for the dark, firm footing of the waterline.

The area seemed populated by three types of beachgoers. Luke first toiled through a crowd of locals. Parents waded knee-deep in the waves with toddlers, and older children buried each other in the sand. Next came the tourists. Men tanned behind sunglasses, many of them impossibly fit and from the nearby gay resort. And young women walked in groups along the water's edge. Lately he'd noticed the dimples—Venus dimples—on some women's lower backs. His gaze lingered now on these hollows of skin—so small they felt like secrets, which was the essence of the turn-on.

But eventually, after a halting, half-mile trek through the masses, the beach gave way to a third place, where the hotels ended at a steep, rocky embankment surrounded by trees. The sand was dotted with loners—some locals, some tourists—who lay asleep on towels or read paperbacks. Shouts and laughter were replaced by crashing water and the call of gulls. Luke opened his bag, removed his towel, and spread it over these sands.

This was the time when most men at the beach would remove their shirts. A few years ago, Luke would have welcomed showing off the arms, chest, and shoulders of his conditioning routine. When his stomach was sheet-metal flat. Now he was that guy who wore a T-shirt when swimming in public.

The Topps Company might bear some of the blame. The baseball card they produced for Luke's rookie year showed him tan and focused, captured in the middle of his delivery—teeth clenched, right arm blurred. At the peak of his powers. It was the default image of himself that he always imagined, at any time, in any situation. So it was always a shock these days when he walked down the street, past the mirrored glass of an office building, and saw his current, authentic self.

He read for about a half hour—the same horrors of the Somme—but the sun eventually bullied him into the sea. A few of the other loners swam as well, the breakers hammering them off-balance. Luke, in his white T-shirt, entered the surf. He'd grown up on Lake Michigan, spending his teenage summer days along the beach, but it had been years since he'd swum in open water. He'd expected the sharp Great Lakes chill of memory, but this was refreshing and comfortable. A wave hit him, and he tasted salt water for the first time in years. Another hit him, sending him on his ass. He came up smiling and braced for the next one. His foot was a useless flipper, making it hard to propel forward with his legs, but with a kind of breaststroke he pushed farther away from shore, until a rip current stoked a subtle panic in his chest, and he edged his way back closer to land.

Standing once more in the shallows—his shirt pasted to his stomach and chest, hair and nipples showing through—he gazed down the coast. Tree-covered hills spiked with radio antennas and cell towers followed the contours of the bay, tucking the city into a long, snug corridor of green and blue. Luke began heading toward his towel but paused and returned to the waves, floating on his back atop the skin of the salt water and remembering what Esteban had said about the ocean being more buoyant. Lake Michigan was fresh like youth, fresh where you could open your eyes underwater without wincing. The ocean was salted like sweat, like the rims of cocktail glasses, but he relaxed now and lay atop the water's skin, trying to detect even the slightest change in sensation.

His bathing suit was still damp, but he'd brought an extra shirt to the beach and was now as comfortable as he'd been all week, sipping Bud Light and smoking a cigarette in an air-conditioned sports bar across from the Malecón. It didn't matter that baseball highlights flashed across the TVs; it didn't much matter that the wall beside the bathrooms was covered in Yankees' pennants and a framed poster of Wrigley Field. Most of the room was strangely decked out in hockey flair. The young bartender with a shaved head was a Canadian named Teddy.

Luke picked up a menu and scanned it only briefly before ordering a cheeseburger. "And can I borrow a pen?"

Teddy retrieved one from over by the cash register. Luke took a fresh cocktail napkin from the stack beside the ketchup bottles. After a few minutes of thought and the remainder of his beer, he wrote:

Goals

Short
More time with Julia and Brie (reading, board games, etc.)
Eat right

Medium
Get in shape! (Swim?)
Job

Long

A moment later, beside the line that read *Eat right*, he added, *(when I get home)*. He'd bought a plane ticket and would leave in four days. Esteban planned on leaving one day prior to attend some meeting at his firm in San Diego.

A couple sitting at a table behind Luke stood up, walked to a window, and gazed upward at something. A few others in the bar joined them at the window and in the doorway; everyone's eyes tilted skyward.

When Teddy brought him a new beer, Luke nodded toward the gathering. "What's going on? We got a UFO?"

"Bird Men."

"A what?"

"You seen the Bird Men yet?" asked Teddy. "They're here every weekend. You got to see the Bird Men."

Luke rose from his stool and wandered over toward the others. There were too many clustered by the glass, so he squeezed past the people by the door and stepped out onto the sidewalk. Above the Malecón stood a towering white pole—maybe fifty feet tall—that he might have noticed before but wasn't sure. Four men in white shirts, red pants, and ribbon-plumed hats dangled, head-down, from four separate ropes that ran between the top of the pole and their waists. They skimmed the cyan backdrop like a dole of doves. In unison, with their arms stretched earthward, they circled the pole, inching closer to the ground with each revolution.

An avian melody floated down with them. Luke scanned the area for a musician before noticing the tiny figure seated atop the pole and playing some sort of flute with one hand and beating a drum with the other, all the while spinning in time with the flyers.

Within a couple of minutes the Bird Men had drifted to solid ground. Tourists applauded, including those watching from the sports bar. Luke returned inside and sat down just as Teddy was serving his burger. "Pretty cool, eh?" said Teddy. "They're natives from over in Papantla."

Luke smiled and shook his head, reaching for the ketchup. "I get the shakes from a Ferris wheel. Those guys got some brass ones."

He happily ate, staring at the list of goals and brainstorming new ones. He glanced occasionally at highlights on TV. Apparently the Tigers were in first place by a game and a half. He'd had no idea. He wasn't even sure how many of his old teammates were still on the roster. There were a few guys he wouldn't mind reconnecting with. Ray Gallegos was solid. So was Shane Saunders.

Luke's phone rang and he answered. "Ready for the shock of shocks?" he asked. "I'm actually watching baseball."

"The shock is what I'm holding in my hand right now," said Shannon. "It's a fucking ream of paper, all of it bills. The girls' tuition. Student loans. Doctor co-pays. Swimming lessons. And our credit cards are *totally* out of control."

He sat back and rolled his eyes. "Jesus, Shannon. Grease me with a little small talk before you lay down the goddamned hammer."

"No. Someone has to finally swing the hammer because we've put this shit off for too long, and it's all jammed up in our faces now." She spoke rapidly. "I don't know what we're going to do. I have absolutely no idea. It's come down to something drastic, like pulling the girls out of Montessori or selling one of our cars."

He tried to lighten the tone. "We could sell some plasma."

"They could bleed us dry, and we wouldn't even come close."

"I'll be home in four days," he said. "We'll figure it out. We always manage. But I can't do anything until I get home."

"That's the problem," said Shannon. "You don't *do anything.*"

Bad back or not, there was little doubt about Luke's lingering arm strength. His phone lay in pieces before he'd registered flinging it against the wall, where it just missed shattering a Heineken bar mirror. He immediately walked over to it, gathering up the pieces and placing them in his pocket. He kept his head down so as not to make eye contact with the people sitting behind him.

"Everything cool, brother?" asked Teddy, standing over him.

"It's cool," said Luke. "Sorry I flared up." He headed back to his stool. "Can I get a whiskey?"

"You sure about that?"

Luke nodded, eyes downcast. "Yeah. It'll calm me down, not fire me up."

He drank the first one neat, the second with ice, and the third with just a splash of water. After paying his bill he stuffed the to-do list into his pocket amid the phone wreckage and hobbled outside. The Bird Men were gone. Their white pole stood solemnly over the colorful crowds.

That shift had come to Luke's head—the wonderful clarity of perception that felt almost tectonic. He'd caught it, and it would be brief, but for now the massive slabs of home and family and body had stopped grinding against each other in his brain and had slipped into perfect grooves where they all fit flush and went still.

A half hour later he was back at the casa, leaning against the refrigerator, finishing off a bottle of beer. He clanked it down on the countertop just as Esteban entered the room. "Another dead soldier, eh Boss?"

Luke ignored him and casually glanced around the kitchen. That shift, that feeling, was slipping away from him. He wondered where Omar kept the vodka. It was almost time for their ritual. The sun was falling toward the sea.

"How was the beach?" asked Esteban.

"Beach was good." Luke squinted and nodded. "I swam all up in those waves."

"Glad to hear it."

Luke took a few painful steps toward the staircase. Maybe Omar was on the patio already, waiting with their drinks. "I could totally feel the salt water. Shit was buoyant."

Esteban nodded and watched him. He crossed his arms over his chest and exhaled deeply through his nose, watching until Luke disappeared around the corner, out of sight, up the stairs.

There was no sign of Omar. The horizon blazed orange as if the bay were on fire, but higher up the sky was such a deep, heartbreaking shade of purple that Luke almost decided to call it a night and turn in early.

Until he heard the shouts on the street. He followed the sounds to the back of the patio and looked down over the iron railing. The same evening crew had gathered below, and as always one of them was on a motorcycle, tracing a tight circuit over the cobblestones. But a mild chaos had broken out. Something wasn't right with the biker—drunk or high, maybe. He steered in a palsied sort of figure eight and then hopped the curb at low speed, right where the others stood. His body lifted off the seat, and he sprawled over the handlebars while everyone else shouted and scattered. The motorcycle's front wheel turned into itself, and the thing buckled, landing on the legs of the fallen driver. Two of the men ran to him, lifting it off, and one of them cut the engine. The dim, narrow road fell silent for a few seconds, everyone seemingly getting their bearings. Then the shouting resumed. The biggest in the group—a guy with a fauxhawk and a huge cobra tattooed on his upper back—wrenched the fallen driver to his feet before slapping him across the face.

Luke pulled a cigarette from his shirt pocket and lit it. After a deep drag he dangled it from his lips, where it seesawed there as his body shook with laughter. He clapped his hands in loud applause.

One of the guys heard and noticed. He spoke in Spanish and pointed up at Luke. The eyes of everyone—including the biker who'd been slapped—shot upward at him.

When he'd wake the next day—sheets sweat-stuck to his body, dried blood on the pillow, and his pores leaking booze—Luke would imagine what he must have looked like then. What kind of crazy fuck slouches there in a bathing suit, giving a standing ovation from his poolside box seat? Esteban had said not to pick at their scabs. But Luke had ripped them off and pissed on the wounds.

He'd tell himself the next day that this wasn't because of the booze or his back or the fight with his wife. It had nothing to do with their drugs or a sense of morality about crime, either. It was the smug certainty of those who think they're untouchable. Just like the drunk guy in Kane County over a decade ago—the one who'd stood in the first row behind the dugout. Luke had given up back-to-back homers, and as he'd walked to the bench the guy yelled, "Your daughter's a flat-chested cunt!" Luke was twenty-one and didn't even have kids yet, but that didn't matter. He picked a ball up out of the dirt and reared back. The third baseman, a guy named Andre Anderson, grabbed Luke's arm and pried the ball from his grip. Luke could have killed that guy in the stands. A fastball from that range? He *would* have killed him and been arrested on the field. But there's something about a man who thinks he's safe behind bulletproof glass, who's fooled himself into believing he's shielded from consequences when, in fact, there's no protection at all.

The guys below sauntered into the middle of the street, toward the casa. A few threw their hands into the air. A few more raised middle fingers. Someone said "motherfucker." They knew his language better than he knew theirs.

Luke was tempted—for one second—to fling his lit cigarette down at their faces. He'd already bought into his own false safety, the one afforded by the fortress-style construction of the casa. He didn't ponder this now, nor even the next day. He only gave them a sort of half salute and then stepped away from the railing, out of their sight, and turned back toward the stairs. The sun was nearly submerged. Omar had never shown.

Down one level, in the kitchen and living room, the street voices were closer and louder. Esteban had stood up from the couch and was squinting through the louvered doors to the outside. "What did you do?" he asked.

Luke wandered near the lime tree, shaking his head. "Do what? I didn't do anything." He peered through the house's open structure, down yet another level, to where Omar was sweeping the floors of the studio. "Hey, Omar!" he called. "You're missing the sun, man. We're missing our little fiesta."

Omar glanced up over his shoulder, faintly shook his head, and gave one more sweep of the broom before walking out of view.

"What's up with Omar?" Luke turned and flinched.

Esteban was standing right in front of him. Right over him. "What did you do?" he said. "What did you say to them?"

"I didn't say a thing. Swear on a cemetery."

"You did something."

Luke took a step back, smirking and turning his head away. "Personal space, man. Respect my comfort bubble."

Esteban lunged forward, thrust his hands toward Luke's chest, and balled his shirt up in his fists. Then he forced him back against the wooden railing—the only barrier to a ten-foot fall. "Tell me," he said through clenched teeth, "or I will split you over those stones."

Luke wrenched himself free and shoved Esteban in the chest. "What the fuck is wrong with you! You going to murder me? You going to fucking *murder* me?" He pressed his hand against his back where the pain had started.

"I am running a business," said Esteban. "I built a place where people come to relax and feel safe." He jabbed his index finger at Luke, and his voice fell quiet. "This city is getting bullshit press. People are already cancelling reservations. And those two-bits on the corner are just worry enough to keep me awake at night." He lowered his hand and stood up straighter and even taller. "You mess things up? Fine. You mess your own things up. But keep your business out of mine."

"What business?"

Esteban raised his hand to his mouth and tipped it back, sipping from an imaginary bottle.

"Oh yeah, that's my business. That's what I'm all about."

"Lately."

"Right. You got me."

"You want to know what's up with Omar? Why he's not watching the sunset with you? Because I asked him not to. You get enough drink all day."

Luke nodded. "You got me all figured out."

"This ain't you, who I'm looking at right now. This guy's angry and feeling sorry for himself. You used to fight and scrap till you won. Now you just trip over your own dick."

"You don't even know. You don't know shit." Luke felt his eyes start to water and turned away. "You can't even begin to begin what I've begun."

"The hell you talking about, man? I can't even understand you." Esteban put his hands in his pockets and stared at the floor. "Why you even here? I thought I'd invite you down for a little sea air, a little change of scenery, you know? Have you cut some stones. Thought maybe we could talk as friends."

Luke just shook his head, still looking away.

"But you don't want to talk with me. You don't want to talk about the game or the old days. Okay. All right. But you don't even talk about your family. Your girls."

"Oh, fuck you," Luke mumbled.

"Okay. Sure. Fuck me. I'm messing with you right now, but you need to be messed with. You need to be shook up so you can shake it off."

Neither of them spoke for a few moments. They avoided looking at one another.

"You done?" asked Luke.

Esteban shrugged. "I don't want to be, but I guess I am. I wish *you* were." He walked over to the dining table and picked up his phone. "I got to call a client back home. Explain to the *tonto* why a hand-carved fireplace actually takes a little time and money."

Luke trudged out of the room, his foot dead and heavy, his back on fire. He ascended the stairs once more.

The sun was gone. The orange had gone purple, and the purple had gone black. The street sounded quiet, but he didn't peek over the railing to check. Instead he approached the red Mayan hammock and gingerly lowered himself into it so that the netting cocooned over his body. Luke rubbed his eyes, yawned, and then stared at a trellis of morning glories. He hadn't noticed any hummingbirds lately.

Subtly—so subtly—a bass beat rose up the hill to him. He felt it before he heard it. It wasn't a tremor, like an earthquake. It was like a war drum. His eyes opened wide, suddenly awake. The bass was clearing his head, calling him down.

The street was still. A rooster crowed nearby though it was just past midnight. Otherwise the only sounds were a pair of low voices near the corner, distant traffic, and the faint but incessant throb of the nightclub. Luke opened the casa's front door just wide enough to peer around the edge and see that only two young men stood under the streetlight at the corner. Both had their backs to him, ambling in the other direction.

He stepped out into the inky air and closed the door as slowly as possible to muffle the sound. After checking the corner once more, he limped down the street in the other direction, holding his snakewood cane but not using it yet. He took the long way around the block, toward the club.

Luke had spent the past few hours nursing a bottle of rum he'd found in the cupboard above the sink. He drank it with Coke while reading in bed, though the words swam across the page and he read little. He switched to playing solitaire with a deck of retired casino cards that he always kept in his luggage. Eventually he showered, shaved, and changed into a crisp, white button up and gray dress pants. Esteban and Omar were in their rooms. At one point Omar played his recorder, the feathery song weaving through the walls of the casa while Luke stared out the window at the lights below the hill, biding his time.

When he'd made the turn and was out of sight and earshot, Luke lowered his cane to the sidewalk to help with the descent. He bit the inside of his cheek without realizing it, imagining women in low-cut tops and skintight dresses. He'd seen just enough flesh on this trip to make him crave more. He'd felt like this a few times in his marriage but had never acted on it. There was a relief in giving in. His head had turned from muddled gray to a pure, starless expanse.

Through the concrete park came the glowing, pulsing sight of El Party. It stood next to a closed pharmacy that advertised Viagra, Lipitor, and human growth hormone. At the club's entrance two bouncers checked IDs. When Luke approached they just nodded and waved him through.

He struggled with the tight bends in the spiral staircase, but when he reached the top floor he smiled and felt a warm tumbling in his stomach. The thatched roof and tiki torches he'd seen earlier were less visible inside at night. Instead, bodies moved as if under dark water, the black lights and dancing creating a sort of liquid humanity. Women lounged on white furniture. Men drank from huge Styrofoam cups. Luke stood at the bar for fifteen minutes before getting a massive rum and Coke complete with plastic lid and straw. He took three long sips with his eyes closed.

He had no idea what should happen next. Luke had started dating Shannon when he was twenty and had remained faithful during all those years on the road. The music almost moved him physically now—almost pushed him forward—through the strobing darkness.

He sat in a lounge chair and slipped the cane underneath. Beside him reclined a young blond woman with hair cut short on the sides and back but with long bangs that fell into her eyes. Her forehead creased as she looked at him. "Are you all right?"

Luke sat up straight, on the edge of the chair. "Doing well. How are you?"

"No," she said, shaking her head and pointing at his thigh. "My cousin was in Afghanistan and got shrapnel in his leg. Were you in the army?"

Luke shook his head. "No, I was an athlete. Played pro baseball in the States. Just a lifetime of wear and tear in cleats."

The woman looked out at the dance floor. "I don't watch sports," she said. A few minutes later she waved at someone across the darkness before standing and striding away.

He sat there through several songs, bodies skimming past him, and finished his drink with a gurgling sound from the straw. A server took his order for another, and while waiting Luke stared at a woman who stood alone against the wall near the bathrooms. Her hair was black and straight, hanging halfway down her back, and she wore a halter top that fell about an inch short of her hips, exposing a band of brown skin around her waist. He wondered if she had Venus dimples. She was younger than him by about a decade.

Luke stood and teetered, bracing himself on the arm of the chair, before walking in her direction. His back barely hurt at all—it felt numb like his entire face. She watched him approach, revealing nothing in terms of pleasure or annoyance.

He nodded and spoke over the music. "This place is pretty great, huh?"

She nodded back. "Pretty great." She had a Spanish accent.

"Are you from here? From P.V.?"

She shook her head. "California."

"God, I love California," said Luke. He could hear himself slurring the words. "Used to go there all the time when we'd play the Angels and A's. I used to be in the major leagues."

The woman glanced toward the bathrooms and crossed her arms. "I went to a Dodgers game once." She shrugged. "They lost."

Luke nodded, turning to see if the server had returned with his rum and Coke. When he faced her again a tall guy had emerged from the men's room. He was young but had the flat nose of an old boxer and an underbite that gave him a long chin. His eyes were distant and squinty from drink.

The woman put her hand on the guy's lower back. "So he just said he was a baseball player."

The guy smiled, looking him up and down. "The fuck he was."

"For Detroit," Luke said. "Starting pitcher."

The guy lifted his chin. "And women get all wet when you tell them that? It works pretty good for you?"

"No, man," said Luke, raising his hand. "It wasn't like that."

The guy stepped forward, about to walk past, but as he did he patted Luke on the stomach. "Keep hustling, champ."

Without thinking, Luke raised his hand up to the guy's face. And then— in a smooth, almost gentle fashion—he palmed it like a basketball before shoving it back on his shoulders.

The fist itself didn't drop Luke. He fell to the floor trying to duck, and his dead foot gave out. For a moment he was on all fours, crawling through a sea of legs toward the bar. Then the guy was standing over him, beating him on the back of the head and neck.

Shouts arose over the music, and the punching stopped. Someone lifted Luke onto his feet, where he wavered for a moment, the room reeling like a ship in storm. Three men had their arms wrapped around the guy. Luke scrambled to the white lounge chair where he'd sat and pulled the cane out from underneath.

The guy had broken free, and everyone in the vicinity just stood back. He charged toward Luke, taking a wild swing that hit him in the chest and another that missed altogether.

Luke stumbled, leaning on his cane before raising it up with both hands and holding it in front of him like a sword. "We're done," he said. "It's cool. We're done."

But the guy lunged forward, and Luke swung the cane, cracking him on the side of the head.

"My ear!" he screamed. "Holy shit! My ear! I can't hear anything!"

Nobody noticed Luke crashing toward the spiral staircase, a white current of back pain sucking the air from his lungs. The bottoms of his shoes were wet with spilled booze, and they slipped over the steps, sending him on his ass, sliding and twisting to the street. The bouncers at the entrance approached him, but he continued past, onto the sidewalk. "I'm good. I'm good," he said before lurching through traffic and frantically clacking his way across the concrete park.

He squeezed himself behind a palm tree, kneeling painfully on landscaping stones, gulping for air in the dimly lit park and staring across the street. He was certain the guy was going to emerge at any moment, looking for him. He clutched an especially smooth and round stone, the feeling against his fingers like a tactile memory. Fueled with this adrenaline, he could have hit ninety on the radar gun right now. Crushed a man's temple in a heartbeat. When enough time passed and no one emerged from the club, he turned and plunged through the trees, headed for the casa. But flashing red lights lit up the night behind him. A police cruiser had pulled up to the front of El Party.

Across from him stood the church, its twin steeples looming overhead. Luke hobbled toward it, bass beats still pounding the sky. Along the church's brick, beneath darkened stained glass, ran a row of broad-leafed bushes. Luke shoved his way between the bushes and the wall and then lay flat on his stomach. The plan was to stay there until the cops left and eventually trudge back up the hill, to safety.

He turned onto his back and stared upward. An old man was speaking rapidly in Spanish, poking at Luke's stomach with his boot.

"What?" Luke said. He sat up, squinting at the man before noticing the light creeping into the sky. Hours had passed. It was dawn.

A ring of keys jangled from the old man's belt. He continued to speak, gesturing at Luke and then at the now-open door of the church.

"I'm sorry," said Luke. "I'm sorry."

His white shirt was streaked with dirt and dotted with blood. Pain stabbed his head, inside and out, and radiated from his old herniated discs to all of the muscles up and down his back. He grabbed his cane, slouched to the sidewalk, and turned the corner of the church. The old man's stream of words faded away, and the city was quiet. No traffic, no music. Just the hollow percussion of Luke's cane climbing the Old Town hill.

• • •

With the stone-carving tools at full volume and the dust plumes rising to his room, Luke sat up, rubbed his eyes, and leaned against the headboard. It was his thirty-fourth birthday. He got up to brush his teeth.

Yesterday he'd slept through the tool noise. Yesterday he'd slipped into the house at dawn, stripped naked from his stained shirt and pants, and slept until midafternoon. Then he'd laid there for a couple of hours, reading but often just staring at the walls, watching another tiny lizard scale the bricks. Or he filled glasses of water at the bathroom sink and gulped down one after another until, by evening, his urine had turned from rust to yellow to white. Otherwise he simply lay in bed, aimed the box fan at his face, and took deep breaths from the cooling rush.

Last night he emerged from his room to eat a small bowl of rice in front of the TV. Omar joined him to watch some *fútbol*, and eventually so did Esteban. While the other two chatted about the game, switching between English and Spanish, Luke kept silent, smiling faintly when the others laughed, even if he hadn't heard or understood the joke.

After Omar and Esteban went to bed, Luke walked over to the lime tree in the dining area. He still had little appetite, but his tongue felt coated in cotton and dried mud. He plucked a lime, pierced the rind with his thumbnail, and peeled it like you would an orange. His fingers stung as the acid flowed into the cuts and scrapes from last night. After taking a bite to cleanse the taste from his mouth, he ran the remaining fruit over the tops of each of his hands, as if applying a balm, and let his flesh burn from the juice for a few minutes before washing up at the sink.

Today he was determined to engage—with others and with his surroundings. Shannon and the girls called the house phone to wish him a happy birthday and tell him they were going to bake a cake when he returned. Then he spent an hour swimming laps in the pool. It was so small that he could only do five strokes before having to make the turn, but by the end his lungs burned and the muscles in his arms trembled. When he returned home, he was going to take his family to Lake Michigan. He'd make it a ritual, every month. Something they'd all look back on when they grew older.

After swimming, he and Esteban walked downtown, shopping for gifts. Luke was leaving in three days and needed some things for the girls.

He bought each of them an embroidered peasant dress, a green national team jersey, a pair of maracas, and a Huichol beaded figurine—a turtle for Julia and a bear for Brie.

Neither Luke nor Esteban made any mention of the last two days. They had argued—nearly come to blows—but were seemingly fine now, both having come of age on playing fields and in locker rooms, where men got angry with one another as a matter of course. Teammates talked junk, made threats, and occasionally blackened eyes. Then they marched out together under stadium lights, taking aim at a common enemy.

As Luke was paying for the girls' maracas, Esteban headed to the shop next door. He returned with a red plastic bag and a huge smile on his face. "I just got you something good. For your birthday."

Lalo usually only cooked lunches at the casa, but Esteban had hired him to make the night's birthday dinner. Luke, Esteban, and Omar sat poolside that evening, sipping Modelo, though Luke had little taste for it. Atop a pedestal near the hammock stood Omar's latest sculpture, which he'd completed that morning. All five plumeria petals were finally complete, attached to a thin piece of metal that served as the stem. The stone flower was so delicate and organic that it looked like it might bend itself toward the sun.

Spiced smoke drifted over the pool. Lalo stood sweating on the other side, grilling chorizo along with corncobs seasoned with *cotija*, cayenne, and lime. The four ate around a small table on the patio, glancing out at the sea while talking and chewing their food. Motorcycles roared back and forth on the street, but Luke ignored them. There'd been no fallout from the other day.

For dessert, Lalo served a tres leches cake with three red candles and four green ones. Omar leaned over the table, lighting the candles with a match. "You outlived Jesus Christ," he said.

Luke shrugged. "I wouldn't know anything about that."

Omar was giddy and a little drunk, celebrating his completed sculpture. Lalo was enjoying sitting at the table for once. And Esteban was just happy everyone was happy, all of which led to them singing *"Feliz Cumpleaños"* and making Luke—embarrassed as he was—blow out the candles.

"We're grown men, for shit's sake." He blew them out but made no wish. As with the torn, smudged to-do list he'd found in his wet bathing suit pocket, it was best not to look too far ahead.

"All right," said Esteban. "Let's get serious now." He reached under the table and retrieved a package wrapped in newspaper. "I saw this and thought of you."

Luke took it from him, eyeing both the package and Esteban. He tore the paper, opened the box, and reached inside. "You thought of me, did you?"

The other three men burst into laughter as Luke held up the gift. It was a white luchador mask, but unlike the others he'd seen for sale all over town, this one was styled as a maniacal clown. Horrific red lips with sharp teeth curled into a smile. Red yarn hung from the back, like long, stringy hair. And at the center of the mask was a round, red nose.

Luke slipped it over his head. "You thought of me," he said, his voice muffled.

Omar clutched his stomach, as if in pain from the laughter. Lalo pounded the table.

"Because I'm a clown but not just any clown. I'm an evil clown."

Esteban wiped the tears from his eyes. He slapped Luke's chest with the back of his hand. "Come on. Don't overthink it." He walked over to a wicker table near the pool and returned with a smaller, unwrapped box. "I got the real gift right here."

Still wearing the mask, Luke held the box toward his ear, shook it, and then flipped open the lid. Inside lay a magnificent Swiss Army knife with a mother-of-pearl handle. He tilted it slowly under the sun to reveal its full iridescence.

"It's got twenty-one tools," said Esteban. "Got a chisel and fish scaler and even a little magnifying glass. Good for fixing shit and solving problems." He patted Luke on the shoulder. "For *mi hermano*."

Luke turned the knife over, where an engraving read: *Don't worry about your ERA. Just get the win.* He nodded, his head sweating now in the mask. "Thank you."

"You going to wear that thing all night?" asked Lalo.

Luke lifted the mask just high enough that it exposed his chin and mouth. He took a small sip of beer and smiled. "There are places I shouldn't show my face."

A couple of hours later he sat alone, smoking and watching the sunset with no drink nearby. The clown mask sat atop his crown, giving the illusion of two heads. He unconsciously played with the Swiss Army knife, flipping the blades and other tools out one by one before returning them to the handle.

A girl appeared on a rooftop a block or two below where he sat. She was tall and thin, probably not yet in her teens. She hung laundry on a line, slowly creating a barrier between the two of them. When she finished, she ran along the line for some reason, flickering between the colorful pieces of clothing. She was visible only in those quick flashes between shirts and dresses, but he saw her entirely, pieced together in his eye and mind, even after she'd disappeared from the roof.

Following lunch the next day, Luke and Esteban played dominoes at the dining table. Powdery stone dust coated Esteban's clothes and face. Lalo scrubbed dishes in the kitchen, America ran a vacuum in the hallway, and Omar had headed upstairs to nap away from the noise.

"I don't think I've ever played the actual game of dominoes," said Luke. "I used to just stand them up and push them down."

Esteban nodded. "You know when fans would do the wave around the stadium? That always reminded me of that."

They'd been talking baseball again. Not so much the game on the field but the stories from the road, about the life. Having to climb the fence and shag home runs because the owner wouldn't buy more balls. Winning a championship in single-A and getting an actual gold ring for it. That feeling of breaking camp with the big boys for the first time.

Because of the noise from the sink and the vacuum, they didn't immediately take notice of the rumbling outside. At first it seemed like one of the garbage or water delivery trucks that always squeezed through the narrow drives. Lalo finished wiping down the countertops and stepped through the louvered doors to smoke on the balcony. He froze for a moment, ducked back inside, and then peered out again, waving his hand frantically. "Esteban! Esteban!"

Luke sprang from the chair, lost his balance, and followed Esteban to the balcony. The three of them crowded for a view, with Esteban's palm already draped over his forehead in horror. Outside, three dark green Humvees idled thunderously on the street. Camouflaged men in helmets and Kevlar vests stood at the ring mounts of the vehicles behind machine guns. Shining ammunition belts lay draped alongside.

Other men had already leapt from the vehicles, clutching assault rifles and surrounding the house on the corner by the pay phone.

"Are they *Federales*?" asked Luke.

"No," said Esteban. "Oh, Christ, no. This is fucking army."

He turned and ran toward and up the stairway. Luke and Lalo followed, and at the top stood Omar. He shook his head over and over, speaking Spanish in a low but frenetic voice.

All four of them ran to the end of the patio and stared down. The troops were barking out commands and pounding on the door of the house on the corner. A young woman in sweatpants and a tank top opened it, hands half-raised, and two soldiers immediately wrenched her arms behind her back, cuffed her, and forced her facedown onto the cobblestones. Four other soldiers charged through the door, leading with their rifles. A few others spread out around the perimeter of the house.

Neighbors along the street leaned out from landings and windows. One of the machine gunners looked up at Luke and the others atop Casa Isabela. He frowned, shook his head, and waved his hand as if pushing them back and out of sight. They followed the order, though Luke lingered for a moment, standing near Omar's plumeria sculpture. He wanted them pulled from the house and arrested. He wanted to see someone he recognized.

Lalo spoke rapidly to Esteban and then ran downstairs.

"What?" asked Luke.

"His brother-in-law's a P.V. cop. He's going to call him and see what's going on."

Omar and Esteban descended the stairs as well, but Luke stayed on the top floor, running his fingers through his hair with both hands. He paced along the pool but stayed away from the street-side end of the patio. In the other direction, the sea lay smooth and coolly blue like a swath of silk. In the foreground, the girl's colorful laundry still hung from the line, unmoving in the windless afternoon.

Voices pierced the air behind him. Luke again crept to the back of the patio to spy on the action.

Wooden shutters slammed open across the street. At first Luke thought it was just another neighbor gawking from a third-story apartment, though in an instant he realized it came from the house under siege. A young shirtless man stood in an open window clutching a black weapon near his hip. He spotted Luke and immediately fired several rounds at him, reports booming through the narrow corridor of houses.

Luke fell from terror and instinct. Bits of brick popped and crumbled around him. His arm got caught in the nearby hammock, twisting up in the red netting as the shots continued. Something shattered nearby—a delicate explosion like glass that he knew at once was Omar's sculpture. It had fallen backward, and bits of the stone petals slid and spun across the patio.

He pulled his arm free from the hammock and crawled on his belly toward the stairs. The street erupted in gunshots, the soldiers firing upward at the open window. Esteban's head appeared in the stairwell. "Come on! Come on!" he screamed as a second spray of bullets swept over the patio, shattering a nearby flowerpot and raining black dirt over him.

Luke tumbled down the first few stairs and then curled into a ball at Esteban's feet. Omar returned, patting Luke's head as the gunfire turned sporadic. "You okay?" he asked.

Luke nodded, a rope of snot hanging from his nose.

Esteban staggered back down the stairs. "No, no, no, no, no." Sweat on his forehead had mixed with the stone dust, and tiny rivulets of mud trickled down his face.

A relative quiet settled over the neighborhood, yielding a quivering, lucid-dream air. The shooting had stopped, and the fighting suddenly felt far away. Luke sat up, wiped his nose with his forearm, and began inching back toward the street on his elbows and knees.

"Get back!" growled Omar. "They're still out there!"

Luke's head gently floated atop the adrenaline, the way it did with the day's first alcohol. He was not brave, but he was unafraid. Like those rare moments as a player when he could tap into calmness amid a shaking coliseum, his surroundings felt cinematic and projected. He wanted to see what would happen next to the men he'd watched every day on that corner.

The gunman had retreated from the third-story window, leaving it black and gaping like an open mouth.

"What are you doing!" said Omar, and even as he said it he began crawling toward Luke.

Below them, the soldiers who had circled the house now stood in the center of the street, pointing weapons at their captives. Five men—some nearly boys—knelt beside the young woman in the sweatpants, their hands cuffed behind their backs.

A muscular man in a black T-shirt and fauxhawk slunk along the far wall of the house, approaching the street, hidden from the soldiers' view. He gripped a handgun, holding it upright near his face. Luke's immediate reaction was simply recollection. He remembered him as the guy who'd slapped the drunken motorcyclist the other day. It was that feeling of recognizing someone you know while watching the local news.

Omar grabbed Luke by the ankle and tried to pull him back toward the stairs. Luke kicked his leg free, rattling himself awake in the process. He rose to one knee. "Look out!" he yelled, pointing at the man.

All of the soldiers and even the captives looked up at him, and then— like a ricochet—followed the direction of his pointed finger. The man with the fauxhawk flashed around the corner, standing in the open air, screaming and firing at one of the Humvees.

A series of blasts from the soldiers followed, and seconds later the man was on his side, clutching his blood-soaked abdomen, the gun laying against the curb.

Omar seized Luke's leg again and pulled, this time dragging him backward over bits of shattered stone.

It had been just a one-day operation. According to Lalo's brother-in-law, the government was doing this all over the country: sending in troops, shutting down roads, and raiding a handful of houses in a city. They were trying to send a message that no place was safe for the cartels or even midlevel players. Yesterday they'd hit towns in Nyarit. Tomorrow they'd strike somewhere else.

But after the army, after the ambulance—after the police and the yellow tape and the dozens of gawkers—came the media. And that's when Esteban became quietly unhinged.

"It's over now, Boss," he said, fingering a bullet hole in the brick. "Got the cameras and reporters down there, filming the casa. Talking about how Americans stay here all the time. You think any tour groups going to come here now? You think any colleges going to send their students here to cut stone?"

Luke sat smoking in a lawn chair, staring at the ground, holding a glass of ice water up to his face. Dried blood, from having crawled over debris, caked his knees and elbows. "People will forget," he said. "That won't last."

"Shit's forever on the Internet," said Esteban, raising his voice. "People type in 'house rentals in Puerto Vallarta,' what they going to see? My name and some picture of an army man with a machine gun? Maybe some gangbanger?" He slapped his hands together as if wiping away crumbs.

Luke said nothing. He blinked away rising smoke but kept his eyes lowered, wondering to himself why he'd relentlessly spied on them across the street, why he'd kept sticking his nose in on that shit. He took a sip from the glass and finally looked up, meeting Esteban's eyes. "It's just water."

Esteban looked bewildered and shook his head. "I didn't say anything." With a kind of wince he bent his face up toward the sky and tugged down on his shirt collar with both hands. Red streaks arose on his neck where his fingernails had scraped the skin. "Shit on their fucking mothers!" he hissed.

Omar patted Esteban on the shoulder with one hand and used the other to gently guide him toward and down the stairs. Maybe it came from a lifetime of sculpture—of practicing an art rooted in touch as much as sight—because Omar so often spoke to men while using his hands. "It's okay," he whispered.

Alone on the patio, Luke leaned back, closed his eyes, and let the smoke unfurl from his nostrils. He kept thinking of the guy who had stood across from him, framed in the window, and how they'd made eye contact in that instant before the explosion of potshots.

Luke figured he'd just startled the guy, that when the shutters had flown open he'd planned on aiming at the soldiers. But maybe it wasn't impulsive. Maybe he remembered Luke from the other day, when he'd laughed and applauded, hip-deep in a bender. Or maybe something else. White guy? Maybe thought he'd turned them all in. That he was DEA or FBI.

Something shattered in the studio below. Luke dropped the cigarette and braced his lower back with his hand. He stood, and by the time he had plummeted down the steps there came three more shatters from below. Esteban stood beyond the lime tree, looking down at the studio, in the very place where he'd threatened Luke with a fall days before. He held a marble bowl over his head—one of the bowls from the shelf above the dining table—and cast it downward.

Omar stood beside him, pleading in Spanish as Esteban scanned the room for something else to destroy. He looked past Luke, into the kitchen, to where the large limestone abstract stood.

"Come on, man," said Luke. "No you don't."

Esteban strode toward it, but Luke stepped into his path—arms outstretched to shove him away. Omar bear-hugged him from behind.

"It's one of mine!" yelled Esteban. "I can do whatever I want with it!"

Between the two of them they shoved him up against a wall. "What the hell, man?" said Luke. "Why are you doing this?"

Esteban pulled away from them both. He set his hands atop his head and vigorously scratched at his scalp as if fighting off insects. "I told you it was over. It's over back home, and now it's over here." He collapsed onto the sofa and buried his face in his hands. "Talk about being ruined. I'm fucking *ruined*."

He sniffed as if he was crying, but he kept his face hidden so Luke couldn't tell for sure. "Real estate's bottomed out. Houses? Bottomed out. You know all that shit. You think people want to spend twenty grand on a marble fireplace? Think they're going to splurge on fountains and columns for their upstairs bath?" He chuckled sadly. "My sister and I been trying to hang on, but we've known for a couple months. We can't pay salaries much longer. We got to shut shit down."

Esteban rose but kept his back to them. He walked to the dining room table and idly flipped through a stack of envelopes. "You guys are standing in the backup plan. Maria and I were going to sell the house in California, move down here permanently, and make this our full-time gig." He wandered into and then down the hallway. "But the backup plan got shot up, didn't it? Backup plan got some holes in it now, boy." His voice trailed away as he entered his room and quietly closed the door behind him.

Luke wished he'd slammed it—rattled the bricks in the walls with his rage. Because that quiet was the quiet of desolation. And that rage? He should have aimed it at Luke. Right between his eyes.

An hour or so later, as Luke spread his bathing suit and towel over a chair to dry, Omar appeared on the patio with two vodka cocktails. "No fresh orange juice. This is out of a bottle. But good enough."

Luke shook his head. "I'm not touching any booze for a while." He looked out at the horizon. "Sun's not even close to going down anyway."

Omar shrugged and handed Luke a drink. "Then just clink glasses with me. Everything is going to be okay. Everyone is alive."

They sat at the table where they'd eaten birthday cake just one day before. Luke raised the glass, toasted Omar, and then set it on the table without a sip. "Esteban ain't okay. Is that why he's going to San Diego in the morning? To start shutting things down?"

"I don't know. I guess so."

Luke stared at his drink. "I'll get up early and see him off." He shook his head and sighed. "It's all on me, man. I dared them to come at me."

Omar frowned as he pulled his drink away from his lips. "No, no. They dared. They dared the army to come get *them*."

Luke picked up his drink and ran his index finger down the condensation before taking a small sip. For a cocktail only barely spiked with vodka, the arrow tip of it still pierced his bloodstream. "I know I've been on the crazy train lately."

Omar smiled. "When you crawled away from me? And started yelling? That was crazy. But you saved soldiers. That was good crazy."

"Loco bueno?"

"Something like that," said Omar.

A hummingbird darted past them. It hovered back and forth between two pots of flowers along the pool.

"Sorry about your sculpture," said Luke.

Omar leaned forward and patted him on the knee. "Sculptures don't last. Wind or rain get them some day. We just sped things up a little." He drank and wiped his mustache with the back of his hand. "And don't worry about Esteban. He's smart and he's tough."

Sunlight through Luke's glass made a spectrum on the table. "Did you have any idea he was that twisted up inside?"

"No," said Omar.

Luke picked up his drink again. "That was hard to watch." He rotated the drink before his eyes, running his finger down it to make ten vertical lines on the cold glass.

Somewhere down the street a metallic rattling faded away, followed by children's screams and laughter. Luke set his right knee atop the suitcase, leaned all of his weight onto it, and managed to run the zipper around its edge. He'd made everything fit by leaving the cane behind, throwing away his stained clothes, and removing the four bottles of premium tequila he'd purchased last week, which he gave instead to Omar. He dragged the suitcase downstairs along with his carry-on and set them by the front door. A taxi would arrive in half an hour.

Esteban had left yesterday at dawn. They'd stood in the doorway, the house still dark save for a small lamp in the hall.

"Thanks for everything," Luke had said, extending his hand, smiling more than was natural.

Their expressions were reversed, and they both seemed to know it. Esteban nodded, grim and embarrassed. "*De nada*, brother." They shook hands, both glancing past each other. "We'll get you back here soon," he mumbled. "Shannon and the girls. We'll get you all down here and have a real good time."

"We will," said Luke. "We'll do it."

Omar was working right now, alone in the studio, sanding by hand. Little noise, little dust. Luke stepped outside into the early heat to smoke. He yawned and stretched his back. He'd slept poorly, the absence of late-night motorcycles leaving a strange hollow that filled with car horns, dog barks, and other new sounds.

Appearing around the corner, having climbed the cobblestone hill, stood two smiling children. The girl was around Julia's age, seven or eight, and wore a pale blue skirt. The boy was a couple of years younger and decked out in Western wear: little cowboy hat, boots, and jeans with a big oval belt buckle. Each held something heavily against their bodies that Luke couldn't make out.

He walked toward them—keeping his eyes averted from the pay phone and empty benches on the corner. The children set the objects they were holding down on the street. They were square wooden scooters with four swivel casters underneath, like the ones Luke remembered using as a kid in gym class. The teacher used to set up traffic cones on the basketball court for relay races, and the wheels had pinched Luke's fingers when he'd tried holding on by the bottom.

The girl sat cross-legged on her scooter and let the hill slowly pull her down. She aimed toward a strip of smoother concrete along the curb, and in seconds she was blurring past parked cars toward the four-way stop below.

The boy smiled watching her and then noticed Luke.

"Hey there," said Luke. "*Buenos días.*"

The boy nodded and stared down the hill again, where the girl lowered her heels to slow down.

Luke pointed at his scooter. "Can I try it?"

The boy looked at him but said nothing.

"Can I try it?" Luke snuffed out his cigarette and pointed at himself. "*Yo?*"

The boy's eyes narrowed, but then he seemed to understand. He smiled and shook his head.

"No?" Luke grinned. "Come on, just one time."

The boy sat down on the scooter, pulling the brim of his hat lower over his brow.

"All right. Giddy-up then."

After pushing twice off the ground with his hands, the boy gained speed. The casters spun beneath him, and he rolled in reverse for several feet before spilling onto his back, his legs somersaulting over his head. The girl jogged up toward him, and Luke began descending the hill as well, wishing he had the cane. But the boy sprang to his feet, beaming, and retrieved the upturned scooter.

Luke watched them climb the hill for a few more seconds before he turned and headed back to the casa. He'd never have fit on the thing anyway, and a wipeout like that would have just meant going back under the knife.

His carry-on sat just inside the casa's door, and Luke knew exactly the pocket where he'd stuffed the clown mask. He bent down with a grimace to retrieve it and then returned to the bright brick street.

The kids sat on their scooters atop the hill, though both glinted with sweat and seemed content to merely roll a few inches back and forth.

"You still can't ride it," said the girl.

Her English startled him. "No, I know," Luke said. He held the mask behind his back. "Tell him I've got a present for him."

"Why?"

"Because I can't speak Spanish."

"Why do you have a present for him?" she asked.

"It's not a real present. It's just something funny. Can you tell him, please?"

The girl spoke in a hushed voice to the boy, who pushed his hat far back on his head and squinted upward.

Luke held the mask behind his back by its stringy red hair, then revealed it with a flourish, shaking it at the kids. "Boo!"

The kids screamed, half in fear and half in delight. Immediately afterward they both laughed, and the boy took the mask.

"I really don't want the thing," said Luke.

The boy stared into its empty eyes.

"Sorry," Luke said to the girl. "I guess it shouldn't just be for him. You can share it."

She smiled. "No thanks."

"Well, *adiós*," he said, stepping carefully backward. "Have fun."

The boy removed his cowboy hat, thrust the mask over his head, and then placed the hat atop his newly deranged clown self.

"*¡Muy malo! ¡Muy malo!*" said Luke, gesturing with his hands for the boy to stay away. Then he waved to them both and returned, one last time, to the casa.

Back inside, he wandered around the kitchen for a few moments, glancing at his watch, unsure of how to spend the fifteen minutes or so before the taxi arrived. He wanted to see the ocean once more, though his heart raced every time he thought about the patio. Pockmarked brick. Broken sculptures. The faint stickiness of spilled drinks. In a matter of days he'd infected this place with ghosts. But he took a deep breath and climbed up anyway.

The ocean was blue the way it was always blue, in a way the lakes back home never achieved. Luke couldn't recall a single cloudy day during the trip. He sat in a white chair to ease his back and watched a flock of pelicans gliding high above the waves.

A hummingbird skirted past Luke's head. He thought at first there were two of them nearby until he realized that this one moved so swiftly that the sound of its wings trailed in its wake. The effect was like that of a ventriloquist throwing his voice. The bird was faster than itself—could leave itself behind. Luke wanted this same power—even more than lightness, more than mere flight.

THE FIRST SEIZURE

I count our strength,

Two and a child.

—Robert Frost, "Storm Fear"

You claw out of sleep as your wife screams 911. A blanket coils around your legs, and you stumble as she runs into the hallway with your daughter cradled in her arms. Your daughter is twitching. Her open eyes move like the wings of spooked sparrows. White saliva bubbles over her lips and runs down her chin. You pick up the phone and dial and follow your wife's strides out the front door of the cabin. Dawn has barely broken the horizon. The surrounding asparagus fields catch the golden light. You stand in the middle of a gravel road when the operator answers. Your wife, Abby, paces along the road's dim edge, near the drainage ditch. For a moment the child goes limp in her arms, limbs dangling. A stand of pines keeps the low sun from touching them. The operator is confused by the rural address but tells you an ambulance is coming.

Your daughter makes a continual popping sound in the back of her throat, like the gulping of a sink drain. Abby repeats your daughter's name into her ear—*Victoria, Victoria*—as if trying to wake her from a night terror. The world is draped in the sheerest white linen. Your daughter's vacant eyes look up past everything, past the clouds and a morning star.

It is summer, daybreak, vacation. And it is lovely save for those eyes and the twitching and the spit-laced esophageal sound. A siren drifts across the flatlands, still miles away. This is how we lose control.

LAST YEAR'S PALMS

arry Jacobson had never attended church after dark, when the stained glass looked dusk-gray and the tug of sleep came from night instead of morning. He'd never attended on a weekday. But that was before Ben swallowed thirty aspirin from a friend's medicine cabinet, and Larry and Elizabeth had to admit him to Pine Rest. The following Sunday Elizabeth walked a couple blocks to this church. By the end of the month she'd persuaded Larry to come along. Outside of weddings and funerals, it had been only the third time in his life he'd stepped foot in a place like this. Now he'd come five times in the five weeks since, all for her sake, and maybe Ben's.

It was dark outside, and the chapel at Northcentral Reformed Church glowed softly orange, lit by two slender candlesticks at the front and the dim chandeliers above. Arched windows and Corinthian columns rose up the walls to the lofty ceiling, which, coupled with the chandeliers, produced the effect of a ballroom. Through the windows, maple branches bent from the windstorm and scraped against the glass. Larry could hear the scraping; there was no music tonight. On Sundays in the sanctuary, the organ triumphantly played the worshippers into the pews. But now Catherine Ferenz, the pastor of discipleship, sat silently in a white chair at the front, smiling and nodding gently at the twenty or twenty-five arrivals. Elizabeth coughed, and it was answered by a few other coughs in the room.

Larry had never seen the chapel before. The carpet and pew cushions were pale blue, and two purple banners at the front read, in gold letters, LOVE SO AMAZING, SO DIVINE. Unlike the sanctuary, which held several hundred people, there was no spacious safety and anonymity in the chapel. He and Elizabeth sat in the second-to-last row behind several old men and women, as well as a few young families with small children. There were no teenagers.

The old men wore dark suits, just as on Sundays. Larry wore jeans and a denim jacket; his thick hair needed combing and hung almost down to his eyes. He glanced over at Elizabeth, who leaned forward, removed her coat, and eased back into the pew with her legs crossed. Larry looked straight ahead and kept his jacket on, though he felt warm and his back dampened with sweat. He thought about The Peacock, a bar on Cherry Street where he met guys from the metal plant on most Wednesday and Friday nights, and about Super Happy Hour, when domestic drafts were seventy-five cents.

Someone struck a guitar chord. Larry leaned forward and noticed Andy Steenstra, the church's baby-faced youth pastor, rise up from the front row with an acoustic guitar slung over his shoulder. He stood in a shadowy corner and played in a way so gentle that it heightened the greater silence.

As he played, Catherine stood up from her chair. She wore a black vestment that hung low off her raised arms. Orange light reflected off her glasses. "Tonight," she said, "we retrace our baptismal crosses and renew our relationship with God."

A few people coughed again.

"On this first night of our Lenten journey, we are reminded of Christ's glorious entry into Jerusalem, reminded of his death on the cross, reminded of our connection to and disconnection from God." She smiled. "As little babies, a minister baptized us and drew a cross on our foreheads with water."

Larry glanced over at Elizabeth, but she stared ahead, refusing to meet his eyes. Neither he nor Ben had ever been baptized.

"And tonight, we retrace that cross of water with one of ash, a symbol of death, but also a reminder that our baptismal cross is still there upon us, that it cannot be washed away, and that God's promises to us are never broken."

Larry leaned toward Elizabeth's ear. "*We* retrace?"

"You won't have to," she whispered. "That's only a Catholic thing."

She had been raised Catholic, her baptism, First Communion, penance, and confirmation all taking place under the roof of St. Mike's in Muskegon. Her marriage to Larry took place at the courthouse. His own parents had been agnostic. He couldn't remember them ever making a single statement of belief or disbelief, just like Larry and Elizabeth themselves by the time of Ben's birth.

"Let us pray," said Catherine. Larry bowed his head like everyone else but didn't close his eyes. Nor did he sing along to the hymns. The deal was that he simply come with Elizabeth, and even that was a Sunday morning deal. He'd considered staying home tonight and killing time like he did many evenings, watching the Golf Channel and drinking screwdrivers before heading to The Peacock. He'd only golfed a handful of times himself and didn't own a set of clubs. But the coverage of the tournaments was calming company. The commentators spoke in whispers, and at this early stage in the season the golfers played in warm-weather states like Florida or California, where the sunshine and green grass contrasted with the Michigan gray out his window. Larry's house had an insignificant yard, and he revered the courses as works of architectural genius. But what he loved most was how a player—when his talents and discipline and unconscious mind aligned—could exert total control over the smallness of the ball and the largeness of the course, arcing a perfect iron shot over the trees and bunkers, onto the green, and settling within a foot of the pin by employing a final backspin that might as well have been the trick of an invisible string.

"God is slow to anger and abounding in steadfast love. Therefore, let us offer up our sins, our broken promises, our broken spirits—offer them up to God, who heals and forgives, who strengthens and refreshes, who gives us new life in this world and everlasting life in the next."

Larry stared at his feet. A white film dusted parts of the floor—salt residue from the long winter. He glanced at the order of worship in the bulletin. Next on the agenda read simply, "Silent meditation."

"Let us pray now for ourselves," said Catherine, "and for those in our lives in need of God's grace."

Larry looked again at Elizabeth, whose eyes remained closed. Creases surfaced on her forehead for only seconds, and then her face relaxed again. He looked back to his feet and then, slightly embarrassed, closed his own eyes.

This was not for Elizabeth's benefit. And he refused to pray for himself, which he considered selfish and weak. It may or may not have been a prayer—he'd never learned how to pray or learned if such a thing was taught at all. No words formed in his mind, only pictures. The first was of that night they left him at Pine Rest, of walking slowly out of the room while Ben's angry screams echoed throughout the fluorescent-white corridor.

Then he conjured up an image from an old photo album: Ben returning home from his first day of kindergarten, proudly displaying his Batman tote bag, his shoulders back and his child's belly roundly sticking out. Next, he tried to imagine Ben at this very moment, sweating and laughing and chopping meat and vegetables around the circular grill at Jimmy's Mongolian Barbeque with the other young cooks. And then he pictured black air in his mind, like space without stars, as he thought about Ben's confession.

It had come in October, at a time when he and Larry were barely speaking to each other after Ben had quit the football team at the start of this, his highly anticipated senior year. He'd returned home, late for curfew and drunk. He'd made sure Larry was asleep upstairs and then curled onto the linoleum of the kitchen floor, Elizabeth lying alongside with her arms clutching his shoulders, as he sobbed and told her of the months of abuse he'd endured when he was six years old.

And now, during this non-prayer, Larry tried again to summon the face of the man—the Who—at the other end of Ben's tragedy. But as always he was just the faceless silhouette of someone Ben might someday reveal to them, though he hadn't yet.

Andy Steenstra played the opening chords of "Beneath the Cross of Jesus" and Larry opened his eyes. Everyone rose and Elizabeth held the hymnal between them to share. But Larry didn't sing. He stared ahead, over Catherine's shoulder, at the gold cross standing between the candlesticks. The non-prayer—like an interrupted dream—still projected onto the back of his skull, and he thought of nothing else for a few moments. Then he scanned through the order of worship. It looked to be a short service, less than an hour. The guys would still be at The Peacock, and Ben would still be sweating at the grill when it ended. After the song would come a responsive reading of Psalm 51 followed by a lesson from Matthew 6. Then, he read, would come the imposition of ashes.

Larry lay the bulletin over the open hymnal in Elizabeth's hands and pointed at the words: IMPOSITION OF ASHES. No longer able to see the music, she paused, mouth still open in song, and read the bulletin.

He didn't whisper. With the risen sound of voices, he didn't have to. "I will leave. I said so."

Elizabeth gently removed the bulletin from the hymnal and seamlessly merged her voice with the other voices, into the second verse. Larry stuck out his jaw, stared at the gold cross, and for a few seconds gave in to his feelings of rage toward the faceless man—the relative or friend or neighbor—who'd made all of it happen. Who'd even made *this* happen: Larry Jacobson standing in a church on a Wednesday night.

The service continued through the Psalm, through the lesson, and then another song. Larry noticed the small silver bowl sitting on a table beside Catherine, and he knew right away it was filled with ashes. Elizabeth could walk up there and do it if she liked. She'd grown up with this—holy water, incense. She'd grown up with ritual. Not him.

The moment finally came when Catherine held the silver bowl in front of her. Elizabeth placed her hand on Larry's knee and rubbed it slowly.

"Next month," said Catherine, "on the Sunday before Easter, we'll all receive a palm frond as we step through the church doors." She dipped two fingers into the bowl. "Afterward, the palms that aren't taken home by people are collected and burned." She removed her fingers. "The ashes are kept for the following year to mark the start of the next Lenten season." She held her hand up to display her blackened fingertips. "These are last year's palms. They were green with life, and now they are dust. We, too, will become dust, but like the palms we will reach, in death, a greater existence closer to the glory of God than we were even in our brightest bloom on this Earth."

Elizabeth's hand slowed, and then she removed it from Larry's knee.

"We invite everyone who so wishes to come forward for the imposition of ashes. An usher will excuse rows, beginning in the back and moving forward."

Immediately an usher in a black suit stepped into the aisle, one row behind Larry. The only person sitting in that row—an old man with a wild sea of white hair—stood and staggered down the pale blue carpet toward Catherine Ferenz and her small silver bowl. Larry wanted to watch him all the way to the front of the chapel, to see the ritual unfold. But then the usher was standing beside his row, and Elizabeth was rising to her feet. She shuffled past Larry's legs while he sat, and then—without looking at him—reached behind herself and took his hand. He was standing. And then he was walking, still trailing behind Elizabeth, holding her hand and approaching the ashes.

The old man had already received his. He turned away from Catherine and began returning to his pew. On his forehead, smeared darkly beneath his white hairline, was a cross. The horizontal was short, but the vertical line ended between his eyes.

Then he was gone and Elizabeth stood before Catherine. Larry watched and listened so that he'd know what to do. He almost turned and walked back to his seat, but a line had begun to form behind him.

"You come from dust, and to dust you shall return."

"Amen."

Elizabeth turned and he tried to see the mark on her, but Catherine—her blond hair, her glasses—loomed. He didn't know what to do with his eyes, whether he should close them or stare into hers. He looked down toward her feet, which were hidden by the black vestment.

"You come from dust," she said, lifting his bangs up and running her warm fingers across his forehead, "and to dust you shall return." Her fingers moved downward, toward his nose.

He lifted his gaze, saw her smile slightly, and because he'd heard Elizabeth say it, mumbled, "Amen."

When he turned and headed back, past the line of people and those still sitting in their seats, he felt the reflexive urge to run his hand across his forehead. He felt ridiculous and certain that the eyes of those he passed were on him. But none of them—the elderly; the young families; or even senior pastor Randall Wierenga, who stood in line like a layman, waiting his turn—made eye contact.

Back at the pew, Elizabeth sat and immediately lowered her head in prayer. Unlike the old man's, her cross was small and compact, deep black like the nighttime windows. Larry sat beside her, but instead of praying he watched the others return down the aisle. Many smiled slightly. Seeing them made Larry smile for a moment, too, because he still felt ridiculous—and the others looked absurd—but since everyone wore the ash cross the embarrassment was finite, like undressing on a nude beach.

Elizabeth finished praying, looked at him, and laughed with her eyes. She dabbed her finger onto his forehead and then touched the tip of his nose.

Not only did they hold hands on the walk home, but they gently swung their hands—something they'd done when they'd dated in high school, like kissing at Elizabeth's locker between classes. The wind had strengthened since before the service. Broken branches lay strewn over the dark sidewalk. If there had been leaves, they'd have been everywhere, but it was March, the season of sticks and mud.

"You going to head to The Peacock?" asked Elizabeth. "It's only a little after eight."

Larry turned his head toward the street and spat. "I don't know. Happy Hour's over."

"So?"

"So."

"So, we're not *that* poor. Go relax a little. See your buddies."

"I'll think about it." He wrinkled his brow. "Want to make sure Ben gets home all right." He looked to see if she'd react to this. But the streetlights were blocked by tree limbs; he could hardly see her face. He couldn't see the ashes.

"He's scheduled until nine," said Elizabeth. "And sometimes he asks to work extra hours. He has friends there. He has fun. You should have some, too. If you wait, the guys at the bar will be gone."

"He shouldn't work so late. Not with school tomorrow."

"Don't worry about that. He's doing fine."

Graduation was just over two months away, and despite failed tests taken during his deepest depression, despite the class time missed while at Pine Rest, he would walk at the ceremony. He'd get his diploma. The medication helped. So did the twice-weekly visits to the therapist. Larry didn't know what they discussed at their sessions. Ben had talked a little with Elizabeth about it, though she'd promised not to tell anyone, including Larry. "But I swear," she'd said to Larry one night, "he's never told me who it was. And if he told me, I couldn't keep that secret from you. But I'd be scared to say it."

"A part of me would be scared to know," he'd said. "Afraid of what I might do."

Things had warmed between Ben and Larry. Quitting football felt like the smallest of things. Spring training had begun, and the two had never had a problem talking baseball. And though they never talked golf, Larry considered inviting Ben out for a round sometime when the weather warmed.

The light over the front door was off when they arrived home, and the place was dark inside. Larry had been trying to cut the electrical bill. Elizabeth turned on a single lamp in the living room beside her favorite reading chair. Two books sat stacked on the end table: Buechner's *Wishful Thinking* and a paperback mystery. She sat beside the only light in the house and picked up the mystery.

Larry looked at his watch. It was closing in on eight thirty.

"What are you doing?" Elizabeth had peeked up from her pages and caught him standing in the foyer, no longer checking his watch but just staring at the door.

"Thinking about what I'll do now," he said. "Watch TV maybe."

"It's early. Go to the bar."

He removed his wallet from the pocket of his denim jacket and checked for cash, as if that were the deciding factor. He did this lately, caught himself—or was caught by Elizabeth—standing in a hallway or staring out a window, not even aware he was passing time doing nothing. It happened most often in the evening, between the time the sun set and the time Ben returned home.

It had been dark that night in January when they'd gotten the call from Adam Haas. Ben and a few other friends had been watching movies at Adam's house. His parents had been gone, visiting family in Scottsdale. Ben left the other guys to go to the bathroom and stayed in there, missing the last half hour of the movie. When Adam and the others checked on him, Ben was stumbling around and began screaming about a piercing ringing in his ears. Then he bent over the edge of the bathtub, violently vomiting over and over. Beside the toilet was an empty bottle of aspirin, which he'd hoped would just put him forever to sleep. Instead, it savaged him.

"Call an ambulance!" Larry screamed over the phone. "Call an ambulance and then call me right back! Don't let him close his eyes!"

It didn't snow that night, but it had snowed all week, and as they backed out of the driveway too fast, Larry plowed into a snowbank. He and Elizabeth probably lost five minutes as she got behind the wheel, accelerating and spinning the tires, while he pushed the front bumper, his boots slipping out from under him, tears of all kinds running down his face.

Larry put his wallet back in his pocket. "I think I'll go," he said.

"Good," said Elizabeth. "We'll both be here when you get back."

He opened the front door, flipped on the front porch light, and stepped out. His hair caught the wind and swirled about his head. The Peacock was a half mile away. He always walked there because he usually left a little drunk. He stuffed his hands in his pockets, shrugged his shoulders against the wind, and headed past the locust trees along his driveway. Tonight he'd just have two beers and come home.

The dimness inside The Peacock nearly mirrored the dark on the street. After eight o'clock, Tina always turned the lights down and the heat up. The place was a dive in the best sense. The carpet was brown to hide the stains. The booths along the walls went all the way up to the ceiling, creating privacy and refuge for couples or for old men who wanted to drink alone. The wreaths had only come down a week before, yet even now in March green and red Christmas lights glowed along the ceiling. The bar was circular and in the center of the room. That was important to Larry. He hated bars that faced walls. He wanted other people sitting across from him. People he liked.

That included most of the regulars at The Peacock, although Danny Verhey sat smoking over an ashtray with both elbows resting on the bar. The guy always laughed too much and liked to stroke his mustache. He still wore his cell phone on his belt like some sad little gunslinger.

But Phil Darnell and Mike Mozart were there, as was Kirby, God bless him. All three had beards, and they all sat opposite Danny Verhey because they said he talked too loud. Their distance just made him talk louder.

"There he is," said Tina. She was blond, with a ponytail, and on certain nights Larry thought she looked young and on others old. She was probably in her midthirties. Tonight she looked twenty-nine.

"I'm here, I'm here," said Larry, tripping over the leg of a chair that he hadn't seen in the dimness.

Kirby smiled. He weighed over three hundred pounds. "Watch your step, partner. The stumbling comes later in the night. Unless you already got a head start on the drinky drink."

"Not tonight." Larry sat between the group of three and Danny Verhey, an empty stool on each side.

"Where you been?" asked Mike.

"Had to help Liz with some shit around the house."

"Your furnace playing games again?"

"No," he said. "Garbage disposal."

He ordered a beer from Tina and happily sipped it in the warm, cavelike room. He let the others talk for a while, but when a stretch of silence finally fell over everyone Larry removed his denim jacket. "God, it's warm in here, Tina."

"Really? I'm cold."

"You're always cold," said Mike. "Every woman I've ever known."

Larry's back felt damp again, and he could feel beads of sweat forming around his hairline. He and the other men raised their eyes to the TVs above the bar to watch *SportsCenter*. The talk was of the upcoming NFL draft.

"That could've been your boy," said Danny Verhay.

Larry didn't realize Danny was talking to him at first. He'd stopped associating Ben with football. "What?"

"Could've been your boy in four years. Big Ten. Rose Bowl. NFL draft." He snapped his fingers and then lit another cigarette. "He ever tell you why he quit? Was it some girl? Or—" he lowered his head and his voice, "—drugs? Something like that?"

"It wasn't drugs," said Larry. He'd never told anyone about Ben, the abuse, or Pine Rest. And certainly nothing about the five weeks of church.

"Lay off, Danny," said Kirby. "The man just got done fixing a garbage disposal. Few things on Earth bring a man such frustration. Let him enjoy his beery goodness in peace."

Vintage Kirby. God bless him. Larry finished his drink, still stricken with thirst. "Seriously though," he said, "it's hot as Hades."

"All right, all right." Tina headed for the thermostat. "I'll turn it down and put my jacket on while I'm at it."

Larry lifted his bangs, wiped the sweat from his forehead with the back of his hand, and then reached over the bar for a dry cocktail napkin.

"What's that?" asked Kirby.

Larry ran the napkin along his brow. "What? Me?"

"Yeah you, partner. What's that?" Kirby pointed at his own forehead. "Looks like you're bleeding."

"Bleeding mud," said Phil.

Larry looked at the white napkin, which was streaked with black. He lunged off the stool, startling the others. He touched his head with his fingers, and they came away black. As he turned and headed for the bathroom, which was off the dark hallway that ran to the kitchen, Danny made the connection. "Those are ashes. My man's been to church!"

Larry tripped over the same chair he'd hit when he'd arrived. The others laughed. "We're cutting you off!" yelled Tina. They all laughed again.

He shoved open the bathroom door, cranked the faucet, and stared in the mirror above the sink. His long bangs hid most of the ashes, but a few dark trickles of sweat had run into his eyebrows and down his right temple. He lifted his hair with his left hand, dipped his right under the water, and tried to wipe the ashes clean. They smudged but stayed visible. He yanked a long strip of paper towel from the dispenser, doused it with soap, and furiously scrubbed. In a few moments the black ashes were gone, leaving his skin a brilliant shade of agitated pink.

Larry tossed the paper towel into the garbage, leaned against the green tile wall, and sighed. Then he checked his watch: nine o'clock exactly.

Like a spy or a thief, he opened the bathroom door a crack and peered through the slit by the hinges, between the door and the wall. He could see most of the bar. Danny was smoking with his back to him. Tina now wore her jacket. Mike was watching *SportsCenter* again. But Phil and Kirby were laughing about something. The guys always laughed around the bar at The Peacock, but the mystery of the punch line, from a bathroom hideout at the other end of the room, made Larry feel sick.

Draped across the back of a vacant stool at the bar lay his denim jacket. His wallet and phone were in the pockets. Larry gently closed the bathroom door and stood under the fluorescent lights, staring at the green-tiled wall the way he'd earlier stood in the foyer at home, wavering. When he broke his stare and looked at his watch it still read nine o'clock. Time failed to move.

After another quick glimpse between the doorway's hinges, Larry slipped into the hallway and headed toward the kitchen. On the wall was an old phone with a sign reading STAFF ONLY. He picked it up and quickly dialed. From this vantage point he could peek around the corner and still watch the bar.

Elizabeth picked up on the other end.

"Is he home yet?"

"Ben? No. Where are you? At the bar?"

"Why isn't he home yet?"

"It's . . . wait. It's only a little after nine. He just got off."

"I'm coming home now."

"Larry, no. I want you to stay there. I want you to hang out with the guys. What I don't want is you pacing back and forth over here. He's fine."

He agreed and hung up, but he'd lied. His beer would go unfinished. His jacket and everything in it would spend the night here. Tina would hold it for him. She'd let him pay tomorrow. And by then he'd have some excuse for why he'd disappeared.

A couple of voices and the clatter of silverware seeped from the kitchen door. Larry pushed it open, squinting from the blinding light and aluminum reflections. Two startled young cooks looked up from the sandwiches they were making. "You can't come in here," one said.

"Emergency," said Larry, and he jogged across the kitchen to a door on the other side of the room. Then he was outside, in the dark and the wind, jacketless.

The branches dipping overhead moved like lake waves preceding a storm. As he began trotting the half mile home, the wind seemed to dig into him, pushing him backward. He leaned into it, and then it shifted directions and came from behind so that he felt in two places at once. Then it calmed, for a second or two, and he stumbled from inertia.

Larry ran faster now, past the church on the other side of the street. All of the windows were dark, and the only light on the property was a spotlight that shined on a golden weathervane, which spun wildly atop the church's copper bell tower. And then he was only a block from home, staring ahead and running now, trying to spot the light above the front porch that he'd turned on before he left. No, it wasn't the light itself he looked for, but the things it might illuminate: Ben's beat-up Mustang or his tall, athletic silhouette approaching the front door. But Larry couldn't see any of these things yet. A few years ago he'd planted three locust trees along the driveway. Elizabeth had always called them ugly and said they were aptly named, for pestilence, because of the seeds they scattered everywhere. But they were fast-growing shade trees, and they'd add privacy to the property and enhance the landscape in so little time.

Less than a block now, and still the locust trees obscured his view, the wind tossing their thin frames frantically back and forth. A car's headlights approached from the other direction, slowed, and turned into his driveway ahead of him. He could walk now, if he wanted. It was all right now. But he kept running. Jacketless, in the cold March wind, Larry Jacobson was sweating through his clothes. He imagined the sweat running black down his face and back and chest. He imagined it running red.

THIRD-DOWN CONVERSIONS

A.J. was the quarterback—the play-caller—so he chose whose hands we'd use for passing routes.

"Willie's."

He held his chewed-up mouthpiece in one hand and Willie's wrist in the other. From inside our front-yard huddle, Mike Mason and I greedily clutched Willie's hand, making his cold, red skin bloom white under our touch. We spread his fingers apart, stretching his palm so that the creases widened.

This was our newest strategy—an inspired Sunday ritual we'd perfected that October. We'd tried *X*s and *O*s on little sheets of paper that we kept rolled up under our wristbands, but our sweat made the ink run. And I'd tried mapping out routes on the sidewalk with a sandstone until Aaron Wexler's dad told us to keep the rocks where they belonged and made us hose off the concrete. Then A.J. got the idea for reading palms as playbooks.

"This line's you, Mike." He pointed with the mouthpiece, running it along Willie's palm so that it left a glassy trail of spit. "This one's you, Sean. And this crease is gonna be Willie. Will, I'm bombing it, so you gotta burn past all those guys. Catch it here, by your middle finger."

Willie smiled, pulled his hand free from A.J.'s grip, and extended that middle finger. "This one?"

"Shut up. Play serious," said A.J. His cousins were linemen at Catholic Central—the Crusaders—and they went to the state championship every year at the Silverdome. He grabbed Willie's finger and bent it backward. Willie screamed, and the other guys got restless.

"Stop humping and hike the ball," said Aaron as he hunched forward with his hands on his knees. He was Jewish, so he got to sleep in on Sundays, watch *All American Wrestling*, and then practice with the other guys on his team. Those others—Joe, Jake, and Jason—ambled along the line of scrimmage, plucking yellow leaves off tree branches, picking scabs from their elbows and shins. They hadn't gone to Mass in months.

We lined up in the wet grass. The teams, as usual, were unfair; we were down by fourteen or twenty-one. Jason should have played for us—he was huge and quick—but both sides agreed there was something cool about having all the Js on one team.

And we all knew how the teams really broke down. Ours couldn't play until twelve-thirty, after we'd returned from St. Mike's and donned grass-stained jeans. By then Aaron's guys were all warmed up, practicing routes now drilled into memory, which didn't require playbooks of any kind.

It was third and long. On our last series, when we'd failed to convert, Joe had beaten his chest and theatrically declared, "Where is your god now!" because he'd just seen someone do that in a movie. Now he started singing "We Are the Champions." He, Jake, and Jason were brothers. Their dad had stopped dragging them to Mass when their mom had moved out and taken their baby sister with her.

"You still have to pray or anything?" I'd once asked.

And Joe had shrugged. "My dad's half Swedish. He says maybe we should worship Thor," which made me think of The Barbarian and The Berzerker on wrestling and was maybe the coolest thing I'd ever heard.

I hiked the ball and then slanted right, following the wrinkle I remembered that bent just below Willie's thumb. And Willie went deep, between the twin maples, slicing left past the yellow fire hydrant, following the imagined crease that ran north to his middle finger. The ball arced over the lawn.

We knew they called it a Hail Mary because it was a prayer—an act of hope. We knew Mike Mason always bowed his head and kneeled after touchdowns because he loved God—and he'd seen receivers do it on TV. And the other guys knew I wore a gold crucifix beneath my sweatshirt—a leash they used for tackling.

If the play drawn from our overturned hands had worked—if Willie had caught the pass?—we'd have put our faith in palms every Sunday. But he dropped it, so we quietly stared down at the grass and lined up to punt.

VIRGIN LANDS

reighters and barges slipped through the locks of the northern industrial borderland. Cory Mattson lurched against his seatbelt and tugged the passport from his back pocket. Steel trusses rolled overhead like waves. The blue St. Marys flowed below. And in the opposite lane, a snake of traffic waited to cross into America. Anxiety foamed up in Cory's chest. He aimed for Canada, rehearsing a white lie.

Sault Ste. Marie, Michigan—the smaller of the fraternal twin cities—receded behind him, arch spans giving way to a view of the Ontario side: smokestacks amid the tree line and the smoldering tangle of the steel plant. And yet beneath the gray of any such town dwelled neon vices a nineteen-year-old man could spot if he squinted toward shore—even if he squinted not from sunlight but, like Cory, from the strange, flulike symptoms of withdrawal.

Maple-leaf flags announced customs. Cory snuffed out his last cigarette and idled up to the booth, where there stood a young blond officer wearing a Kevlar vest over her uniform and a handgun on her hip. He rolled down his window, early July heat pouring into the car, and provided his passport, which he'd applied for months ago so he and Mike and B-Rad could legally drink in Canadian bars. The officer scanned his document at a computer. "What's the purpose of your trip today?"

And here came the white lie—one he didn't really have to tell. This was a legal mission, if not a noble one. But any lie to Border Services made Cory think of holding cells and two-way mirrors. He fidgeted with the bill of his Red Wings hat, which he always wore to cover his thinning hair. "The casino," he said.

Cory expected suspicion. Why leave one country for the next? The provincial casino had the same games as the Kewadin in Michigan. And with the currency exchange, you'd lose money from the start. But she just smiled. "Any alcohol, tobacco, or firearms?"

"Nope," said Cory. Something like pride swelled up inside him. He was a fine citizen and noble American envoy.

A sharp wave—faintly electric—ran through Cory's body, from the top of his head through his torso and arms. It was a side effect of antidepressant withdrawal, competing with other sensations across and beneath his skin. Prickly flesh. Pain where his hair met the scalp. A hum in his brain that made his skull feel tight, his face contract, and his eyes squint. Sudden sentimentality. And the half seconds of missing time, like skips in a video, when a wave shot through him and he went from suddenly there to suddenly here.

Beneath these sensations stirred a sexual arousal he hadn't felt since Cuppa Joe had put him on sixty milligrams of Cymbalta last year. Cuppa was actually Dr. Simon Moss, a rangy milksop of a man whose first comment during their first meeting was to nod knowingly at the travel mug in Cory's hand and ask, "Cup of joe?" It had been the high-water mark of their clinical relationship.

Cuppa had warned him that SNRIs often came with sexual side effects. Delayed ejaculation, especially. Cory had refused to ask him a follow-up question and instead asked the old leather-faced pharmacist who liked to wink when he talked.

"Delayed ejaculation?" The man had chuckled. "That's deadwood. Trouble pulling the trigger." He shrugged. "But what are you? Twenty? Twenty-one?"

"Nineteen."

"Nineteen!" He leaned forward with his elbows on the consultation counter. "When I was nineteen I could've gotten off by walking head-down into a stiff breeze." He winked. "You'll be fine."

Cory wasn't, and at first that was okay. The root of his depression had always been sex. He'd gotten Kaitlin Connolly pregnant when they were both fifteen. The pills killed his libido, kept him from coming, and managed the guilt that always followed: the thoughts of the newborn boy Kaitlin had given up for adoption.

But a year had been enough. He'd begun pulling apart the green-and-blue capsules, pouring out roughly half of the tiny white spheroids inside, and swallowing what remained. He'd cut his dosage from sixty milligrams to maybe thirty and now to nothing. The withdrawal had led to this hyper arousal—skull tightness and shock waves—but a return to lust as well. Girls had terrified him for three years. So had other things. But he wanted to feel the true *everything* again. Not prostitutes; he feared the law. But he wanted a trial run—an anonymous return—to the world of lust. For most of the two-hour drive, Cory drove with half a hard-on.

The officer smiled, returned his passport, and wished him good luck. Moments later he was off the bridge and onto Canadian soil. The casino was just ahead, but he turned north, toward the strip club.

Club Z could have been just another warehouse—three stories of brick and right angles—except for a thread of pink neon and the purple awning that read simply SEXY. He'd noticed the place once while barhopping. There were no such clubs in the Upper Peninsula. He'd driven a hundred miles for this and now plunged into the gravel lot amid a flurry of dust and crunched stones. Only one other car was parked there, a wine-bottle green minivan with its left front tire tottering on a concrete wheel stop. Cory squinted beneath the blue sky—his forehead tight and buzzing as he scanned the area for witnesses. There were none. Beyond the surrounding warehouses ran a rusted bascule railroad bridge and, beyond that, the steel plant's anatomy: conveyor belts, blast furnaces, and great piles of iron ore. A seagull swooped down to the sidewalk and then rose, a plastic straw in its beak.

Cory removed his driver's license from his wallet and approached the door. Bass beats pounded distantly on the other side. He'd been to a strip club only once before—last year, for his cousin's bachelor party in Kalamazoo. He'd spent the night sipping Coke in a dark corner, his Red Wings hat low over his brow, peeking at girls from a sliver under the bill.

Now his skin tingled—from the withdrawal, but also from a wonderful anticipation as he reveled in the first dimly lit step inside.

His equilibrium vanished. Hip-hop boomed from speakers. A long, black hallway stretched ahead, and Cory ran his hand along its brick wall for balance. It opened into a lounge area where two dancers in fluorescent bikinis played pool. One of them, tall and pale with a sleeve of tattoos, turned and smiled as he passed. Black lights illuminated the adjacent room, and red Christmas lights ran along the stage. The stage was triangular and vacant save for three brass poles rising from each vertex. Two bearded men sipped beers at the far end. There was no one else.

Cory sat at the room's edge, at a wooden table upon which past men had carved rough-hewn tits and cocks and balls. Under the black lights, his shirt was suddenly flecked with iridescent lint, and a large mystery stain surfaced on his pant leg—luminous, amoeba-shaped, and invisible in daylight. He licked his fingertips and started wiping at it.

A server in fishnets with a glowing green tray took his drink order.

He slid his leg beneath the table. "Just a Molson, I guess?"

"A Molson you guess?"

He nodded, and after she turned to the men at the stage, Cory noticed he still held his driver's license. There had been no bouncer; no one had asked for ID. He slipped it in his wallet, with its baby-faced image of his sixteen-year-old self.

The music shifted to some party-barn country tune. An unseen deejay unfurled his low, smooth voice throughout the room. "Okay, boys, let's give it up now for the *lov-el-y* Savannah."

A girl wearing a pink bikini top and microskirt stepped through a bead-curtained archway onto the stage. And she *was* a girl—probably eighteen. Younger than Cory. His entire teenage life he'd thought of naked women as older than him. But here was this girl, rail-thin, with angel wing tattoos on her upper back and clear platform heels that flashed red and blue lights with each step, like the sneakers advertised on Nickelodeon.

She wrapped her thin legs around one of the poles and slowly twirled—once. Twice. The two bearded men opened their wallets and set down cash on the stage. Cory was relieved when the server returned with his beer so he had something to do besides simply stare. He gave her his debit card and started a tab.

The first song ended and another began and the girl removed her top. His arousal—which had gone dormant while he'd settled into the place—returned, though only for a moment. There was something about her face—the sharp jawline and narrow nose—that reminded him of Kaitlin. He hadn't seen her in two years. She'd moved to Wisconsin with a friend, and somewhere out there a three-year-old boy—who was now neither his nor hers—tottered the Earth.

Cuppa Joe wrote scrips but proved worthless as a confidant. Cory lived with his mom, but he'd never relive these things with her. Nor with Mike and B-Rad, who were basically kids when it all happened and kids to this day. But now four years later—a topless girl dancing before him—he wished he could lean toward another person and relay the memories she now triggered of pink sheets with plush unicorns at the foot of the bed. Of how Kaitlin's parents both worked swing shift, and to ward off silence she'd catch crickets out in the bushes and release them in the house. Of how, that one night, as they fumbled with each other's bodies, a cricket in the laundry room had serenaded them.

An R&B tune began. Savannah dropped her skirt and thong. And Cory finished one beer before quickly downing another, transfixed by memory and skin. When the song ended she gathered up the few bills, slipped them in a tiny purse, and disappeared behind the beaded doorway, her shoes lighting up red and blue in the distance.

With the stage now as empty as the rest, the place had a film of gloom over it, as if Cory could run his finger along a table and leave a trail. With it came an echo in his brain that was separate from the humming sensation of med withdrawal and which went something like, *Why the fuck are you here? Why the fuck are you here?* The prospect of being back in Haymaker, sitting in a basement beanbag chair playing *Call of Duty* with Mike and B-Rad, suddenly seemed reputable next to this solo mission being piloted by his groin. He ordered a third beer.

The woman's arrival nearly blinded him: white-blond hair, white fishnet dress, and white knee-high boots—everything glowing purple beneath the black lights. She sat beside him and crossed her legs. "How you doing, baby?" Her words were laced with a Russian accent. She winked and shook his hand. "I am Nika. You like dance, baby?" She nodded toward an even darker corner of the room, divided into cubicles, toward which Savannah now led one of the bearded men.

Nika was much older than him, well into her thirties. "Maybe later," he said. "I'm just relaxing now." He sipped his beer.

"No problem, baby." She reclined. "But I still sit here, though. My legs are tired, and there no other men to work." She looked him in the eyes, then scanned his whole figure, then returned to his eyes. "Why you here, all young and clean? You from up here?"

Cory shook his head. "Up here, but not Canada. I'm American."

"Ugh," said Nika, snorting. "It look ugly over in America."

"Across the river?" he asked. "It's a big country. That's just the part across the river."

"I never been, but I see enough. I see Detroit from across river. Buffalo across river. I am from Toronto but do these sort of tours." She shrugged. "I like America growing up. I love freedom. But I do not like some things you do lately. I do not like war."

The deejay announced the arrival of Nixie onstage. She was the woman with the tattoos who'd been playing pool.

"What you do for job?" asked Nika.

"It's exciting. You ready?"

"So ready, baby."

"Check out. At the grocery store."

"We all do jobs like grocery when young. Me, too. Then I got degree in Russian literature. No lie. Soon I be paramedic. Strip and make money and drive ambulance." She shrugged again. "I am happy."

"I was thinking about joining the army," he said. He'd considered it briefly, and it felt right saying it now, to her.

Nika rolled her eyes. "Oh, that will make the baby the big man."

The server returned. "Another Molson you guess?"

Cory nodded, and Nika ordered a Red Bull. "I like wine, but it make me horny."

"Wouldn't that be good for your job?" he asked.

"Would be most awful shit for my job. Most awful shit."

Nixie held the pole with one hand and walked around it, not really dancing.

"Where are *you* from?" he asked Nika.

"Russia. I get back two months ago. Have my teeth fixed." She smiled, the two rows bright blue under the lights.

"They look great. Where in Russia are you from?"

"Kazakhstan."

He frowned and tilted his head. "That's not Russia. That's Kazakhstan."

Nika leaned forward and rubbed his knee. "That's because you smart, baby. Most men know shit about Kazakhstan. Just know *Borat.*" She rubbed his thigh.

"Well, your teeth look great."

She sat up straight. "I get my eyes fixed next."

"What's wrong with your eyes?" he asked, but he already knew.

"I have Russian eyes. Men say I look sad. Nobody want dance from mopey stripper."

The server returned with their drinks. Cory raised his beer, his fourth one. He hadn't eaten all afternoon. "Cheers."

"Happy Canada Day," said Nika. "Did you know this? The holiday? That's why it so slow. Manager say men at picnics and bullshit. They come after fireworks. Get drunk and look at pretty lights in the sky and then come look at pretty girls."

Cory shook his head. "I don't even know what Canada Day means."

"Me neither. Maybe something with the freedom."

Songs played and girls danced while she began talking about her homeland. About a cousin who'd died in protests. About marching for freedom herself when she was young.

"How young are you?"

"Nineteen."

Nika gently closed her eyes and held them closed for a few seconds, a strange smile creeping across her lips. "Try not to throw up when I tell you. I am thirty-eight. Twice you."

"No," he said, faking it. He was mildly drunk and turned on from her hand on his leg and from the word *baby.* Her breasts were round beneath her dress, and her skin looked smooth and bronze and smelled like cotton candy. But he saw the lines at the edges of her mouth, the creases in her eyes, and he wanted to tell her right then about Kaitlin and other secrets.

"Look at this," he said. He removed his hat, revealing his thinning hair. "I think you look pretty great. I wouldn't worry about it."

Nika squeezed his knee, patted it, and dropped her eyes. Then she began a long monologue about Kazakhstan, half personal history, the other half just history. She said it was the ninth-largest nation in the world. She mentioned the Cosmodrome, from which the Russians had launched

Sputnik and still sent men into space. "They leave Earth from *our* land," she said, picking at a tabletop carving—a stick figure with a huge erection. And she described something called STS, where the Russians had tested nukes on Kazakh land, poisoning the people and the soil.

A half hour passed. Maybe more. It turned out she was part Russian herself, her grandparents immigrating to Kazakhstan as part of some huge agricultural initiative. "Khrushchev want more wheat. Send hundreds of thousands to cultivate steppe. Called it Virgin Lands. Because if Russians had never been there, must be new. No?"

Cory shook his head. He had no idea what she was talking about.

Nika spread her arms wide to depict something huge. An expanse. "All new start. All new beginning." She dropped her arms to the table. "It work for little while. Then, not enough wheat. Khrushchev need to buy wheat to feed people. And from where? From Canada. So, Happy Canada Day." She looked around the room. "I need cigarette."

Cory removed a lighter from his pocket. "I'm all out." He felt the urge to tell her about his pills and Cuppa Joe and he began rubbing her leg, shocked by its softness. So different from her eyes. He pulled his hand back.

"Is okay," she said. She smiled and placed his hand back on her leg. "You are nice and quiet and young. I tell you if you do something wrong. This nothing. In private dance, men touch anywhere." She raised an index finger. "Except one place. I had man tried to lick me there and I kick him," she said. "In the face. With my boot." She extended her sleek leg toward him. The boot was laced up to the knee. Something a pro wrestler or superhero would wear, but with heels. "Broke his nose and cut his lip. Blood all over these boots. These amazing boots, baby."

He nodded and grinned. "Good for you."

Nika winked at him. "You remind me of friend of younger brother." She glanced at the stage, where a girl was finishing. Cory didn't know how many had come and gone during their talk. "I am next," she said. "Come up to stage. I dance just for you. Like free private dance."

Nika stood, crossed the room, and disappeared down a back corridor. Cory returned the lighter to his pocket, ordered another beer, and bellied up to the stage. About five minutes later the deejay introduced her, and Nika strode out to the industrial hammering of an old Nine Inch Nails song. She loomed over him, grinning slyly, ignoring the two bearded men downstage. The song was fast, but she moved slowly, her eyes fixed elsewhere, to a horizon that couldn't possibly exist in the dark room.

The song abruptly transitioned to some cheese pop Cory might have heard during a halftime show or a Sprite ad. As it did, Nika slowly slid the straps of her white fishnet dress past her shoulders and pulled the top down to her hips. He stared at her breasts and sighed—a trace of a moan slipping out from him. They were firm and smooth as the rest of her body, further betraying the subtle lines on her face. He thought of how, in junior high, he'd popped the head off his sister's Barbie and replaced it with the head of Cruella de Vil, and he instantly knew the connection to Nika was horrible and mean. He began to slip outside of himself, staring at his beer, but then forced himself to really feel the guilt. To feel all of it. The true *everything*.

Nika crawled toward him on all fours, her eyes infused with a lust that part of him believed was real. She lowered her face to him, breathing warmly into his ear and rubbing her lips on his neck. "You like, baby?"

He did but said nothing, aware of all the flashes of thought at his mind's edge—Kaitlin and Cuppa and the Barbie doll—before sealing them off from this pure essence of pleasure. His eyes were closed. Her hair fell over them.

The song ended, and an awkward silence settled over the room. Nika stood and began to fully undress, pulling the dress to her ankles and stepping out of it. A man's whistle came through the speakers, alternating with a quick, soulful guitar riff.

Cory smiled and shook his head as the singer began crooning about the Moskva, about Gorky Park. It was "Wind of Change," an old song from around the time he was born, but Cory knew it well. Mike's dad owned *The Very Best of Scorpions* CD and always listened to it on repeat while working on his car.

Nika removed her white thong and now wore nothing but the superhero boots and a gold belly bracelet he hadn't noticed before. As she danced, she no longer looked at him nor off toward some indoor horizon. Her eyes were closed.

The man sang about soldiers, about two sides finally feeling like brothers. Cory and Mike had watched the video on YouTube. Grainy Cold War footage. Shots of tanks and jets. The Berlin Wall in pieces. And they'd always laughed their way through it. The bad perms. The dopey crowd waving sparklers. The lead singer's whistling of the melody, so earnest it was hilarious.

Nika's eyes remained closed. Her dancing was not seductive now but almost operatic, slow and soft until the chorus, at which point she'd shimmy up one of the poles, hang upside-down, and whip her glowing white hair over the stage. The refrain thundered through the dark room, the impassioned singer going on about magic and glory and children's dreams of the future.

For years Cory and the guys had had a bet. If either he or Mike or B-Rad could whistle the entire chorus of "Wind of Change" without laughing, the other two guys would buy him a steak dinner at The Venison. No one ever had to pay up.

Cory grinned, remembering these things, happy for the first time today. He was loose and drunk, a woman dancing naked before him, a woman he would talk to further after the dance. He removed the lighter from his pocket, sparked it into a flame, and raised it above his head. As the chorus ended, Nika returned to her feet and turned toward Cory, where he sat half grinning, half whistling while waving the lighter over his head in an orange arc.

The whites of her eyes dimmed. Her smile caved in. Nika stepped backward, away from him, and turned her head away as if about to spit. She stood downstage near the bearded men and danced for them. She never looked back at Cory.

He recognized it at once, that old familiar feeling—the drenching shock of fucking up. The guitar solo hit—the most stirring moment of the song— but Nika barely moved now. She stared at her feet, even as the chorus again declared the magic and glory of a people's joyful tears.

Cory reached for his wallet and removed a ten-dollar American bill. He set it in front of him on the stage and waited for her to see it, to look his way again. But when the song ended she marched to her clothes, gathered them up in her arms, and left through the beaded entranceway. His money lay there like litter. He stood up, crammed it in his pocket, and stumbled into the lounge area, looking for her.

A panic that he'd once had under control gathered in his chest. He inhaled deeply—and again—still unable to catch his breath. The room tilted. He set his hand atop the bar for balance, aiming for the hallway that led to the back.

The woman tending bar approached. "You can't go there."

A door flung open, and from the darkness strode Nika in her white dress, her eyes furious. "Get the fuck out."

"Wait. What?" He spread his palms as if showing he was unarmed.

She pushed past him and whispered something to the bartender, who nodded and said, "You have to go."

Nika spun around and jammed her index finger in his chest. Her mouth barely moved as she spoke. "I pay for your drinks. Just leave."

The bartender watched him, a phone halfway to her ear.

The sun was low and the sky was dim, cirrus clouds tinted to purple and pink. Cory staggered to his car, his eyes wet with tears as anxiety overtook him. He was drunk and afraid to drive, especially through the high tension of American border security, where they made him feel like a liar when he just stated his real name. And he'd told a lie tonight—white or not—and felt just now that he'd told many others, though he couldn't figure out what they were.

He drove the back roads to the OLG Casino, using cruise control to avoid erratic speeds. A little shock ran through him, followed by one of those skips in the video. Suddenly there to suddenly here. The place was busy the way casinos are always busy, and he continued taking deep, controlled breaths to allay the rattle of dread in his bones. With a wince he passed through the sliding glass doors into the clamor of gaming: bells and buzzers and flashing lights like miniature heat lightning in the clouds of smoke. Cory's skin hurt. His skull felt tight.

In a corner was a counter with free beverages where he drank two cups of lukewarm coffee to clear his head. He finished the second while gulping for breath, as if surfacing from a deep swim, and wandered unsteadily through the dazed populace. A row of ATMs lined the far wall. He'd play the slots a few times to extinguish the white lie as he sobered up and then head home across the bridge.

He remembered a half second before spotting the absence in his wallet: his debit card was still behind the bar at Club Z. Amid fear and regret and the casino din, there arose a trilling hope.

His head felt as clear as the sky where stars appeared above the gray city. It was just light enough that he could make out the silhouettes of the blast furnaces but dark enough that, as he approached the club once more, the pink neon outside reflected off of street signs and broken sidewalk glass. There were five or six cars in the gravel lot now. Cory parked and walked again toward the door and the bass beat, but he turned when the club and cars around him glowed in an instant, purple light.

Pink bursts, like flowers, followed. A giant green spider. A series of golden willows that tapered into falling light. The fireworks had begun.

He spotted Nika immediately, framed by the vanishing point of the long entrance corridor. She smoked and smiled and crossed her legs. About a dozen people, dancers and customers, now lingered in the lounge area, including a thirtysomething man with thick, dark hair seated beside Nika.

Cory ignored her at first. He rested his elbows on the bar, casual as could be, waiting for the bartender to see him. She looked up while rattling a martini shaker and frowned. "She paid for your tab."

"But I need my card," he said, and out of the corner of his eye he saw Nika standing and approaching. She blew smoke in his face. "Fuck you doing back, little boy?"

"I need my card," he said again. And then, "I need to talk to you. Just for a second."

Nika shrugged and shook her head. The man behind her was staring at them. "I got better people to talk to now," she said.

Cory lowered his voice and leaned toward her. "Please, please, please." He could feel his eyes going wet again.

She turned and snuffed out her cigarette before giving him a single nod. "You get one minute." He took his card before following her to the exit and the parking lot.

The sky lit up red, then gold. "I'm so sorry," he said. "I didn't mean to insult you. But I did, and it was stupid and I'm so sorry."

She hugged herself, chilled in the open air. "The world is big. You must grow up."

"I know," he said, stepping toward her. He had to tell her right now about Kaitlin. Then they could talk, and she'd understand, and maybe they could talk again tomorrow night. "I was on these pills, but now I'm not. I probably need to go back on them. I'm just feeling kind of crazy. But not like that. Not *crazy* crazy."

She tilted her head, confused. "I am going inside."

Nika turned to the door, and Cory grabbed her arm to stop her. She glared at his hand and then his face. He released her. "I'm sorry."

"Don't ever touch me like that."

"I'm sorry. I just—" He removed his Red Wings hat and ran his fingers through his thinning hair. "I have a kid. A little boy. He was adopted and everything, but I just wanted to tell you that."

She smirked and shook her head while stepping back toward the door. Her face and hair momentarily glowed with blue light. "So the baby has a baby. Good for you."

Time didn't skip this time, but the anger seemed to come from nowhere. He grabbed her arm once more. It was smooth. He had to talk to her.

Nika wrenched her arm free and then flung it backward, her elbow smashing his eye. Fingernails slashed the right side of his face. He fell backward over a wheel stop. Through gapped fingers he saw her huge white boots stomping at his head. The door to the club slammed shut behind her, and he lay there, still covering his face, the world bright as day but only for seconds at a time.

His heartbeat throbbed in the cuts on his face. Below ran the dark ribbon of water. Above stretched the darker expanse of sky. A white flash from a security camera made him blink and see colored spots. Let it see him. He was hiding nothing now. This was the true *everything*.

The American Border Patrol agent was tall with a shaved head. He took Cory's passport and asked the usual questions. Tobacco? Firearms? The purpose of your visit?

"I went to the casino."

The agent stepped outside with a flashlight, shined it into the backseat, and asked him to pop the trunk. Cory couldn't remember what was inside. Ice scraper and jumper cables. Maybe some fast-food wrappers. Nothing to hide. The guard slammed it shut and approached him to return the passport. The flashlight blinded Cory, and when he shielded his eyes with his hand the guard recoiled.

"What's that on your hand, son?"

"Blood." He turned his head slowly to reveal the cuts on the right side of his face. "A woman scratched me, but it's okay." Of all the day's sensations, this pain with each pulse felt best. He hoped it would last the drive home. He would creep quietly to bed, not waking his mom, and he'd hold off on taking the pills a little longer. He'd lie in bed feeling and remembering everything.

The guard stepped back and spoke into his handheld radio. A garbled, crackling voice came in return. Like the words from a foreign speaker, it made no sense.

SAY NOT REALLY

Today's garbage day, and there's a windstorm. Torn envelopes and food wrappers scurry through the neighborhood like tumbleweeds. Trash bins lie in the road with their lids agape. Warren steers wide around them, headed home from the post office, where the woman behind the counter told him they couldn't just stop Beverly's mail from arriving. "You have to go online, to the Direct Marketing Association's Deceased Do Not Contact list."

"On the computer?" he said. "I'd rather kill myself."

And he could almost hear Beverly's voice then, whispering into his ear: *Say, "Not really."*

At home, there's paper sticking out of the brass mailbox. It had come in the ten minutes he was gone.

He parks, gets out, and removes advertising circulars, Valpak coupons, pre-approved credit card applications—all in Beverly's name. Warren holds them above his head before liberating them like frantic release doves. "Fly, you fuckers!"

He cleans his glasses on his coat and heads inside. It's only three thirty, but he wants to drink until he blacks out and maybe sleep forever.

Say, "Not really."

Beverly was a habitual finger-crosser and wood-knocker who refused to stay on the fourteenth floors of hotels because she knew they were really the thirteenth. When the disease stole all but the last of her memories, she'd still make Warren say "not really" to quash the bad luck of his black humor.

When he cut his finger with a kitchen knife and joked he'd bleed to death.

Say, "Not really."

When he mused that the Chinese would enslave us within a decade.

Say, "Not really."

There's gin and bourbon in the kitchen, but he runs cold water and makes coffee instead. While it brews, Warren gazes out the window above the sink. Along the fence runs a hard-packed stretch of dirt that had once been Beverly's garden. In the perfect purgatory of her disease, when she remembered past blooms but not the words *iris* or *dahlia*, he'd pierce the dirt with the plastic stems of silk flowers, and she'd stand before this window and smile.

The first sip of coffee fogs his glasses so that, for a moment, he's lost in a cloud only he can see. He ambles down the hallway to his small study, sets his mug on the desk, and opens the lowest drawer, removing matches and his usual stockpile of candles: pillar and taper and votive. A half-dozen tea lights Beverly once put in jack-o'-lanterns. He arranges some on the desk and the rest among bookshelves. After lighting all of them he shuts the door, closes the curtains, and turns off the lamp.

Among the dim orange light, Warren sips coffee and reads the newspaper while, outside, wind-thrashed branches rasp against the siding. Soon the room's air has burned so thin he feels high as if on wine. It's something like amnesia. He breathes deeply, head floating, wanting to be blessed the way she was cursed, with a mind scrubbed utterly free.

But not really. Not really. Not.

LIGHT YEARS

You step onto the front stoop, shielding your eyes from the sun, and there's this white stretch limousine idling along the curb, taking up all the space between your driveway and the neighbor's. Eric Kellogg is leaning against the hood, wearing a Michigan State tank top and teal swimming trunks. He crosses his arms and grins. "What you say, Angie? You want to go to prom?"

He's forty-one, you're forty-two, and though you'd never gone to any dances together, you'd dated for six months during your junior year of high school. Lost your virginities to each other. You reunited by accident last week, at your niece's wedding reception where Eric worked as a deejay for his company, Live-It-Up! Productions. After talking and laughing over drinks from the open bar, you made plans, and today you're going for a swim—your first date together in over twenty-five years. Your first date together since you'd broken it off all those years ago and began to worry that—maybe, in some small way—you'd added to all of his adolescent tragedies.

You cross the front yard barefoot, over dead grass sharp as pine needles. The temperature's ninety-three, the heat index a hundred. You wear a pair of khaki shorts over a black one-piece bathing suit, and within seconds your skin films over with sweat. You shake your head at the sight of the limo, although a smile creases your lips. "What are you up to this time?"

Eric's high forehead gleams under the sun. There may be traces of gray along his temples, but he's still such a towhead that it's hard to tell. He makes a joke of buffing the car's hood with the bottom of his tank top. You'll catalog every joke today—study his face, his mood—looking for signs that he's damaged or healed. And you'll fight the old guilt that rises like bile from your gut. It's fine. He's fine. Everyone's older, but everyone's fine.

"It's one of my old rentals," says Eric. "Air conditioner in my Camry just died, so this is our only chance to stay half-cool."

"What about your *new* rentals?" you ask.

"One's in the shop. The other's at some daddy-daughter dance."

The limo's well maintained, but the boxy chassis gives away its age. "How old *is* this? Abe Lincoln take it to homecoming?"

In the yearbook Eric was voted class clown. Senior year, he drove an old tricked-out hearse with the vanity plate MEATWGN. "It's a '91 Lincoln Town Car Executive," he says. "Built right about the time we were dating."

"So it's ancient," you say.

And you're just about to put an end to this and suggest you take your Civic when Eric jogs around the front and opens the passenger side door for you. "It'll be fun," he says, gesturing with his hand like a spokesmodel. "Fine leather interior for a fine, classy lady."

You roll your eyes before returning to the house and checking your ash-brown hair in the mirror. If you tuck it behind your ears your eyes look brighter, but then the creases fanning toward your temples lay exposed. You let the bangs fall back over your face, slip on some sandals, and return to the heat wave with a pink gym bag slung over your shoulder. Eric opens the passenger door, bowing while you slip inside.

Before he shuts it, you motion him close with your index finger. His lips purse ever so slightly for a phantom kiss. But you stop him short, resting your finger on his chin. "Unless you want to make her feel old," you say, "don't ever call a woman a *lady*."

Then you wink and smile. Because it's fine. You're fine. Everyone's older, but we can joke about it, right?

• • •

Eric's parents took him to the Muskegon Air Show for his fourteenth birthday. During a loop maneuver, a vintage T-6 Texan flew too low, clipped a power line, and smashed into the runway, scattering flaming wreckage over the grandstand. Twelve died, including Eric's mom—killed instantly by shrapnel—and his brother, Gregory, who survived three days in the hospital before succumbing to burns.

Eric—in line at the Port-A-Johns with his dad—emerged unscathed.

"Look at these kids," he says now, grinning while pointing out his window. As you leave, two boys run alongside, waving at the limo, and Eric drives slow enough so they can keep up for a ways.

The plan is to swim at the YMCA downtown—which has hot tubs, waterslides, and a lazy river—before heading out for burgers and beer. Over your left shoulder sits a row of silver toggle switches. As Eric turns onto 36th Street you twist around in your seat and tinker with them, raising and lowering the partition, flashing the dome lights in the back. Eric glances over: once at your breasts, once at your legs. Your suit's a Speedo that tucks, slims, and holds everything in place, concealing your entire backside and most of your cleavage. The last time he saw your skin it was porcelain-smooth, splayed out on your childhood bed, and surrounded by your stuffed turtle collection.

It's your turn to glance. His chin's doubled, his belly's grown, but his eyes—even more than his mouth—hint at a smile always simmering beneath each expression.

You cross Division, passing a vast lot of concrete slab and weeds. Chain-link and barbed wire line the perimeter. GM closed the metal-stamping plant here in 2009, and the demo crew that followed left nothing behind but the pedestrian bridge. Eric became a press operator right out of high school and walked this bridge every day between the employee lot and the factory floor. "Looks stupid, right?" he says as you pass beneath it. "Connected to nothing?"

"Bridge to nowhere," you say.

"Like a big old high five someone's left hanging." Eric shrugs and reaches to turn up the air conditioning, though it's already on full blast. "But if it hadn't happened I'd never have started my business." He delivers a slow-motion punch to your arm. "Wouldn't have met up with you again, hey?"

He started Live-It-Up! two years ago, hiring old friends from high school to help with emcee duties, lighting design, and limo rentals. You, on the other hand, shield your face at the mall when spotting former classmates. You refuse to attend reunions, and except for the wedding reception and this very date, you've had no real contact with anyone from that past. A few months back, on a date with an industrial designer you met on eHarmony, the guy mentioned attending his college homecoming. You'd had three Chardonnays. With a slow shake of your head you eyed him sideways and said, "Nostalgia is puke."

Yet here you sit, in a limousine, with the man you loved when he was just a boy and you were just a girl.

"How about you?" asks Eric. "How long you been at the credit union?"

"Like, eight or nine years. Wait—no." You count silently, moving your lips. "Twelve! It's been twelve years now."

When you reach the Y, Eric slows the limo to a crawl before turning sharply, hopping the curb along the way. The lot's empty and the building's dark. He pulls up along the front walk and reads the posted hours before checking the dashboard clock. It's almost seven thirty. "Shit, it's Sunday, ain't it. They close early on Sundays." He pulls the limo forward, turns around, and amid the vast emptiness of the lot performs a series of slow but enormous figure eights that make you mildly, comfortably light-headed.

Were this a real first date, it'd tumble into awkwardness here. What do you want to do? I don't know; what do *you* want to do? But you've got history, even if it's twenty-five years in the past. Even if you have to feel along its edges, sift through its sediment, and see what, if anything, remains.

You slip into the leadership role—same as always—and tell him to get on the highway and drive to Grand Haven, to the beach forty miles away.

"Are you chipping in for gas?" asks Eric.

You rub his knee. "Drinks on me. How's that?"

The two of you ease up the on-ramp, headed west toward the lake and the late-day sun, and begin narrating the high points of your lives to each other. When he asks what you do for fun, you merely shrug and don't mention the fact that sometimes you sit on the front porch wearing sunglasses and waiting for the young, shirtless cross-country runners to gallop down the sidewalk. Or how, twice a week, you go to hotel bars—where there's no shame in being alone—to sip wine in the company of a crossword or your Kindle, telling any men that approach that your husband's in the fitness center and will be joining you for dinner.

Eric smiles uncomfortably when you speak of your daughter, Haley, who's a sophomore at Western and the result of your failed marriage to Jeremy Bates. You went to senior prom with Jeremy while Eric went stag, sipping from a flask and then break-dancing amid wild cheers before vomiting, staggering through the exit, and blacking out in the country club's hedges.

Drinks on me, you'd just said to him. Maybe he still has a problem, although he seemed fine at the wedding's open bar. When he was sixteen and you were still together, his dad converted him from son to drinking buddy, buying him beers down at The Peacock and, at home, mixing vodka with Hawaiian Punch. His dad was a late bloomer as a drinker. Barely touched the stuff until jet wreckage decimated his family.

"I didn't take the transfer to Flint," Eric says now, peering down the highway. "Just collected unemployment and read a lot."

He's been talking, filling in the gaps of decades, and you've missed it.

"Books on nature," he continues. "I got a big garden. Bought a couple apple trees, hoping they'd cross-pollinate, but it's been four years and still nothing."

"So you never married," you say.

Eric shakes his head. "Not even close, really. But I always sort of wanted to." He glances out the driver's side window, beyond the silos to the landfill where seagulls float above on invisible currents. "When it comes to relationships, I got black-cat luck."

You rub his knee again. "It's luck, is it?"

He nods and smiles. "I'm a two-leaf clover."

You study that face—the eyes, especially, through which you can detect his real smile from the clown one. All of those frantic high school dramatics were, you understood later, a false joy. Playing banjo in the cafeteria. Dressing up as Napoleon for the history exam. Streaking across the football field in a thong.

All of it a bullshit salve. Had you been older you'd have handled it better, listened more. You'd have noticed the blazing, five-alarm signs and steered him to counseling. You'd have said the right thing that day in Spanish when Señora Jenkins asked everyone to repeat a series of innocuous phrases, including the one that made him bury his face in his arms and bawl at his desk.

No puedo encontrar a mi madre. No puedo encontrar a mi madre.

I cannot find my mother. I cannot find my mother.

The lake fills the view, a shade neither emerald nor sapphire but of a jewel not yet dreamt up. You lean forward, placing both palms on the dash, the vents pouring air over your arms. "It's so damn beautiful," you say. "Why don't I come here more often?"

The limo eases around a sharp turn, the narrow road now running along the shore. "Because of this," says Eric. Bumper-to-bumper cars stretch into the distance. Hundreds—thousands—of people clog the beach. Parking here's a nightmare on summer weekends, when even compacts have to shoehorn into spaces. Part of you suddenly hates the clown side of Eric and this enormous clown car of his. But it's immediately followed by guilt and your memories of his teenage grief, foolishness, and rage. Memories of the night the two of you, headed to the movies, came upon a car wreck: police, ambulances, bloodied victims. Spectators ogled from the curb. Eric parked the car, leapt out, and ran toward the crowd. "Take it in, you fucking gawkers! Suck it dry, you vampire pigs!"

Later that night, the phone trembling in your hand, you finally told him, "I think we need a break from each other." And a month later he bought the hearse, the MEATWGN. Funny, right?

The limo inches forward in the lakeshore traffic. You take a deep breath through your nose and exhale slowly through your mouth. In the distance, shirtless young men and bikinied young women tiptoe the water's edge.

After a half hour navigating the crowded streets you're now on the commercial strip, which is to say you're nowhere. Eric pulls into a Meijer parking lot and idles there, far from other cars, the limo straddling three spaces. You fold your arms over your hollow stomach, hungry but in no mood to eat at some Applebee's.

The sun slowly arcs toward the horizon. Seagulls circle a cart corral. "I'll be right back," says Eric, unbuckling his seatbelt and slipping outside. But he's gone for nearly twenty minutes, during which you pass the time by playing some more with the special limousine switches. The partition rises. The partition falls.

He returns slinging four plastic grocery bags and motioning for you to come join him. "Let's treat ourselves. We deserve it," he says as you step out into the heat and follow him into the back compartment of the limousine, that place normally reserved for prom queens and brides.

There's a bar area with two empty decanters and some tumblers on a tray. Eric immediately removes the items and sets the tray on the floor before unpacking the contents of the grocery bags: hummus, cashews, blue cheese, olives, a long baguette, a bag of ice, Ocean Spray Cranberry Juice Cocktail, and a fifth of Smirnoff Red.

You lean back in the rear-facing seat, charmed by the tiny orange lightbulbs that line the ceiling—sort of like a stripper stage, sort of like Christmas decorations, but mostly like the rows of votive candles you remember from your grandparents' church. They circle an overhead mirror.

There's another control panel back here. You turn on the radio and find a station playing old, smoky jazz. Then you turn another dial, lowering the dome lighting so that a soft orange glow—a virtual twilight—settles over the compartment. Above you is your inverted, reflected self. You tuck your hair behind your ears so that your eyes glint. A dark line of cleavage runs down your chest.

Eric lays the food out picnic style on the floor and slices the baguette with a Swiss Army key chain. You join him, sitting cross-legged with the banquet between the two of you. The limo's old engine rumbles away, the vents still blowing half-cool air. He hands you a cocktail, makes one for himself, and then he sips. It looks like Hawaiian Punch. You lean forward, kissing him on the cheek. Unlike earlier, when you motioned him close and he pursed his lips, he assumes nothing this time but merely closes his eyes for the moment. What you feel is like the pull of a distant sun.

When he finishes eating, Eric reclines on the floor with his legs up on the seat and his hands behind his head. He barely touched his drink. You join him without thinking, tucking into his body, your left ear pressed against his chest as it rises and falls with his breath. "God," you say, "it's been so long since I've heard your heart."

You lift your head, touch his face again, and then kiss him deeply. For a moment you're breathing in his exhalation. The sudden light-headedness is a high—from the lack of oxygen but also from the sense that you're thieving some inner part of him. You haven't breathed him in for twenty-five years, and now it's so familiar it might as well come from your own girlhood lungs. When you finish you lay your head on him again and listen.

The first time he undressed in front of you he was so skinny that his heart showed through his chest, gently lifting the skin beneath his nipple, in pulse time. You mention this to him now and he quietly laughs. "It ain't there no more. Maybe if you shove the fat out of the way."

And just like that you're both laughing, comparing your bodies to the ones you once knew. "My pubic hair fundamentally changed after pregnancy," you say.

Eric arches his back, howling. "Changed how? What does that even mean?"

"Like, longer," you say. "And thicker."

He wipes tears from his eyes. "But, baby, you haven't lived until you've sat on a toilet and your balls hit the water."

The laugh that escapes you is so pure that it's silent. Your body shakes. You slap his chest with your hand and then lie on your back next to him. When you settle down you simply stare up at each other's reflections, side by side but making eye contact.

"If you'd had some crystal ball when you were sixteen," he asks, "would you have looked inside to see your future?"

You roll your eyes. "Aw, come on. Yuck."

"Is it that bad?" he says.

You're not sure what he means. "I just get freaked out by the entire concept of time."

"Like the past?"

You shrug.

"I work school dances and weddings every weekend," says Eric. "That puts things in perspective."

It wouldn't surprise you if Haley soon made that leap from dances to marriage. For a year she's dated a boy named Austin who comes from one of those families who plays board games together and celebrates half birthdays. "I hate the future, too," you say. "Not necessarily *my* future but the *whole* future. I'm freaked out by the concept of infinity."

"Really?" He gently rubs your knee.

"And outer space. The idea of the universe. Galaxies after galaxies."
You shiver for effect. "The planetarium's like a horror show."

He nods slowly, smiles faintly, and you study his face in the mirror.
Subtlety has vanished amid the car ride, the food, the kiss. Later you'll
see this question as selfish and heavy-handed, but you ask it now anyway:
"What bothers *you* these days?"

Both of you turn onto your sides at the same moment, ignoring the
mirror and looking directly into each other's eyes. Although not a parent
himself, Eric's smile contains a fatherly kindness and patience, aimed as
if at a child who thinks she's figured out the world. "I'll be right back," he
says softly.

After exiting the limo and opening the trunk, he returns holding
a smooth, black object resembling binoculars—something a sci-fi
character would use to view the horizon. "It's a Scatter Star," he says. "A
laser machine."

"Which you just happen to keep in your trunk," you say.

"You should see what's back there. Disco balls. Fog juice. All the tricks
of the trade."

He plugs a cord into an outlet beside the control panel and then turns
off the radio and all interior lights. Outside it's dusk, and with the tinted
windows the compartment goes black. "I've done this a few times when
I needed to disinfect my head." He sits cross-legged, aiming the device
forward. "You ready?" he asks.

"I don't know. What's happening?"

Needles of green light pierce through the darkness. They fan out over
the seats and windows and doors. Eric adjusts something on the device,
and the needles cluster together to make circles of green light that
slowly pirouette. Then they speed up, their dance frenetic. He adjusts
something again so that their pace relaxes once more, slipping into a
gentle rhythm.

"Oh my God, this is freaking me out," you say through laughter.

He switches it off, the dark returning, and lies down beside you. "Just
relax. I won't make it go crazy like that anymore. Just stare up at the
mirror."

"It's too dark to see it."

"Good," he says. "It's better if you don't even realize it's there."

The green laser needles return. This time Eric aims them upward so that—with reflection—they multiply, filling all the dark space around the two of you, covering your bodies with green stars.

You squeeze his arm, slightly hyperventilating. "I have no idea why this weirds me out." And suddenly it's not funny anymore. You squeeze your eyes shut as your breath quickens and your throat tightens.

"Pretend you're floating."

"That's what's weird," you say, your fingertips tingling. "I feel like I am."

"Or that you're swimming," he says. "Like you're in a lake at night, floating on your back over the waves. That's what I do."

You're only half listening to him, thinking for some reason of those young couples you saw earlier along the high-water mark. Thinking of Haley, how she turned twenty last month. She's already outlived her teenage self.

You shoot up—your eyes still shut—and fumble for the door.

"Are you okay?" asks Eric, touching your back.

You run your hand down the window until you find the door handle, and when you do your hand rests there, and you pause, and you take a deep and cleansing breath. Outside, the air will be hot and syrupy. Outside, the green stars will vanish forever.

"I'm fine," you say, still touching the door handle, happy to know it's there. "It was just a shock at first." Your eyes remain closed, but you can make out the needle lights through the lids. You find his hand with yours, and he gently leads you back to where you were just before.

The first time you held hands you sat beside each other in the dark, fingers slick with sweat and popcorn butter, staring at a giant movie screen. Now your eyes are still closed, but when you finally open them again the two of you exist in your own private universe. Galaxies after galaxies. Each star is an illusion, of course, its light a ghost from a past age and a source that no longer exists. And yet it has found you—here, today—in this soft and quiet place.

CORONATIONS

I sweep toys away with my foot—puzzle pieces, Candy Land cards, a few Weebles—and unfurl the jumbo checker mat over the worn carpet. My four-year-old, Victoria, picks up one of the red checkers, stretching her fingers to the edges. It's the size of the plastic plates stacked on the toy kitchen beside us.

"Do you want to be red or black?" I ask. I know the answer but have learned, with her, never to assume.

She raises her right hand, holding the checker. "Red." Then she lowers it and holds it close in front of her face, noticing, for the first time, the little ruts and teeth along its edges. She drags her left index finger along its red circumference.

Red's her favorite color. I've never known a little girl with red as a favorite color. She shrugs off purple and pink. She loves her Christmas dresses and wears them in June.

When I was young I had a fear of the color red. It's the kind of thing eradicated with time and pills but which still appears like a ring of spilled wine, unnoticed, until I raise the glass and see it there on the white tablecloth.

It wasn't really a fear of blood. In fourth grade, on a field trip to Lake Michigan, my friend Jason Crawford was running down a sand dune. A decayed, half-buried section of fence stretched along the edge, meant to slow erosion. Jason's leg caught on a nail, and it tore open to the tibia. I stood at the bottom of the dune and could see the white of the bone.

But the phobia didn't arise then. It surfaced a couple of days later, while visiting him in the hospital and seeing the kid he shared a room with. The kid had accidentally shot himself and now had instruments measuring his heart rate and blood pressure and breathing. What I hated was the thought of those pulsating organs inside of him. Inside of me.

From then on—for at least a year—I had the same two images pop into my head while saying my bedtime prayers. First: a person biting into a human heart, like a crisp apple, making a cracking sound. Second: a person holding a firm red artery at each end, like a single piece of uncooked spaghetti, and snapping it in half.

My dad's favorite toy growing up was a set of Civil War army men. He'd kept it and passed it on to me. Half the men were blue, and the rest were gray. But all of them were splashed with red—my grandmother's old nail polish, which he'd painted onto their heads and abdomens and the tips of their bayonets. Setting them up on the table or on the floor, I made sure that none of their guns ever aimed at me. If they did, my chest would feel tight; my pulse would race.

And so I never wore red clothes. I cheered for the Tigers and Lions and Pistons, but I hated the Red Wings because of their uniforms. In fifth grade we'd watch videos about current events: Reagan and Gorbachev and thermonuclear weapons with red Soviet flags.

Red meant sirens. It meant fear. Vader with his red lightsaber. And I was never one of those kids who'd felt invincible. Even as a teenager—the height of this illusion for most people—I felt I could go at any moment. A bloody red nose on the basketball court infecting me with AIDS. An icy road, a learner's permit, and a flashing red stoplight.

A decade later my wife, Abby, would tease me during our birthing classes because I'd turn away from the films they'd show. I've never fainted in my life, but she was sure I'd black out in the delivery room. And yet when Victoria arrived I snipped the cord with scissors and helped wipe

away blood and vernix and even watched as the afterbirth spilled from
Abby's womb.

• • •

Our cat, Little Man, steps over the large checkerboard mat and paws at it
briefly before leaving. Then Bruin, our black Lab, sniffs the rows of pieces
until I nudge her out of the way with my shoulder. I'm busy teaching rules.

My daughter points to the board, counting silently to herself. "They're
all little squares," she says, "and the whole board is a big square."

"You're right." I show her how the pieces must stay on the black squares,
though she wants them on the red. They must move diagonally, to adjacent
squares, but they can't move backward yet. We take a few turns each, and
then I show her how to jump. Her forehead wrinkles when I take her red
piece and set it beside me on the carpet.

We continue to practice. I let her jump one of my pieces. "Good job."

She sets the black piece next to her. "Did you let me?"

She's a poor loser, crossing her arms and pouting in an over-the-top,
cartoonish way. But I shouldn't have let her take the piece. I want her to be
tough—tougher than I was growing up. So on my next turn I jump another
red piece. Then I double jump and land on her side.

"King me," I say.

"What's that?" She winces, and I assume it's from losing.

"I'll show you." I reach for my captured black piece, but she grabs my
wrist. "It's okay," I say. "It's how you play the game." I stack it onto my newly
kinged piece, fitting tooth into groove. "See. Now it's a king. It's wearing a
crown. It can go anywhere it wants now. Forward or back."

I win this game, and she pouts. We play a second game, and the result's
the same. We play a third, and now she's getting it. I'm winning, but I'm
getting lazy, half watching a football game on TV, and at one point she
actually double jumps my pieces and lands on my side of the board.

"Queen me!" She stands up, shaking her hips in a dance. "Queen me!"

She inherited my wife's curiosity and focus. She inherited my eyes and
nose. And I want to think some trace of her boldness is mine. But I don't
recognize the voice or the proud posture of this girl who sees the world as
a conquerable place, who will move through it with grace and ease.

She crowns her queen in red and then stands, arms crossed, over the
board. And I know now why we named her Victoria.

MERCY MERCY ME

I was fourteen, sitting cross-legged atop my canopy bed with the laptop warming my bare knees. Glowing on the screen was a topless image of my mom that Dylan Haney, a giggling twit from school, had forwarded to me and about a dozen classmates. I shook my head slightly before typing: *Yeah. Pretty hot, huh.*

My mom's the former actress Rachel Dawn Rice, and the image was a still from her 1992 debut film, *The Harpsichord*. In the scene, she's changing her bra in front of a vanity and is naked for about a second and a half. The picture's so grainy that her small breasts might as well be some trick of light and shadow. But for boys like Dylan—and like their dads in dark theaters twenty years earlier—this glimpse of flesh was like a firefly they wanted trapped in a jar.

The Harpsichord was indie, low budget, and critically acclaimed—easily my favorite of her seven films. Ed Harris stars as a widower piano technician repairing a music school's antique harpsichord. He falls in love with a teacher, played by Julianne Moore, who guides him through his grief and helps mend the frayed relationship with his daughter. Rachel Dawn Rice, then nineteen, plays the daughter. It was her first time on-screen.

I stood and carried the laptop across my room. Although eight o'clock on a September evening, the sun lingered like the last person at a party. I drew the blinds so that, other than the monitor illuminating my arms and chest, the only light came from the zebra-striped lamp on my nightstand. The walls, dimly pink, were covered in ballet posters, framed prints of the Louvre and Eiffel Tower, and a mirror above my armoire that read LA BELLE ÉPOCHE. Beside it hung a corkboard with postcards, school certificates, and photos in which me and my best friend, Hannah Kosten, stuck out our tongues, made peace signs, and pulled our noses into pig snouts. Hannah always teased me about how my room hadn't changed since fourth grade. Hers was an altar to pop culture, actors and singers plastered everywhere. Beautiful boys with beautiful eyes that followed you as you moved. My mom hated shit like that. She'd never have allowed it.

"Just because *she* was famous?" Hannah had once asked.

And I shrugged and went silent because it was that simple until it wasn't. I was just starting to seriously dig into my mom's past: her fame and how it ended. I kept trying to fill the gaps she hadn't yet explained to me herself, especially involving her affair with Gordon Shultz—my father, the phantom I'd never met—and his wife at the time, Oscar winner Patricia Gray.

I sat amid the pink-and-beige pillows I kept heaped in a corner of the room, tucking my long dancer's legs beneath my body. I flipped the hood of my sweatshirt up over my head and pulled the drawstrings so that it cinched around my face, leaving a hole smaller than my fist to stare through at the nude image of my mom's younger self. Then I once again went to IMDb and read her profile.

Born: Rachel Dawn Rice, March 1, 1973 in Grand Rapids, MI, USA.

She'd never used her middle name before Hollywood; it was a union issue. And when—pregnant with me—she'd fled Hollywood to return to Michigan, she never used it again.

A photo on the page showed her at twenty-five, toward the end of that brief career. The deep red backdrop and slanted typeface suggest some red-carpet shot from the *Mercy Mercy Me* premier. She wears a white strapless dress by de la Renta. Her enormous brown eyes, blessed with their own gravity, tug at the camera lens. They were her most famous feature, followed by the boyish haircut, always short, dark, and parted to the side. Entertainment writers loved describing her with the word *nymph*. "*Rachel Dawn Rice, with her nymph-like features and impish charms . . .*"

I scrolled down to the filmography, which I knew then by heart. I'd watched them all, streaming them late at night in bed.

Actress (7 titles)	
Mercy Mercy Me	1998
Edge of Moonlight	1997
Albuquerque Baby	1995
The Butcher and the Baker	1994
Party Down Under	1993
Shadowfalls	1993
The Harpsichord	1992

A series of thumbnails ran across the page. I clicked one, enlarged it, and lazily skimmed through the slideshow, the pictures moving backward in time. Many of them were publicity shots. Production stills of Rachel Dawn Rice facing down Kevin Spacey's handgun in *Mercy Mercy Me*. Pursuing a criminal alongside Tommy Lee Jones in *Moonlight*. Seated around a dinner table with the cast of *Albuquerque Baby*.

All the way back to stills of *The Harpsichord*. Filmed in Big Sur and Monterey, every frame resembled a watercolor. My mom—nearly a girl, a little younger than I am now—clutched her knees to her chest, gazing out at the sea, brushing stray hairs from her face. And because I was fourteen, whenever I googled her past and stared at that beautiful young face on-screen, I wasn't looking for similarities to the forty-two-year-old Rachel Rice raising me at the time. I was looking for traces of myself.

I stood with the other girls along the barre, in fifth position with our legs crossed at the knees, toes inward. We faced the floor-to-ceiling mirror while Mr. Fishman, the mustachioed pianist in the corner of the studio, played "Waltz of the Flowers." Outside, the leaves had barely begun to yellow. The late September sun still grew warm in the afternoon. And yet we, once again, had begun our three-month slog toward *The Nutcracker*.

In the mirror's reflection, through the glass wall behind me, I glimpsed my mom entering the lounge area. For all the elegance of the ballet company, this section of the school wing remained a cinder-block gloom.

She wore her sleek black yoga outfit and removed her sunglasses to peer into our studio, that bright cube of light.

She did yoga six times a week—an essential element of her post-acting life—along with regular sessions of meditation, mindfulness, and distance running. She'd never worked once she quit film. (My grandpa, her financial advisor, mentions "investments.") So as I grew older she filled her days with self-improvement, home restoration, and occasional volunteering.

Her hair, falling past her shoulders, was the longest it had been in her adult life. She stepped now past some waiting, middle-aged parents who read paperbacks or played with their phones, and then sat opposite a group of young, ponytailed mothers who waved at their pink preschoolers in the adjacent studio and jockeyed for position to photograph every tiny arabesque and dégagé.

Our ballet mistress, a woman we girls secretly referred to as The Anguish, clapped her hands and barked instructions as I capered along the marly floor, stepping as if I were glancing across a pond of thin ice. As I performed a pirouette, The Anguish waved her hands above her head, Mr. Fishman halted play, and I scampered back toward the barre before attempting again.

I stole another glance through the glass wall to the lobby, where my mom remained the only parent watching us teenagers in Ballet 7—we who wore black, not pink. Even from that distance I could sense a watery, melancholy look in her eyes, as if she were watching not the actual me but a video of my youth. Nostalgia in real time.

I sensed her studying my body, as well. This was back when she and I would go to a restaurant or to the mall together, and she'd observe the nearby men and say, "They're staring at you from behind. They think you're a college girl. But when you turn and they see your baby face it freaks them out and they drop their eyes."

I was a couple years from noticing the perpetual leers of men. A couple years from appreciating how, in that ballet class, we all seemed to exist in the realms of both child and adult. The boys had slim waists but shoulders and arms like pro athletes, like soldiers. And we girls had long, muscular legs stretching from our slippers up to hips that barely hinted at the curves of grown women. Sometimes after class—with my hair, of course, in a bun—my mom would put her arm around me in a hug and then slide her hand up, tenderly pressing her palm against the back of my neck. "You're so elegant," she'd say. "Like a bud vase." And then she'd sort of pull away, afraid,

I think, of making me conscious of the physical: of my looks and my body. Because that would be so *Hollywood*. Although at fourteen I still mainly thought of my body as a vehicle for dance.

That September day, amid the tinkling notes of Christmas time, we continued performing a small, precise number of steps while The Anguish clapped her hands, barked out orders, and sent us back to the barre again and again. I grew both so focused and exhausted that I forgot anyone might be watching. Toward the end of class I stood facing the wall of mirrors, my hands on my hips as I caught my breath. When the knocking started I figured it was just some excited toddler watching us through the glass wall. But when I looked up the mirrors revealed my mom, standing pressed against the door, rapping her knuckles on the glass and frantically waving to get my attention.

I turned, and as she entered the studio—staggering slightly as she approached—she held her phone out in my direction and shook it a little. Amid this moment of shock her famously large eyes had turned wider, grotesque. "I'm sorry," she said, glancing at The Anguish. Oblivious, Mr. Fishman continued playing "Waltz of the Flowers," but The Anguish and the dancers and the parents in the lobby went rigid and stared at my mom's sudden appearance, her sudden affliction.

She fell against me as if exhausted, accidentally shoving me against the mirror and the girls next to me. "Oh my God, Ellie." She spoke with a frantic, though whispered, urgency. "Patricia Gray died!"

Which meant nothing to me, at first. I just stood there, overwhelmed by her isolated chaos. A cyclone dropped from a clear, blue sky.

I held her as she raised the phone up to my face and spoke in a choked strain. "It's *everywhere*."

I helped her stand upright, both of us holding the barre for balance and facing the mirrors. The music finally stopped. A sea of dancers in black—awestruck and terrified—reflected back at us. My mom turned and surveyed them, confused as anyone by her sudden presence in the studio. She squinted from its shimmering light.

Bleeding from cuts on her face and knees, Rachel Dawn Rice sits up, struggling to drag herself to safety as her arms tremble, her shoes slip on broken glass. Kevin Spacey looms over her—a silhouette in the dim, abandoned factory—pointing his handgun. "*What a sad little ending for you,*" he says with a charming smirk. "*All of that pain. All of that suffering. And in a flash of lead and fire—in a flash of blood and bone—it's all over.*"

I lay in bed with the lights off, wrapped in a cocoon of dark with my laptop and a pillow on my chest, headphones snug in place. *Mercy Mercy Me* was a completely ordinary thriller: Rachel Dawn Rice as the young widow seeking the truth about her murdered husband, and Kevin Spacey as the prosecuting attorney—and the real killer—who's arguing for the sentence of an innocent man. With most of my mom's films I could never think in terms of character names. I saw *her*. I saw *actors*. Only with *The Harpsichord* could I lose myself in the dream of the story.

My father, Gordon Shultz, had directed *Mercy Mercy Me*. I'd watched it just once before, and that time I'd focused less on the lame plot twists than on the fact that this was how my parents had met—how their affair had started—and I'd kept reaching for epiphanies that didn't exist.

With slow, deliberate steps, Kevin Spacey's black loafers crunch over the glass. "*Say hello to your husband for me.*"

Though she still wore her hair short in the back, as was her trademark, my mom's bangs had grown long by then and hung over her eyes. No longer nymph-like, those eyes in her final film appear hollow and hungry. It was more than just makeup and lighting and the demands of the scene. This came at the tail end of the grunge scene, when Rachel Dawn Rice epitomized heroin chic. When tabloids said she weighed just ninety-eight pounds.

A close-up of her right hand, the fingers slowly grasping a knife-sized shard of glass. She slashes his Achilles tendon, and in a flurry of shots she lunges for the gun that's clattered to the floor; then she stands over him, a swinging lightbulb glowing above her like a broken halo. "*No,*" she says, "*say hello to the devil for* me!"

The booming gunshots made me wince and turn down the volume. The carnage itself happens off-screen, the camera lingering on Rachel Dawn Rice's face as she fires and the tendrils of smoke drift across her face.

And while I watched her there on-screen, the real-life Rachel continued to diminish downstairs, curled up on the sofa in a tangle of blankets like someone sick with the flu. The other day, when we'd come home from ballet after learning the news—the car straddling lanes as she drove—she'd disappeared into her bedroom and locked the door. I'd seen her a little bit the last two days, mostly after school, as she drank wine and flipped through TV channels, wearing the same yoga outfit she'd worn when the Patricia Gray news broke. When I asked her this evening how she felt, she said she hadn't slept in three days.

On-screen, she places a crimson rose atop her husband's gravestone before the scene fades to black, the credits roll, and the music swells—the title song, of course, but a baffling choice in terms of tone and subject matter. After all the film's violence and heavy-handed emotion, Marvin Gaye effortlessly croons the opening lines. And yet I loved the melody so much that I didn't care that it made no sense to have a song about environmentalism play after a factory shootout. I'd downloaded and would listen to it on my way to school. That first verse, where he wonders about blue skies, was perfect for late-winter Michigan mornings, when I measured sunlight in monochrome degrees.

I closed the movie, removed my headphones, and searched the entertainment sites for the latest on Patricia Gray. The funeral had been that day, and on *Radar*, between a story of a musician entering rehab and a story about an actress's post-pregnancy bikini beach body, were photos of the ceremony. The casket was silver, draped in a spray of white roses, white lilies, and white orchids. Among the pallbearers were two men at the front, both in their late twenties, wearing black suits and grim faces. They were my half brothers, Allen and Richard, sons of Patricia Gray and Gordon Shultz. Just as I'd never met my father, I'd never met either of them; I've still never been to California. After my parents' affair and his divorce from Patricia, my father had married again and had a baby. He'd started yet another family.

And there he stood in one of the photos: slim, wearing an immaculate black suit and pair of Ray-Ban Aviators. His goatee was neatly trimmed, his skin tanned faintly orange, and his short-cropped hair looked not white but silver. Only his hand—resting on Allen's shoulder, covered in liver spots and huge, wormy veins—revealed his age. He was almost as old as my grandpa.

According to the article, Patricia, living alone in Beverly Hills, had suffered a stroke while floating on a raft in her pool. Her body had apparently slumped, tipping the raft, and she'd splashed unconscious into the water. A pair of landscapers, arriving hours later to replace some fieldstones near her koi pond, found her at the bottom of the deep end.

Even though later toxicology results would prove she was clean, the last line of the piece read, "Gray's brief stint in rehab over a decade ago came soon after her divorce from director Gordon Shultz and was followed by rumors of depression and self-medication in the ensuing years."

They made no mention of Rachel Dawn Rice here, but other sites included her as a footnote. I went to TMZ, where they'd posted a still from *The Butcher and the Baker*, my mom in flannel and ripped jeans. The heading asked 'MEMBA HER?! and the caption read, "In the '90s, Rachel Dawn Rice was an iconic face of Generation X before leaving Hollywood amid scandal. Guess what she looks like now!"

And when I clicked on it, a contemporary image of my mom appeared. She's smiling under a blue sky at some park, her long hair pulled back in a ponytail. "Rachel Dawn Rice—now 42—was photographed looking bright and sunny!"

I had no idea who'd taken this or how it had made its way to TMZ. But at least she was smiling and looking healthy, giving people the false impression that she'd achieved some carefree, post-Hollywood life instead of her actual drifting through days, devoid of any social life, exercising and meditating until school got out so she could furtively study the changes of her teenage daughter. Always best, as an actress, to play a part.

I did yet another image search of her, scanning through the photos I'd come to know so well. Sipping hazy pink cosmos at after-parties. Jokingly wearing prop-department clown masks with Jeff Goldblum. Walking down a Manhattan sidewalk in a ball cap and sunglasses, carrying Starbucks with lipstick on the lid. And all the old red-carpet poses, sometimes with an actor on her arm. Christian Slater, Kiefer Sutherland. Keanu Reeves, whom she'd dated for six months. Beautiful boys with beautiful eyes who'd hung from girls' walls in the nineties.

But then I stumbled on a few I'd never seen before. Posing on a Paris balcony for a Chanel ad. Reaching across David Letterman's desk for a kiss. And another, which made me sit up in bed and lean over my laptop.

My mom looked a little off at first glance, a stiffness to her posture and a greasiness to her skin. But when I clicked on it I realized it was actually a replica of Rachel Dawn Rice, a sculpture on display at Louis Tussaud's Waxworks in Niagara Falls, Ontario. She wore a pale flowered sundress and canary-yellow cardigan, just like her outfit from *The Harpsichord*. And though her lips were pursed strangely and her nose was too large, the sculptor had managed to do the impossible. Her eyes—the eyes as they'd been in *The Harpsichord*—were nearly perfect. The wondrous, sweet, dewy eyes of that place and time I knew from so many viewings—they existed, right there, in an otherwise synthetic self.

A little while later I went downstairs for a glass of orange juice, and the house was so dark I had to run my hand along the wainscoting to find my way. The place felt empty and bleak, the way it had when I was little and my mom had it under constant construction, its meticulous restoration serving as her full-time job, her full-time diversion. It's a Georgian Revival in the Heritage Hill neighborhood of Grand Rapids, where she still lives. Other than my college education it's the one thing I've known her to spend big money on. When I'd ask, she'd never tell me her net worth.

Sweeping, cinematic music played at the other end of the house. I stepped through the foyer, running my hand along its polished hardwood columns, past the parlor and the library to the sitting room, where we kept our piano and had mounted a huge TV above the fireplace.

My mom sat cross-legged on the end of the camelback sofa, swathed in two enormous fleece blankets that circled her lower half like an eddy of fog. A news program about an orchestra in Congo ran on TV. The amateur musicians lived in shacks with scrap-metal roofs built along garbage-strewn roads, and the story spliced this imagery with clips of war. The musicians played warped violins and dented flutes, a warehouse for their concert hall. But they all wore black suits and dresses as they sent *Carmina Burana* thundering through our sitting room.

I watched from the piano bench for a few minutes, oblivious at first that my mom had sheets of tears running down her face like rainwater. "Oh my God." I stumbled across the dark room to the sofa and wrapped my arms around her. "Mom, are you okay?"

She shook her head before supplanting the movement with a nod. After struggling through fluttering, paper-thin breaths, she said, "It's just so beautiful." Then she looked at me and placed her palm on the back of my neck. "*You're* so beautiful."

"What?" I said quietly. "No." I pulled back a little, confused and embarrassed, but that only made her cry more.

"I'm sorry," she said, rubbing her eyes in huge circular motions, maybe to hide her face. "This insomnia's making me really raw. Like my nerve endings are raw." She shook her head again. "Like I feel everything twice as much."

Two empty wine bottles remained on the coffee table, along with a sleep mask, a white-noise machine, and a plastic case of melatonin tablets. They all lay scattered around the potted lemon bonsai tree that was older than I was—the only thing from her California life displayed in our house. A single, full-size lemon grew on it, its weight making the tiny tree slouch toward the table. Only one fruit ever grew at a time, and when it turned ripe she'd always juice it into a shot glass, silently toast the tree, and toss it back without a wince or a shudder. It had something to do with energy or purity.

She lay back and struggled to pull the blankets out from underneath her. A pillow muffled her voice. "I'm being an awful mother. I'm an absentee parent right now."

I muted the TV. "No you're not. I'm fine. I just want *you* to be fine."

"I know. You're growing up," she said and then sighed. "Friends are most important. I totally remember those days." She laughed softly, turning onto her back with her arm draped over her eyes. "That's my ego talking. Thinking you need me. Like your world would fall apart without my help."

I was supposed to say something here, tell her my world *would* fall apart. But for the first time since Patricia Gray's death, I was angry. I felt, just then, like my mom was reading off a script and feeding me lines.

"I have an appointment Monday with my therapist. She'll bend me back into shape." Her arm slid away from her wet eyes, and she rolled onto her side. "I've been worse off. When that whole storm broke years ago, I didn't sleep for a full week. The paparazzi had a dozen cameras out on my street, and I swore they had special lenses that could see through walls."

I lay down, tucking myself between her and the sofa back, and rested my head on her shoulder. Though my eyes grew heavy, I stared at the bonsai tree and listened to her exhausted but ethereal voice tell these stories that I always craved.

"I didn't fall asleep till I got back to Michigan. Till I got back to Grandma and Grandpa's, in my old bedroom that they'd hadn't changed at all. It was kind of like a fortress. Like the Midwest was a moat and nobody out west could follow me. They couldn't touch me."

I closed my eyes, hoping in her restlessness that she'd narrate all night. Then I slipped my hand beneath her hair, lifting and draping it over my face, so that the dark beneath my lids grew darker, the intimacy of her words grew warmer. And maybe she did talk all night. But without meaning to— of all times, when my mom yearned for it herself—I sank into sleep.

I stepped onto our back deck, amid acorns and dead leaves. My mom, overlooking the yard in an Adirondack chair, glanced at me and faintly smiled before taking a deep breath through her nose. The world smelled like tanned leather and sweet rot. She held a coffee mug in both hands, steam rising from it, mirrored by her breath in the chilled air. "Everything packed?" she asked.

It was late November, the Tuesday before the holiday weekend, and she'd pulled me from school a day early for our road trip. My family rotates its Thanksgiving gatherings. The previous year we'd celebrated at my aunt's in Illinois. The year before that, people stayed with us in Grand Rapids. But that morning my mom and I were headed east, where my uncle and his husband lived just outside of Boston. Normally we'd have flown, but she hated the madness of airports this time of year, so when I suggested we drive she surprisingly agreed. She'd turned a corner recently, an Ativan prescription leveling her out while she increased her therapy visits, and as Patricia Gray faded from the headlines my mom became, if not joyful, at least comfortably back in her routines, treading days like water.

I sat on a bench beside her and hugged my knees. Oak leaves fluttered downward, and with the trees nearly naked the yard had become hollowed out, our dog-eared fence fully visible. The previous fence had been replaced in sections, over a few years, so that this one had aged unevenly. The east side had turned gray-green. The north, pale and sandy. The west side, which was newest and received the most shade, remained nearly golden.

Eventually we shoved our bags into our Prius and set off across the state, passing through Canadian customs a little before noon. A week earlier she'd suggested breaking up the drive with a night in Toronto, to sightsee or catch a show. I was the one who'd mentioned Niagara, claiming I'd always wanted to see the falls, and in a burst of improvisation I was stringing white lies like pearls.

Of all my mom's online images, I'd become most obsessed with the one that wasn't actually *her*. I could only find that single photo of her wax sculpture, but when I realized Niagara was on our way to Boston I started fantasizing about seeing it in person, standing across from my mom's *Harpsichord* self.

I kept all of this secret. For the first part of our five-and-a-half-hour drive we talked about things like school and *The Nutcracker*. I tried texting Hannah but remembered she was in class. And as we cut through Southern Ontario my mom settled into a show on public radio while I played games on my phone, relieved by her seemingly balanced state of mind but also worried it wouldn't last. A couple of times in recent weeks I'd caught her drinking and watching TV in the dark again, and once *Edge of Moonlight* played on HBO. Rachel Dawn Rice, the twenty-four-year-old rookie cop, loomed over our sitting room. "This is always so weird," said my mom, not taking her eyes from the screen. "Totally frozen in time." She took a long sip of wine while staring at herself. "I just realized that during the Oscars, when they show the people who died this year, they're going to show Patricia Gray."

I sat on the sofa opposite her.

"Do you think," she asked, still watching TV, "that when I die they'll show *my* face?"

I opened my mouth to speak, but all the things I almost said got tangled in my throat.

"Even if they do," she continued, "it won't be my *real* face. The face of whatever I'm like when I die. It'll be my old face." She finally looked at me. "You know what I mean. My *young* face."

Which is why I was afraid to mention the waxwork to her. I didn't think she even knew it existed, but I'd come to believe for some reason that she should see it, too. I'd been watching some of those intervention shows on TV, and my feeble, adolescent plan was to surprise her with the sight of it, like somehow—by viewing her beautiful past on display amid other celebrities and icons—she'd feel proud of what she'd achieved. Maybe she could reflect on that time without the incessant regret. That was my plan.

At one point during the final leg of the drive I turned my phone off and asked her a few direct questions about how she broke into the business. She'd seemed calm and happy, laughing at something on the radio, so it felt safe. I knew she'd modeled locally as a teenager and done a few commercials,

but I'd never realized she'd had an agent who took her to New York for the
IMTA competition. There she'd read a monologue from *The Crucible* that
drew wide attention, becoming part of an audition tape that made its way
west, where Michael de los Santos, director of *The Harpischord*, viewed it.
A year later, at eighteen, she headed west, as well.

"I was so young," she said. "And my parents took it on faith that people
there would take care of me, you know? But a couple years later I'm making
more money than they'd ever dreamed of themselves. So everything's
distorted. You see your whole life through fun-house mirrors."

My mom talked the rest of the drive. And I simply sat there, absorbing
new stories, while the highway lines marked time like a metronome.

"You're told you're beautiful. Nonstop. Young and beautiful. And you're
so naive that you just smile and nod and agree to everything. Make this
movie. Take this pill. Come home with me tonight."

She started to cover her mouth like she'd shocked herself—said too
much—but then tried to hide it by simply touching her lower lip. "You
probably know so much about me," she said, nodding at the phone in my
lap. "I don't even want to know what you know." She squeezed the steering
wheel with both hands and sat up straighter. "I realize I get a little weird
sometimes about you growing up. I've talked with my therapist about this.
I'm working on it. But I look at you sometimes and you're more a woman
than a girl, and I see an old movie of mine on TV, and that face on the
screen looks more like you than me, you know? And so I'm not just feeling
guilty about stuff from my past, but I'm also sort of terrified that a little
while from now you'll make the same mistakes." She winced and kind of
shivered. "But that's controlling and it's wrong and you deserve to make
your mistakes. Or not make them."

About fifty kilometers outside of Niagara she began to obliquely talk
about her old drug use: mostly pills but occasionally cocaine. Heroin
just once. She referenced a six-month stretch of bulimia, and how an
Edge of Moonlight producer once squeezed her belly flesh and shook
his head. All of this—including the eventual talk of Patricia Gray—
came unprompted, with me nodding, staring at the road, my fingertips
tingling from shallow breaths.

"She was like our national saint for a while," my mom said. "Our
national martyr. Your dad and I were the ridiculous clichés. The older
man and the pretty little ingenue. And when we got caught it was like

everyone wanted to burn me at the stake. Gordon got off easy. They
went after me. And when they found out I was pregnant?" She took her
hands off the wheel for a moment and made a gesture like an explosion.
Like a mushroom cloud. "Which is kind of where my head's been since
all this got dredged up in the news."

Looking back at it, what I asked next seems sort of cruel, but at the
time it stemmed from my own flickering panic, the words spilling from
trembling lips. "So do I make you feel guilty? Like, just by looking at me
are you always thinking about this stuff?"

And my mom took the kind of deep, purifying breath I imagine her
taking while meditating or doing yoga. "I see you dancing? Or when
I see you laughing with Hannah?" She looked at me. "Or when you
rest your head against me?" She put her hand over her heart and then
pantomimed another explosion.

A half hour later my mom stood in front of our hotel room window,
pausing for a moment before flinging the curtains open with theatrical
flair. She audibly gasped. "Oh, come here, Ellie."

The Horseshoe Falls consumed our panorama, the sheets of foaming
water like a white skirt on the gray sky. For a woman who never flaunted
her wealth, my mom had surprised me by booking us a two-bedroom
fireplace suite on the forty-third floor of the Hilton Fallsview.

"I'll just stay inside," she said, though her smile revealed her teasing.
"Order room service. Gaze out the window. Sip wine in the Jacuzzi
bath." Because for someone who claimed to hate West Coast elites, she'd
described most of Niagara as "tourist trap swill."

After a short rest we put on our winter coats and headed down to the
falls. I still had this nebulous plan in my head, but it had suddenly become
impossible to imagine my mom's *actual* self entering a wax museum. As
we rode the elevator to the lobby I told her, "After we see the falls and get
some dinner you have to do one stupid tourist thing with me."

"I'm not going on one of those boats where you wear the big rain
jackets."

"It's too cold for that," I said as the doors slid open. "But you have to do
something." We crossed the lobby, her heels clicking over the marble floor.
"Because I'm growing up and you want to make memories with me."

She laughed and put her arm around me and told me to shut up, and as we marched down the hill against a cold wind, I figured I had her.

But her easygoing vibe evaporated when we approached the falls up close. Under this off-season sky, the few tourists scattered about crammed their cold hands into coat pockets. Several shops and concession areas were closed until spring. And the bare tree branches creaked as they bent against their will. Because of the surging white noise of water, my mom and I spoke very little, instead staring down at the enormous churning cauldron and eventually wandering a little ways from each other. A haze, like a low-lying cloud, hovered over us, and even at a short distance I almost lost sight of her. But at one point she clutched the handrail and peered down at the watery cliffs, and the thin crease of her mouth gave a sense of someone brooding. It was a rare moment in real life where I felt I was watching her on-screen.

When we eventually turned our backs to the falls, crossing the parkway to find a restaurant, we discovered that a silver mist, sheer as gossamer, covered us both. The droplets were so fine that, even under the clouds, her hair shimmered a little, like a dark field of grass veiled in dew.

While my mom used the restroom at the Boston Pizza, I stood waiting outside a gift shop, staring at salt and pepper shakers in the window display. Two were shaped like headless torsos with huge breasts, the word *Niagara* painted where the waists would be. When she emerged from the restaurant we walked together up the sidewalks of Clifton Hill—the pure, plastic essence of the town's kitsch. Strike Rock N' Bowl. Captain Jack's Pirates Cove. Ripley's Believe It Or Not, which was fashioned like a tipped-over Empire State Building with King Kong on its spire. Above everything, lazily rotating as if exhausted from another year, loomed the SkyWheel. In the summer heat the place was probably filled with families in sunglasses basking in the waffle-cone air. But this was November and a Tuesday and we did not bask.

"So for some reason," said my mom, "I agreed to let you cash in a golden ticket." She rolled her eyes. "To which of these tawdry showplaces will you drag your poor mother? And don't say Castle Dracula. Although it's probably better than whatever you've got planned."

I shot her a look. "I don't have a *plan*."

"Oh sure." She smirked. "You've got something."

The road split and we veered right, around the corner of the 4D theater, where a timber-framed, faux Tudor house stood beside its enormous neon sign: LOUIS TUSSAUD'S WAXWORKS.

My mom shook her head. "No way." I grabbed her by the hand and pulled her toward the entrance, and though traces of a smile laced her voice, my neck and back muscles had gone tense like when I sat to take an algebra test. "I have witnessed my end," she said. "Death by tackiness." If nothing else, I realized she had no knowledge of her own sculpture inside.

Behind the ticket counter, between enormous wax replicas of Hulk Hogan and Andre the Giant, sat a teenage girl with her legs crossed, staring at her phone. We bought our tickets from her and then plunged into the first of the museum's many dim rooms, my mom giggling a little, enjoying herself, while I slipped into a nervous tic I had, repeatedly swallowing as my mouth turned dry.

We pressed through the first display, all of it devoted to Canadian celebrities—John Candy, Alanis Morissette, Wayne Gretzky—most of whom I didn't know. Then on to the next room, where I rounded every corner with anxious dread, expecting to encounter my mom in her *Harpsichord* dress, knowing full well this was my goal but now overwhelmed with the reality of it. As for my plan, it ended with the sculpture's discovery. I had no idea what came after.

"So why this place?" she asked.

I shrugged. "I don't know. It's just kind of funny in a stupid way. The bad ones are funny."

She studied the grimaced smile of Prince William. "They're all bad ones," she said.

The interior of the building, like the sculptures it contained, continued an illusion and actually felt like a real Tudor house. Dusty old furniture and floral wallpaper provided a home for the waxworks. Accentuating the eerie setting was the silence permeating each room. Other than the girl who sold the tickets, we hadn't encountered another real person.

Each time I crossed a threshold I felt the subtle shock of expectant new faces leering and smiling: Gandhi, the pope, Bill and Hillary Clinton. The rooms were themed—World Leaders to Sports Heroes to Music Legends—and I knew at any moment that we'd arrive in Hollywood.

The route led to a staircase resembling ours back home, wainscoting and ornate banister, except that along the wall as we ascended hung a series of life masks: celebrity faces with closed eyes that made it seem as if the people themselves stood trapped on the other side, pressing themselves against the wall, suffocating. "This is creepy," I whispered.

My mom seemed to deliberately avoid looking at them. "Reminds me of the makeup effects on set."

At the top of the stairs the room opened up into a vast space with a high ceiling, a banner overhead proclaiming MOVIE MAGIC. My mom paused for a moment before slowly shaking her head. I wondered if she sensed a trap. "Maybe I'll see some old friends," she said.

Dozens of figures inhabited the room, and I had to do a double take to ensure that none were real people. The scene played out like an Oscars after-party, the stars holding trophies, posing for photographs, and patting each other on the back. Julia Roberts laughed with Tom Hanks. Will Smith shook hands with Brad Pitt. When I saw Keanu Reeves I expected to see my mom on his arm, but no.

Each face was vaguely misshapen, and the hair appeared stringy and translucent under the lights, fake like fishing line. My mom wandered to the left, examining Golden Age stars like Clark Gable and Elizabeth Taylor, who talked amongst themselves as if in a separate clique. And I took that moment to literally jog from waxwork to waxwork, desperately searching for Rachel Dawn Rice.

I looped past all of them twice before my mom approached without me seeing her and placed a hand on my arm. "What's wrong?"

I struggled out of my winter coat and let it fall to the floor. Sweat began streaking down my forehead, and I actually stomped my foot like a pissed-off toddler. "I can't find you!"

She said nothing but softly rubbed my arm and watched me the way she sometimes did through the glass at ballet. Nostalgia in real time.

"You're supposed to be here," I said, my limbs suddenly numb from an adrenaline crash. And then I confessed it all—the entire half-assed plan designed to accomplish some abstraction that I'd never actually determined.

Her hand, as it so often did, rubbed my back before rising and warmly settling on the back of my neck. She kissed the top of my head and must have figured I was burnt out, ready to leave. But when we navigated through the rest of the museum and returned to the ticket counter, I nearly pounced on the girl staring at her phone. "You advertised some that weren't here." I actually jabbed my index finger in her face. "Someone's missing. There are supposed to be others. Where are the others!"

I laugh about that now, especially because they sounded like lines from one of my mom's mediocre thrillers. But they had the desired effect. The girl scrambled off to some back room and returned with the manager, a middle-aged man with damp eyes who kept cleaning his glasses on the bottom of his shirt.

As I rattled off the situation to him, my mom edged toward the exit, shaking her head at the floor and mumbling. "It's fine, Ellie. It's fine. We don't— He doesn't even know—"

The manager politely nodded the entire time, sneaking looks at her, maybe trying to recognize her face or recall her name among the sea of formerly famous.

"I'm relatively new," he said, placing his hand over his heart, "so I don't know precisely what was here before. But we do, from time to time, make changes to keep the exhibits fresh and current."

My mom stepped farther away.

"There are always new ones," he said. "And when new figures are delivered we have to find space for them, which means removing some already on display." He glanced at my mom again before lowering his voice. "I don't mean to sound cruel. And this is embarrassing. But please understand it's a matter of both space"—he dropped his eyes—"and giving customers what they want."

"Ellie, I'll wait for you outside."

"Wait!" I said. And as a tear raced down my cheek, the manager's jaw fell loose, pained, as if I'd slapped him. He must have had a daughter. "Do you get rid of them?" I asked. "Or do you keep the old ones somewhere?"

For the first time during that conversation my mom looked up at us.

"I can't make any promises," he said. "I'm not exactly sure what's down there. And customers should never be down there themselves." He set his glasses atop his head. "But I'll make an exception. Considering," he said, nodding at my mom, "who you are."

Whether he actually knew who she was, I don't know, but he led us back behind two closed doors, through the office area, and to a third door, where darkened stairs led to some kind of basement. As we descended, my mom, behind me, placed her hand on my shoulder for what I assume was balance. And I actually reached out and touched the manager's back, frightened and disoriented myself. The room was pitch-black when we first reached the bottom. But then he said, "Watch yourself," and a series of fluorescent lights blinked to life from the low ceiling, casting a soft green tinge over everything below.

"Oh my God," I said, shocked by the sight, jumping backward into my mom, who wrapped her arms around me.

Dismembered waxworks lay strewn over tables. Decapitated bodies, nude and sexless like giant Ken dolls, leaned against the walls. On a shelf sat a row of heads, their names written on masking tape stuck to their necks: John Wayne, Jimmy Carter, Audrey Hepburn. I pressed my face into my mom's chest.

"It's okay," she said quietly, pushing forward into the room while I clung to her, the three of us wading among boxes, wax baseball players, heaps of clothes like at a thrift store. More bodiless faces stared from the shelves—faces I only vaguely recognized. My mom gently pulled me free and then kept pressing ahead, following the manager through the storage disarray.

"Is this—?" he said once, glancing back and forth between a brunette sculpture and my mom. "No, this isn't you, is it?"

"No," she said calmly, still walking, looking to her left and to her right as if examining paintings at a gallery.

"She had short hair," I said, stopping momentarily. I didn't want to go farther into this place, but it went deeper than I thought, and as the two of them navigated through the junk I became terrified they'd duck behind a shelf and I'd lose them, having to wander alone in this room of heads.

When I caught up to them the manager was scanning another shelf, as if parts of my mom might be there, but she herself now stood still, gazing at a row of waxworks against the back wall. "I found her," she said.

The cardigan was missing, but there she stood, in her sundress, with her pixie haircut. Her impish charms. There she stood against gray cinder blocks, between some guy in a top hat and a little boy with a pet dog. The large eyes of Rachel Dawn Rice caught the flickering fluorescents enough to seem alive even atop the dummy body with the crooked neck.

I started weeping, wanting to rush up to my mom and embrace her but also afraid to go near for some reason.

She stepped forward until face-to-face with her likeness, resembling a mother beside her daughter if her daughter were a broken doll.

The manager stood as silently as I did, waiting for my mom to say something. Instead, she simply placed her hand on the back of the waxen neck. She closed her eyes. And then, delicately drawing close, she kissed herself on the lips.

ACKNOWLEDGMENTS

Never-ending thanks to Jennifer and Elizabeth for the real-life stories we share.

A special thank you to Dan Mancilla for providing feedback on nearly all of these stories.

Thanks to those friends who provided assistance with specific stories, including Amy Bailey, Matt Brown, David Greenwood, and Robert James Russell.

And thanks to the crew at Switchgrass Books/NIU Press for believing in my work and fighting the good fight.

Note: Some details used in "Witch Whistle" were derived from Antony Beevor's *The Battle for Spain: The Spanish Civil War 1936–1939* and especially from Geoffrey Cox's excellent *Defence of Madrid*.